I0676345

Monty

Leigh Leslie

Published by Nolan MacKenzie Books, 2024.

MONTY

First edition. April 2, 2024.

ISBN: 978-0473740610

Written by Leigh Leslie.

Also by Leigh Leslie

Lady Winscombe's Parure
Monty

With gratitude to David Boughey

AUTHOR'S NOTE

One day, while walking down a country lane in England with my daughter, we came across the name of a property that sparked the idea for this novel. Initially, I used *Monty* as a working title, but in my mind, I thought of it as *Letting Go*. However, it was soon pointed out that such a title might be mistaken for a self-help book—which this novel is not, though it certainly could be for its main character, Monty.

Over the years, the characters and plot gradually took shape, and *Monty* remained the title. Despite my initial intention to avoid writing anything that required extensive research, I ultimately spent several years immersed in it.

My sincere gratitude goes to Lesley Morgan, John Kappes, Jane Carpenter, Iain of the

Customer Care Team for Greggs, and Rosalie Cumming who all furnished me with suggestions, advise and help in my research. A majorly big thank you goes to David Boughey, Service Assistant (National Trust, Anglesey Abbey) who went out of his way to provide me with information related to Monty's visit to Anglesey Abbey. Special thanks also to both my editor and beta reader—both of whom know who they are – who helped me to write out the wrinkles in this novel.

All characters in this novel are entirely fictitious, as are the locations, except for Anglesey Abbey and Brighton. Any inaccuracies are mine alone, and I sincerely apologize for them.

ONE

Charles Montgomery Chinthurst, named after his father Charles and his father before him, and Monty to his many friends, always knew that one day his past, or part of it, would catch up with him. But it still came as a shock to be confronted with it like this.

Monty was definitely what most women would call 'hot', a fashion-plate. Nudging 6 foot, he had a build that, while natural, could have been an ad for muscle supplements or gym membership. His hazel eyes were so spiked with yellow that at times they looked golden, and he wore his dark blonde hair short in a conservative manner to match the conservative cut of his suits. His perfect teeth smacked of expensive orthodontic work, and he had a perpetual tan that came naturally. To top that off he was also a smart dresser, equally at home in the business suit as he was going casual.

He sat motionless at his desk, his face masked of emotion, and stared at the envelope that his PA had placed before him.

"What do you want me to do with it?" Melanie asked. She stood back from the desk and watched her boss as his face paled. She thought that she had seen all his reactions to the mail that passed across his desk, but this was new to her. She tried to decipher his thoughts from his eyes, but today their hazel brilliance betrayed nothing.

The envelope was addressed to Charlie Hirst. The writing was in dark blue ink. Bold. Capitals. To Melanie it gave nothing away. But not to Monty. He knew.

Though he did not recognise the penmanship, and there was no return address, he still knew. Only two people knew Charlie Hirst. He had no need to guess who the sender was. He picked up the envelope, marvelling at the fact that it didn't burn his hand, and he tapped the corner of it on the polished surface of the mahogany desk that spread out before him.

Melanie made to move beside him to console him from whatever it was that, by all appearances, was disturbing him, but something held her back.

"Well? Who is he? Do you know?" she asked, her voice alternating between petulance and concern.

Oh, he knew all right. But no one else needed to. Not ever, or at least not until he had opened the envelope and seen what the contents were. He could feel the palms of his hands starting to sweat, along with an increase in his heart rate. He wasn't sure the reason why he was reacting this way. Was it dread or exhilaration? He took a deep breath and willed his heart to stop racing. The past was in the past and he was no longer young and brash. He had buried his misdemeanours and did not want to confront them again. Why would Teddy be writing to him now, after all these years?

He pushed his chair back and stood up. Melanie watched him as robotic-like Monty moved around the end of the large, polished desk, and walked past the wall-to-wall floor-to-ceiling bookcase that was filled with books and trinkets from his travels, all fighting for space, to the large plate glass window. He stood there, left hand fisted in his trouser pocket, his fingers rolling frantically in the ball; his right hand tapping the envelope against his right leg. Grey skies settled threateningly over the red roofed, tree dotted Cambridge cityscape that spread out before him, but all he saw was a brilliant canopy of cloudless blue reaching down to caress a vast expanse of barren red sand.

"Charlie is someone whom I used to know, but he isn't with us anymore," he mused, half to himself.

"What do you want me to do with it then?" Melanie asked as she walked across the Ocean Deep Axminster *Devonia Plains* carpet to stand beside him at the window. Her head almost level with his, thanks to the aid of her high heeled shoes. She ached to comfort him, but resisted touching him, uncertain of his mood. One she had never witnessed before. "Shall I open it?" She reached for the letter, but suddenly pulled her hand back as Monty spun round quickly and confronted her in such a manner that she momentarily shrank back.

"For a return address?"

"No."

Monty strode back to his chair, spun the envelope onto the desk and placing his hands on the edge of the desk, hooked his right leg around the leg of the buff camel coloured leather upholstered chair and pulled it towards the desk, letting the seat-edge collapse the backs of his knees and he sat down.

"Leave it with me, I'll sort it."

Melanie looked at him, one perfectly curved dark eyebrow raised in question. A question that he chose to ignore. He glanced up at her, half a foot shorter than him without her shoes, with dark, wide-set almond eyes that matched her raven hair. Svelte, competent well-dressed Melanie. A complete contrast to his ex-wife and now the only woman he thought he wanted in his life. He ought not to have snapped at her. It wasn't her fault. The letter.

"I'm sorry Mel, I should not have yelled at you like that. It's just that the letter caught me by surprise. I never expected it. Never expected to see that name again."

He sounded bitter, and Melanie wondered who Charlie Hirst was, and what he had done to upset Monty in this manner.

"That's all right," she hesitated, "Monty."

Monty looked up at her in surprise and she felt an infusion of blood seep into her complexion.

"Sorry, Mr Chinthurst," she corrected herself and Monty nodded. It was not like her to forget her place, or their agreement. "I understand. You've had a shock, that's all. Can I get you something?" She made to move towards the drink cabinet set against the wall opposite the bookcase. "A drink maybe? Or a coffee?"

Monty had the grace to smile at her before returning his gaze to the elephant in the room. The envelope. "No thanks." What he really wanted were several stiff drinks, enough to totally obliterate the day so that he could wake up and find the envelope gone. But that was not going to happen. The last time he had been that inebriated to lose a day had been the catalyst for where he was now, staring his past in the face.

Eton had not guaranteed him entry into any of the prestigious universities, and he'd only scraped into a recognised tertiary institution where he failed miserably both socially and academically. Socially because he simply did not fit in, and academically because he expended his energies in trying to fit in. It had all come to a head as he approached his 21st birthday. In an attempt to keep his two lives, home and study separate—heaven forbid that the members of his parent's social circle should catch a glimpse of his erstwhile fair-weather friends from the wrong side of the tracks—Monty had arranged a night out on the tiles the week before his much acclaimed "official" birthday party. Unfortunately, for all concerned, the night ended rather abruptly with his parents being summoned to the police station in the early hours of the morning followed quickly by his summary departure overseas, without chains, but shackled all the same, the mantle of shame foisted on him a weight that he was uncomfortable with and determined to shake off. He belonged to the upper echelons of society, and society decreed that he confine himself to its tenets of behaviour. There would be no more rollicking with the riffraff. It was, until the arrival of the envelope, a period of his life that he had succeeded in erasing.

He could feel the intensity of Melanie's concern and looked back up at her "I'll be fine." He smiled at her again, hoping that it was convincing enough for her to leave.

"Is there anything else that I can get for you? Do for you?"

"No, all's good. If you can get those letters sent out." He waved his hand in the general direction of a pile of paper at the end of his desk. "And when Gregg Wilson gets here, just send him straight in."

Monty watched her covertly from under the hair that had flopped down over his eyes as she glided across the room to the office door. She moved like a leopard, gracefully and silently, on the prowl. And no doubt she had the spots that didn't change to go with it. He could wear that; it could be interesting. He still found himself drawn to her like he had no other. No other since ... But no. He dared not go there. That was in the past, along with Charlie. And Teddy. Oh why did they have to surface at this point in his life? Why did they have to surface at all?

Melanie pulled the door behind her as she left the office wondering who Charlie Hirst was.

Maybe, could it be ...? It was before she started working for Monty, but it had not been long before the grapevine brought her up to speed. Monty's wife had left him and taken the children with her. If ... no, *when*, Monty was hers, there would be no way that she would relinquish her hold on him. No way.

Rumour was that there had been another man, a partner in the firm. Could that have been Charlie Hirst? That would explain the letter turning up at the office, and Monty's adverse reaction to its arrival—someone that he had known, and now no longer here. Here being the office. Or did 'no longer here', mean that he was dead?

With the closure of the door Monty dismissed Melanie, the letter, and Teddy from his thoughts. He opened the Wilson file and started to refresh his mind about the case at hand. But Teddy wouldn't leave his thoughts alone.

The letter had to be from Teddy, no one else knew Charlie, other than Ralph Delany, and he had no cause to be writing to him, or to Charlie Hirst. Unless it was a joke. But then, Ralph Delany was not a joking man. So it had to be from Teddy. But why? And why now? And did he have time to open the envelope before Gregg Wilson arrived? Monty looked at his watch, Ten minutes. That was plenty of time to run through the file before he arrived, and to open the envelope.

His hand hovered over the envelope. What could Teddy want? Had something happened to her father? And how did Teddy know his address? It had been, what, 15 years since they had last had contact. And it hadn't been at all pleasant. In fact ...

Monty found himself heating up at the memory, as guilt filled his being. He had tried to forget. Had hoped that Teddy would forgive him. But he could never forgive himself. He'd been stupid, and naïve, and embarrassed, and guilty as hell. So guilty in fact that he had run. Run, and tried never to look back.

But now it was all catching up with him. And the questions kept circling in his mind. What did Teddy want? After all these years of silence what could Teddy possibly want? If it was an apology, then he would give it. But apology alone could never be enough. How could it after what he had done? That would always be there with Teddy. A daily reminder of what an arrogant dickhead he had been. Totally unforgivable, no matter how many times he apologised, no matter how much he apologised.

Slowly he drew the envelope towards him. The quiet schluff of quality paper against the polish of the desk the only sound in the room. He picked the envelope up and turned it over. Nothing. There wasn't even a postmark. Well there was, but it was so smudged that any time or place was obscured, but he noted that the stamp was British. What could that mean? He tapped the envelope against the tip of his aquiline nose. Dare he open it? Who knew what was locked inside? What secrets might escape when he did?

Thinking better of the situation he pushed his chair back and, still tapping the envelope to his nose, he moved across the room to where his briefcase lay on the sofa facing the window. He opened the briefcase and dropped the envelope inside. Tonight. Plenty time tonight. Or tomorrow. Who was to say when the envelope had arrived in his possession? If he had been out of town on business for the week, then he would not have received it till he'd come into the office next Monday.

That meant that he could happily leave the envelope where it was for the next 6 days. Monty snapped his briefcase closed and returned, a much happier man, to his desk and bent his head to Gregg Wilson's file.

TWO

The light was fading into early evening when Monty cleared his desk for the day. He walked over to the sofa, reached over the back and picked up his briefcase. While this was a familiar routine, for some reason tonight it reminded him of the same actions the previous week, when Teddy's unexpected envelope had been in the briefcase.

So much had happened since then. Mostly good. No, he corrected himself, it had all been good. A whirlwind of good that, if he played his cards right, would be culminating in an even better good tonight. Smiling broadly at the thought of how his evening might end. Monty made his way to the door, leant the briefcase against the wall and shrugged himself into his coat that had been hanging on an ornate hat stand. His hand on the door handle, he turned around, a cursory look over the office showed that all was in order. He opened the door, strode through, closing it behind him.

Melanie was still at her desk, and he could see beyond her that while she was not alone in the office, the other staff were not nearby.

"We're still on for dinner tonight?" he asked quietly as he walked past her. He wasn't sure exactly why he felt the need to be secretive. The firm did not have a policy that frowned on extra-curricular fraternising with the staff, and it wasn't as if he and Melanie had not socialised before. But that had always been work orientated. This was different. This was an official 'date'. Something that he had not indulged in for a while now. And he felt different. Almost like when he had been on first dates as a teenager. He felt his skin prickle at the memory of some of his adolescent attempts at dating. Not always pleasant memories.

"Of course." Melanie smiled demurely for the benefit of anyone who might have been observing them. From the very beginning of her appointment as Mr Chinthurst the third's PA she had slowly and calculatingly been insinuating herself into his life, and tonight she felt sure she was going to hit paydirt. She was feeling excited, and smug. Monty had been emotionally all over the place since she had handed him the envelope addressed to Charlie Hirst. She still had no idea who Charlie Hirst was, or the hold that he had over her boss, but since its arrival she had made sure that she was even more indispensable to Monty. Always there, and an oasis of calm, just as any conscientious PA with higher aspirations ought to be. She was looking forward to tonight.

"Good. I'll pick you up about 7," he said, and strode through the remainder of the open plan floorspace imagining that all the incumbents were following his passage, knowing that he and his PA were embarking on a 'first date'. He could not get out of the place quick enough.

He walked comfortably down the pedestrian walk that had once been a main thoroughfare, before the advent of modernisation. Thank goodness for forward thinking councilmen. The narrow, cobbled street might have been adequate in years past before the appearance of the horseless carriages, but it, and so many like it, was no place for today's hustle and bustle. Besides, a little exercise was good for the soul as well as the physique.

The locals were familiar with Monty, his stride, dress and manner all alluding to his status, and many were the greetings that he exchanged as his regimentally shined shoes clipped over the cobbles. All that was missing were the top hat and silver-crowned cane. Debonair, and proud of it. He mentally wrinkled his nose as he passed 'the local' from where raucous bellowing issued, and he side-stepped, as was his habit, the not so elderly homeless woman who was bedding down in the doorway of a building.

His only concession to normality was to then catch the bus home. He stood in line with the other commuters, barely acknowledging their presence, paid the driver his fare and sat, as usual, halfway down the bus in an aisle seat, so as not to encourage interchange with others.

After Lyndall had taken the children and left, he had remained in their family house. It was too large for him, on his own, but it provided him with stability and a sense of belonging. The two of them had spent a long time looking for the 'right' place, and now, having found it, despite him being on his own, he was not about to relinquish it. It suited his 'standing in society' as his father had been wont to state, and who was Monty to disagree with that sage? Especially if the alternative was to accept the frequent offer to return to the family estate. Returning to live at home with his parents was not something that he could envisage. But latterly the invitation had been sugar coated with the news that his parents were planning on reopening and modernising one of the wings – one where he would be quite separate from them and the main living area – and he was finding the idea mildly enticing.

Melanie, on the other hand, was only too anxious and willing to help him find alternative accommodation. A place that was more in keeping with her lifestyle. Not that she had any complaints about the calibre of lifestyle that Monty enjoyed, but she was more into modern than traditional. She was of the opinion that if you had money, then you ought to flaunt it.

Thus, rather than the sedate Georgian house that was Monty and Lyndall's castle, Melanie was all for bold, square steel, concrete and glass. Something that shouted "Look at me! I've made the rich list."

As Monty walked up the garden path of his domain, he marvelled that someone as beautiful, talented, worldly and tantalising as Melanie could also be so judgemental and superficial. He could not understand how she didn't appreciate the history and charm of the older style houses, and traditions.

For all her airs and graces, her breeding, for want of another word, showed through the veneer every so often. Nothing could really hide the fact that she was not brought up in the privileged strata that he and his family had enjoyed for generations. He'd never really made a serious study of his family history, but for as far back as he knew, his ancestors had enjoyed an elitist life. As had Lyndall. Not so Melanie. Melanie was a product of nouveau riche parents, and only too happy to splash her family's wealth around.

He would have been the last to recognise the distain with which he viewed some aspects of society. Except for the lapse in his late teens-early twenties, he was the epitome of the British stiff upper lip landed gentry, and proud of it.

THREE

"So, are you going to tell me who Charlie Hirst is?" Melanie asked coyly, a smile on her face. She looked, beautiful. Her long hair, normally held back in a clip, was let loose, framing her heart-shaped face with an interesting allure, falling over her shoulders. And her usual austere tailored blouse and skirt that was her 'uniform' at the office was replaced by an alluring scarlet jersey figure-hugging dress that left little to the imagination.

They were seated at a corner table in The Willow Tree, a quiet, intimate restaurant in a little village about eight miles outside Cambridge. The wall to one side of them was papered to appear as a bookcase straddling an open fireplace, a decorative display of pinecones in the grate. It hadn't been many months since it had been blazing, throwing out a wonderful heat, flames reflected in the myriad of mirrors gracing the other walls. A candlestick flickered from its holder on the bare wood top of the round table that was theirs for the evening, the flame, and those on the other tables sparked off the crystals hanging from the chandelier in the middle of the room.

The other patrons scattered around the room did not interfere with the intimate atmosphere that made the place so sort after. The eclectic collection of furnishings added to, rather than detracted from, the restaurant's quaintness and was complimented by the menu.

Monty played his fork through the turnip puree of his venison haunch, trying to think how he could best answer. He looked up at Melanie, his eyes brimming with amusement. Her heart melted, as it did every time he looked at her, and she knew that he wasn't going to answer.

"Okay," she said then pouted.

Monty gave a soft chuckle. Melanie knew she ought to feel resentful with his dismissive attitude.

"Then tell me, have you opened the envelope?"

His mouth twitched, and she leant forward and touched the corner of his mouth with her finger and smiled again.

Monty put his fork down on the side of his plate, lifted his hand and held her wrist then slowly brought it before his mouth. With deliberate slowness, he pressed a soft kiss to the tender skin on the inside of her wrist, before placing her hand on the table. He could smell her perfume ... a soft musk mingled with something floral. He wondered what it was, not sure if it appealed to him or not.

"We, we have been invited to the opening of an art exhibition." He smiled at her as though he had just delivered the present of her dreams.

"What?" Where on earth had that come from? An art exhibition! She shuddered at the mere thought.

"We have been invited to the opening of an art exhibition." He continued to smile.

Melanie sat back in her seat and stared at Monty. Whatever could have possessed Monty to even entertain the idea that art would be of any interest to her?

"The envelope." Monty looked at her, wondering why she wasn't responding in the manner that he had imagined she would. After all, it was an opening. Not everyone was invited to such a prestigious event, and here he was. He had been invited, and to bring a guest. And who better to have on his arm than the delectable Miss Melanie Carpenter? He leant forward across the table and reached out for Melanie's hands, taking them in his and giving a slight tug. "The one you have just asked me about. The one addressed to Charlie Hirst."

"You did open the envelope!" She pulled her hands out of his grasp, looked around, then leant in closer. "That's illegal. It was not addressed to you."

Monty could not decide if it was a whisper or a hiss that escaped his lips. "What would you have had me do?" He raised an eyebrow at her, his smile challenging her, but Melanie chose to take the question as rhetorical and simply glared at him. He smiled sardonically, which made her more incensed.

Monty had opened the envelope. In the security of his home, he had opened the envelope. With trembling fingers he had fumbled with a letter opener in the form of a medieval knight's sword. Slowly he'd passed the opener along the upper edge of the envelope and slit it open. What he'd found was a bit of an anti-climax.

He wasn't sure exactly what he had been hoping for, but it certainly wasn't what he slid out of the envelope. He turned the envelope up and shook it, but nothing else came out. All it had contained was sitting on the kitchen bench in front of him. An invitation. An embossed invitation on quality paper, made out to "Charlie Hirst and Guest. To the opening of an art exhibition. A simple card was clipped to the invitation saying, "As promised, Teddy."

Monty looked down at his empty hands and picked up his fork then speared a piece of venison, swirled it through the puree and slowly manoeuvred the whole to his mouth and chewed. He swallowed then smiled at her again and shrugged his shoulders. "Does it matter?"

Monty sopped up the remainder of his main, placed his knife and fork together on the plate, leant back in his seat and mopped his mouth with his napkin. "Beautiful!" He indicated Melanie's empty plate opposite him, not so long ago it had been the receptacle of a rather expensive sea trout on a peach, baby spinach and champagne risotto. "Dessert?"

"Oh, Monty! Really?" How could he think about food when she had introduced his felony to the table. Here she was, sitting at a table with a criminal, a common lawbreaker and all he can talk about is dessert. She thought she knew the man, but he was impossible. Here she was, thinking 'her Monty' to be a cultured law-abiding citizen, one favoured to be sought after by her. What could she have been thinking? She certainly was not recalling offering to open it herself, in search of a return address.

"Yes, really. Would you like to order dessert?" He chuckled quietly, amused by Melanie's reaction.

"But the envelope Monty, you opened an envelope that was not addressed to you," Melanie shook her head in disbelief. If Monty was going to go down as a criminal the best she could do was support him and join him in his misdemeanour.

"Charlie Hirst is no longer with us, so it is now a moot point. Besides, his loss is our gain. Now, dessert. I recall seeing chocolate mousse on the menu."

Melanie still could not believe Monty's audacity, but the mention of chocolate mousse momentarily distracted her. She could come back to the envelope and Charlie Hirst. But chocolate mousse?

"Hmm, chocolate mousse? Are you going to indulge in dessert too? I don't want to appear a pig."

Monty laughed, but not loud enough to disturb the other diners. "There is no way that you could ever be mistaken for a pig." He raised his arm and called the waiter over with his fingers and asked for the menu. "Well, when I was spying the chocolate mousse, my eye also caught mention of a passionfruit & orange cheesecake with orange sorbet & orange crisp," Monty said, hoping to keep the conversation on the lighter side of things.

Melanie, however, was not to be so easily side-tracked, and she was not going to let Monty off that lightly. "So, tell me about this invitation."

FOUR

Melanie, feeling slightly confused after the partial revelations over dinner, and dejected when her subtle invitation on the doorstep had been rejected, still managed to go to sleep dreaming of what to wear to the swanky opening night the following month in London, the West End no less. There had to be opportunities there, even if it was an art exhibition.

Monty was not sure if he'd call the 'date' with Melanie a success or not. After the debacle of the invitation over dessert, the evening had deteriorated such that it was almost a relief to drop Melanie back at her flat declining the night-cap invitation. He had then continued the drive to his parent's home where he was residing for the weekend – just to try out living in the refurbished private wing of the family mansion, and there recall his first meeting Teddy.

The gate, like just about everything else on Calinda, *had been made on the property. It was an iron pipe bent into a rectangle with the ensuing space filled in with chicken wire laced in place by thin wire. Hinges were welded into place along one of the longer sides, with a bolt on the other side to match up with the latch on the fence post. There was a kick-plate affixed along the bottom, theoretically to keep the livestock out and the domestic animals in. But years of it being used as a literal 'kick' plate had rendered it useless for either task. At the moment a scrawny kid was hung over the gate, head tilted to one side and resting on arms folded across the top, one foot resting on the bottom of the gate, the other gently kicking the kick-plate, the thwock of the shoe and the squeak of resistant wire on metal creating an interesting welcome.*

As Charles Montgomery Chinthurst made his way across the dirt yard from the shed that constituted the garage and workshop, he was hard pressed to determine whether it was a girl or a boy making up the welcome party. Not that it mattered, he would find out soon enough. Obviously it was Teddy. The child that he had been engaged to tutor for the next three months, with the option of an extension.

He looked beyond the child on the gate, to the house that stood behind what he assumed was a front fence. The house, like the fence, was hard to distinguish, covered as it was by what looked like grape vines gone rampant. An oasis of green in an otherwise barren red world. But he could see that the house was on one level, and had a wide veranda that appeared to run along three sides. He presumed that there would be no reason for the fourth side not to be similarly clothed. He could hear a foreign noise, over and above that coming from the gate. A plaintive slow squeak. Scanning his head and surroundings and attuning his ears he discovered, set behind and rising above the roof of the house, the skeleton of a tall narrow metal pyramid, the struts of which appeared too frail to support the large wheel and tail set at its apex. A windmill, the kind that he had only ever seen before in glossy travel brochures of the Australian Outback. The vanes of the wheel were slowly revolving, emitting a squeal as they did so.

He could feel the scrutiny of the eyes at the gate boring into his being. Stripping him of the clothes that he now was feeling rather uncomfortable in. Not just because of the scrutiny, but because he could feel the perspiration trickling out of his pores and congealing in the small of his back, and under his arms. He took a look at the man beside him. Cool as a cucumber. Cream moleskins over brown elastic-sided ankle boots and a checked, open necked short-sleeved shirt. A worn Akubra on his head. Why couldn't he be as casual?

Teddy swung on the gate and stared at the men making their way across from the ute that her father had just driven into the shed. For the life of her, she had never seen such a spectacle. Not that she had had much of a chance to experience all that the world had to offer. At just eleven, and rarely off the station, her knowledge of male fashion was very much dictated by her family and the farm hands. Casual. Of course, she had seen her brothers, father and other male members of her family togged out in 'good clobber', going to a wedding, or funeral, or her brothers heading off to boarding school. But this new man took the cake. For a start, he didn't wear a hat. No one went bare-headed in this place, even if it was just a faded much washed terry-towelling cap. No hat smacked of stupidity. So this new man was already so labelled. And he looked so out of place, and decidedly uncomfortable in a dark grey jacket and ... what was that he had around his neck? She cocked her head to one side and gaped. It looked like a bunched up patterned scarf tucked into his pale blue shirt. A man, wearing a lady's scarf? She almost laughed, but then remembered that she was meant to be on her best behaviour. His trousers matched his jacket and had a hard crease down each leg, and were held in place with a black leather belt, the same shiny black as his shoes would have been if they weren't being scuffed through the dust.

She mentally shrugged to herself and waited.

Monty could feel the child staring at him, and it made him uncomfortable. He was tempted to stare back, or even poke a face, but his upbringing and position here didn't allow such actions, so he dismissed the thought. Instead, he looked down at his feet. His brilliantly polished shoes were longer sparkling black, but coated with a sheen of red. He stopped and shook one leg, then the other, that did nothing to dislodge the dust. Already he was starting to question the wisdom of his being here. Not that he had had any say in his being here. That had been all his father's doing. His father. He fumed and, like a petulant child, kicked the dusty ground before realising that the action was not helping him keep his shoes shiny.

He was here, and it was only for three months. Three months of purgatory. He sighed. Out here there was nothing he could do about the predicament, so he supposed he would be a man and with a stiff upper lip he would endure it. He grimaced, hefted his shoulder bag further up onto his shoulder and dragged his suitcase behind him, getting ever closer to the child on the gate, and the next three months of his life.

Fat lot of help wheels were in this dust. He mentally swore to himself. If he had known rebellion was going to be like this – isolated, dry and dusty – he would not have 'taken up with the riffraff of society' and 'gone off the rails' as his father had raged when he'd stood up to his father and told him that he didn't want to go into the family business. At the same time, he knew that there was no way that he was going to be doing anything other than following his father into the business. Any dreams that he might have had of making his own way in a world of his own choosing had never had the chance to be more than that, dreams.

"There has always been a Chinthurst heading this firm, and there always will be." His father had been more than emphatic. Dictatorial. Like his father before him. There never had been, nor ever would be, any question of debate, discussion or decamping. Monty had tried, and look where that had got him. Everything was orchestrated by his father.

He supposed he loved his father, as best as one can love a father. He knew no different so never questioned the status quo. It just went with the territory, and one got on with it. Stiff upper lip and all that tosh. Generations of breeding, reinforced with a public-school education and there was no room for contention among the ranks. It was just the way it was done. And Monty knew no different. The migration of liberalism along with feminism and all the other 'isms' of the 20th century by-passed the likes of the Chinthursts and their ilk.

The little bit of rebellion that Monty had tried to implement had landed him here. Miles from home, and equally far, or so it seemed, from any semblance of civilization. Well, he would do his penance and return home duly chastened, with his tail between his legs and assume his responsibility.

"Theodora Delany," said the man at his side. Monty stopped in his stride and looked up. "My daughter Teddy. Teddy this here is Charles Chinthurst."

Now that Monty was close up he could see blonde plaits poking out from under the straw hat that was pushed down hard on Teddy's head, that she was a girl. Pale blue eyes pierced through him and he felt that they had found him desperately wanting. There was no way that his tongue could function, and it was not only the heat that was striking him dumb. The stare that this young girl generated was enough to strike any man silent. He tried to read the message that the eyes contained. Arrogance? Defiance? Resentment? There might even have been a bit of curiosity, but he couldn't be sure.

Ralph Delany reached over the gate, released the latch and swung it open, his arm across Teddy, and holding the gate open for Monty to pass.

"That's a stupid name. A stupid name for a stupid person."

"Now Teddy," said her father. "That's not a nice thing to say to your tutor."

"Well, it's the truth. Charles whatever-he's-called-hurst. Who's called "Charles" these days? Other than the Prince. And he," she said, waggling her finger at Charle.

"Doesn't look like Prince Charles at all. His ears don't stick out for one thing."

Ralph stifled a laugh by turning it into a sigh. It was long past time that someone of substance took this child into hand and cultivated her. Since his wife had died when Teddy had been but a toddler she'd been the only white female for miles. She'd be off to boarding school soon enough and she needed to know some decorum before then. He stole a look at Monty and wondered if he had done the right thing by engaging a male tutor for his daughter, rather than a female.

But a female, he theorised, would have created more problems than the effort would have been worth. Unless of course the female was a decrepit old hag. That would have solved the potential problem with the station hands, but not with the training of Teddy.

No. Much better this way. A young man with breeding behind him. An inbuilt knowledge of social graces that came naturally, rather than the pretentiousness of local society, or even society from further afield.

"His name is Charles, and you will be calling him Mr Chinthurst, my young lady."

Teddy dropped down off the gate and walked over to Monty who by now had dropped his shoulder bag onto the concrete path that bisected the only patch of green that he had seen since leaving the city. She stood in front of him, hands on her hips and, looking up from beneath the brim of her hat, stared him in the eyes.

"No I'm not. His name is Charlie Hirst and that is what I am going to call him. Ain't that right, Charlie? Come on, I'll show you your room." *With that she slipped her hand into his and pulled.*

Monty, taken aback, turned to see Ralph once more covering his mouth with his hand to hold back a laugh, while shaking his head.

"You'd better do as she says, my boy. No peace otherwise. I'll see you shortly in the office. Teddy," *he called after the retreating pair,* "you mind now, the office, as soon as you have shown Mr Chinthurst his room."

And so Monty became Charlie and entered employment on "Calinda" as a tutor to Teddy. He really had had no conception of what it was that he was embarking on back in England. All he knew was that he had been told by his father that if he was to take his place in the family firm, then he jolly well needed to buck up and mend his ways; and that he thought the best way was for Monty to see the world a bit. And that this transformation was going to take place on the outback station of an acquaintance of an old friend who was owed a favour.

FIVE

The first morning Charlie dressed carefully, as was his wont, in his grey slacks and a clean light blue shirt. His hand hesitated over whether to wear a cravat or a tie, and then decided that he needed to initiate a segue into station life and leave his collar open. Even if it did make him feel naked.

After the reception this attire received from all and sundry, it did not take Charlie long to mend his ways and relegate what he considered to be his informal clothes to the bottom of his suitcase and acquaint himself with the station store, kitting himself out with less conspicuous moleskins and cotton open-necked shirts. Jeans and tee-shirts were really taking casualness too far.

Charlie's life had been one of privilege, but with his family no longer having need of live-in servants, he was not used to being waited on or having his bed made and room cleaned. That made him feel decidedly uncomfortable. And despite having been there for a week, he still wasn't used to the customs of the place. The predawn chorus of unfamiliar bird song, if one could call the raucous cacophony 'song' was followed by a general melee of sound from the kitchen in the house, and the various buildings and yards which surrounded the immediate area as the variety of inhabitants roused themselves ready for the day's work ahead.

His days started, as did everyone else's, with a cooked breakfast, served in the dining room of the 'homestead', not the 'main house' or even the 'house'. He still felt himself colour as he remembered the ribbing Teddy had given him over that gaff. There was an entire new language to be learnt. And he had thought that Australians spoke the Queen's English like he did. Not only was the accent one that he had not encountered before, but the words were all wrong too. And, he was learning that the language Teddy used was not always the same as that

23

used by her father, or that he heard wafting across from the station hand's quarters.

Station hand. That was another new term that had brought Teddy to what he was starting to call her 'rolling on the floor' stance. She would put her hands on her hips and roll her eyes in total and abject horror at his ignorance. "P-leease! Charlie, really!" Then she would release her hips and bend over double and let fly with such a belly-laugh that it would be all he could do to not join in. But instead he would stare at her reproachfully and hope that his embarrassment did not manifest itself in too deep a hue to his face.

After breakfast it was time for the day to start in earnest. While Ralph went into his office to give the overseer the day's instructions, Charlie and Teddy would retire to the schoolroom for the morning. In Ralph's youth the schoolroom had been furnished with a pedal radio and not much else. Now it had been decked out with a computer, printer, comfortable chairs and tables, not to forget the comfort of an air conditioner. Really, all that Charlie had to do was supervise Teddy, ensuring that she kept on task. Which she did readily. Though the thought had crossed his mind that the diligence with which Teddy pursued her scholastic endeavours was simply part of a ploy to get out of the classroom as soon as possible, and back out into the world in which she was most at ease, and where she wanted to be.

A routine had quickly settled, and to his surprise Teddy had not been the handful that first impressions had been unkind enough to generate. She was a pleasant child and one that was motivated in her structured lessons and eager to acquaint herself with the niceties that society would expect of her once she left the relative isolation of home. Outside of the classroom it was a different scenario.

Not that Charlie blamed her. While the room was comfortable, the outside provided far more stimulation and excitement than any computer game could ever offer. He himself wasn't one of the generation that had grown up with X-boxes, Playstations and video games, so *naturally his interests lay not with an LCD screen and joysticks, but with what was on offer in outdoor pursuits, his 'Three Rs' had been rugger, rowing and riding.*

For Teddy, when the outdoors called she saw excitement, adventure, and danger. Every day there was something new happening on the station, be it at the homestead, or further afield. Movement of stock, comings and goings of people, the unplanned accidents to humans, stock and wildlife alike. Then there were always the domestic animals – the horses, the working dogs, the chooks, the cat, and the fluctuating population of orphaned and injured wildlife.

The first shared outdoor activity, which Charlie had designated as a sports period, was horse-riding. Being seated in the saddle was something that Charlie was comfortable with. And he liked the idea of being able to show off his expertise. Something that had been sadly lacking in his endeavours to acclimatise himself into station life. He felt quite elated at the prospect, and he wondered what sort of bloodstock the station had to offer. He had seen the work horses – sturdy and stocky Quarter Horses – and he could see that they would be most suitable for the close stockwork that the station demanded, but he didn't fancy riding one himself. He was used to the finesse of the thoroughbred.

Charlie walked from the classroom back to his room to change, and thought of Nero, the black stallion he had left in the stables back home. Now there was a horse. Would his horse here be its equal? He doubted it but looked forward to meeting his mount all the same.

Kitted out in his riding gear, Charlie confidently walked across to the stables to meet Teddy. Halfway across the yard he saw Teddy assuming her 'Roll on the floor' stance. He stopped mid-stride and wondered what had brought it on this time. Bringing his feet together he looked down and frowned at the coating of red dust that had settled on his knee-high riding boots. This cursed place and its dust, he thought. But that alone, surely, had not brought on The Stance. He sighed. Well, better get on with it.

Teddy watched from her pozzie on a stack of hay bales just inside the stable doors as Charlie marched across the yard. She could not believe her eyes. He was going to go riding, in that? Who dressed like that to go riding? Here? She might be a country kid, but even she knew the difference between riding on the station and riding at Badminton. And here was no Badminton, but someone had obviously not told Charlie that fact. She jumped down from the bales and stood in the doorway. Peering out she put her hands on her hips and burst out laughing.

"Hey Charlie! Did you take a wrong turn somewhere?"

Honestly, Charlie was so stupid at times, Teddy thought as he stopped in his tracks and looked down at his feet. And her father thought that she needed a tutor. Charlie was supposed to be the adult, teaching her, but here he was, once again, having to have her tell him what to do. "Didn't anyone tell ya? This is Calinda, *not Badminton."*

Teddy burst out laughing.

Charlie still had no idea what faux pas he'd committed this time. He was wearing his riding outfit and they were going riding, weren't they? He looked down at his camel breeches with knee patches, tucked cleanly into his black, equestrian boots. He settled his helmet on his head and tucked his crop under one arm to facilitate putting on his riding gloves. Maybe the gloves were a bit of an overkill, but no self-respecting rider would dare venture out not properly attired, though he had relinquished his show jacket to the wardrobe as a concession to the ambient temperature.

Then he looked back at Teddy. The only compromise she had made to them going riding was to pull on a pair of weathered elastic-sided boots. Other than that, she was still wearing her 'uniform' of faded denim jeans, checked shirt and straw hat. Maybe her riding hat and crop were inside. He unconsciously tapped his riding crop against the side of his boots in agitation and resumed walking towards the stable.

"What do you call all that clobber then?" Teddy asked as she came forward to meet him and escort him into the stable.

"This? This is what I go riding in. Don't you have riding gear to wear?"

"All I need special is these boots, so that my feet don't slip through the stirrup. See," Teddy lifted her right foot behind her and twisted round to show Charlie. "This here heel stops my foot slipping through so I don't get caught up and dragged head under the horse's arse." She dropped her foot and skipped down the walkway between the stalls.

Cautiously, because of the dimness in the stables that he had not entered until now, Charlie followed. The stables were surprisingly small for the size of the station and the number of horses that he had seen in the yards, with only four stalls. At the entrance there was an open space for the tack, and access by a wooden ladder to the overhead loft. The loft did not extend fully across the building, rather it was in two parts either end of the stables, leaving the stalls open to the roof some considerable height above. At the far end doors opened out to the yard beyond. Everything appeared to be immaculately clean and tidy.

A welcoming whinny, followed shortly by another, came from the further stalls. Charlie peered through the dimness to the end of the stables.

"Come on!" Teddy skipped back to his side. "Grab your gear and let's go."

She went over to the wall and hitched down one of several bridles that hung there and handed it to Charlie before taking down another one. Then hefting a saddle from off another wall she started down the open space towards the whinnying.

Charlie followed suit with a saddle and trailed Teddy, wondering what his mount would be like.

"Here she is! You can ride her." Teddy had stopped outside a stall with a dapple roan horse. She then went to the opposite stall, released her hold on the bridle by tossing it across the stall door and did the same with the saddle before returning to Charlie and his mount. "Her name is Rosie." She scratched Rosie's muzzle "She's quiet and can be trusted.

Aren't you girl?" Teddy asked as she planted a kiss on the roan blaze that ran jaggedly down the horse's nose.

SIX

It was on a typically damp London evening that Monty and Melanie found themselves standing outside an unimpressive doorway down a lane in the vicinity of Carnaby St.

"This can't be right Monty." Melanie clung possessively to Monty's arm as she looked disdainfully at the entrance before them. It was narrow, dark and uninviting.

Monty gave a quiet chuckle and squeezed Melanie's arm against his side. "It's the right address and then there is that sandwich board there." He pointed to an amateurish cardboard sign leaning against the wall beside the doorway proclaiming the venue to be that of an opening art exhibition.

Melanie gave a sniff. "Not very impressive, is it? Not after the embossed invitation. You do have the invitation, don't you?" She pulled away to look up at him, anxiety etched across her face. She was starting to think that she might have miscalculated the calibre of the event. What if she was overdressed? On the strength of the invitation, she had splurged on a spending spree hoping to dazzle Monty and anyone else who might be present. She had fallen in love with the emerald green velvet dress as soon as she had seen it. The possible incongruency of it being floor length, sleeveless and with a plunging almost to the waist neckline and in velvet didn't enter her head. But now she was beginning to doubt her choice.

"Come on," he answered, catching her hand in his and pulling her towards the opening. "It can't be all that bad once we are inside."

Monty led the way down a narrow corridor, the eerie echo of their footsteps and the ethereal fairy lights that were strung along the wall at ceiling height gave Monty had a faint feeling of déjà vu, but he could not place it immediately, although as they progressed he had flashes of recollections of glow worms on a mild night. He shook his head, not sure that he wanted such memories invading his thoughts.

Tonight, he felt, was going to be a big enough experience without flashbacks to haunt him.

The muted babble of distant voices wafted towards them as they walked further along the corridor and a faint beam of light could be seen shining around a bend, and Monty increased his pace. Melanie reluctantly following him, wondered what the other women would be wearing.

When they turned the corner they were greeted by a cacophony of voices and a pool of brilliant light spilling out from the foyer of the gallery. Melanie let out a breath that she hadn't been aware she was holding, and felt herself relax. She leant into Monty and squeezed his hand. "I think we have found the place," she whispered in his ear. "Will you look at all these people? I doubt that we will know any of them. It's not as though you move in the arty circles, I wonder who they all are?"

Then, before he knew anything Monty was being pulled into the room by Melanie. He was surprised to see her exuberance. He smiled and looked around. They were standing in the small foyer, with no artwork to be seen, anywhere, except for a small commercial display set up just inside the door—advertising, brochures, postcards and art inspired nick-nacks for purchase by those whose pockets were not sufficiently deep for the originals. Positioned discretely beside the display unit stood an attractive young woman dressed in a smart business suit and holding a leather folder close to her chest. She smiled at him.

"This is a private function sir, do you have an invitation?"

Monty reached into his inside jacket pocket and produced the requested embossed card.

The woman took the card, looked at it and then at Monty. "Mr Hirst?"

Monty inclined his head, grateful that Melanie, busily occupied observing the other guests to be seen mingling in an anteroom, had not heard. Explanations were not what he wanted. Not tonight, and hopefully not ever. It was just typical of Teddy. In his head he saw the mirth with which Teddy would have penned her name for him on the invitation, and he felt a prickle course through him. He turned to watch as Melanie sashayed towards the adjacent anteroom. Anyone would have thought she was the host and this was all for her benefit. And at the same time, he wondered where the real host was.

The door attendant ran her finger down the list of guests in her folder, found Monty's name and put a small tick beside it before handing the invitation back.

"Thank you, Mr Hirst." The attendant's voice drew Monty's attention back. "And welcome to this evening's event. I am sure you will be much inspired by Ms Delany's talent, as we all are. Please, help yourself to refreshments," she indicated the anteroom. "And take a stroll around the gallery. The formal opening will be taking place shortly, in the further most room."

Teddy, standing beyond the anteroom, was watching. It was almost dé·jà vu seeing Charlie walk in, clean cut, dressed to impress and with the curls that he had left Australia with, which used to hug his collar, replaced by the same regimental haircut that he had arrived with. Then again, she smiled, what did she expect, her pigtails had also departed fifteen years ago.

Monty thanked the attendant and stepped across the foyer and entered the anteroom. The room was smaller than he had imagined for an art gallery would be, but then again, the small circles of guests scattered about did nothing to increase the apparent dimensions. The walls were a stark cream and the bright lighting came from a myriad of downlights set in the ceiling. Demure, black-uniformed waiters stood sentinel at a couple of damask clothed tables covered with canapes and punchbowls while two waitresses circulated with silver trays of fluted glasses.

He looked around for Melanie and saw that she was at the table. He smiled and his heart swelled. So far, of the women present that he had seen, she was most definitely one of the more attractive. He went to join her but felt someone touch his arm. He turned to see who it was and stopped. He blanched, swallowed and took a step back.

"Char ..."

Monty grabbed Teddy's outstretched hand in both of his and looked over his shoulder for Melanie, but she was not concerned by his absence. "Actually it's Monty now."

"Monty? Oh my God, you have to be kidding me. Right?" Teddy released her hands from Monty's grasp and brought them to her mouth to smother a laugh. "Monty? As in Montgomery? Wherever did *that* come from?"

He grinned sheepishly and nodded his head. "It's what all my friends call me."

"Oh my goodness! What? No Charles? Not even a Charlie?" She stepped back and stifled another laugh behind her hands which she had once more clasped over her mouth. The attempt to hide her amusement was not effective. She lowered her hands, raised one finger to her chin, placed the other hand placed cynically on her hip, stepped back on one heel in a classic comic pose reminiscent of 'The Stance' and looked him up and down.

"Charles is my father."

"I guess that would be about right, no room for a Charlie among the British Upper Crust, hey?"

She took in his appearance. Casual yet almost Saville Row, if such a thing still existed. Broad shoulders filled the smoky grey jacket that he wore over a dark blue vest and pin-striped paler blue shirt. Dark blue trousers, caught at the waist with a conservative belt, fell to the tops of his black loafers. A man comfortable within himself and able carry it with total aplomb.

She smiled to herself, thinking how similar his attire was to what he wore when he first arrived at Calinda – grey and blue. Yet, here he was. She let her eyes appraise him, stunned to see that there was not even the skerrick of a vestige of the contrite larrikin that had left without a goodbye. Instead, the man standing in front of her was a mature version of the stuffed shirt she had met and ridiculed all those years ago. And she wondered briefly why that should surprise her. Her lips broke into a smile. "Monty hey. Yes, I can see how that works!" Teddy took hold of Monty's hand and pulled him away from the crowd in the anteroom and towards the doorway that led to the gallery rooms beyond.

Teddy's controlled mirth was transmitted to Monty who grinned back. "Yeah, that's about right," he said, unconsciously falling back into the manner of speech he had not used since leaving Australia.

The fact was that once he had returned to England, the stuffing had been shoved back in so tightly that any semblance of Charlie had been totally dissipated without any trace. And Monty had liked it that way. Till now.

Now, standing beside Teddy in a small room, surrounded by the display of her artwork, all of which seemed to depict some aspect of her homeland, he suddenly felt as alien back here in England as he had all those years ago when he had first met Teddy at the homestead gate of *Calinda*. And that memory was not sitting comfortably at all.

Monty was saved from his memories as he saw Melanie coming towards them. He leaned close to Teddy, smelling the freshness of newly washed hair unadulterated by products. "Please, no Charlie here." He looked towards Melanie and Teddy followed his gaze. "Gotcha Ch... Monty. Sorry, that just sounds so foreign!" She laughed, then quickly composed herself as Melanie caught up to them.

"Monty, you'll never guess who I've been talking to."

Monty reached across and slipped his hand under her elbow, drawing her closer, in an attempt to move her to his side so that he could introduce her to their host.

"Mel ..."

Melanie turned back to where she had come from and waved to a circle of people, glasses in their hands, in animated conversation that gave every indication of irrelevance to the surroundings. "See? You must come and join them."

"Mel, I'll come, but first ..."

"Oh do come on Monty, you must join them. It will be great PR for the firm if you are spotted with them by the cameras. Come on." She paused and acknowledged Teddy's presence, taking in her outfit and inwardly congratulated herself on her own attire. What the woman in front of her wore was hardly *haut couture*, not even last season's. Dressed like that the woman could only be the talent behind the art they had come to view. Melanie took another look and supposed if that was the case, that being an artist precluded her from being endowed with fashion sense, though she did have to grudgingly admit that the lavender calf-length dress was rather becoming and suited her dusky blonde hair. Still, it was nothing compared to her own fashion statement which, thankfully, fitted in with the other female guests.

Teddy could sense, and was amused by, the other woman's mental pigeonholing and knew that she was being brushed aside as easily and effortlessly as an unwanted piece of lint.

"But Mel, this is ..."

"Oh do come on Monty, you don't want to miss this opportunity. Do you?"

Monty pulled Melanie tighter to him. "We are here for the opening of an art exhibition, it is not a business convention for meeting and greeting, Mel."

"If this is the opening, then the art will be here for a while, this might well be the only opportunity to meet and mingle socially. Look at those who are here, this is an important opportunity for you. You don't want to miss it."

Monty looked at Teddy, unsure what to say or do. Whatever he said was going to offend one or the other of the women. And he didn't want to do that. He had to work with Melanie, and they were just embarking on what could be a wonderful future. Teddy on the other hand ... Teddy. What was Teddy? She was simply a part of his past that he wanted to forget. No, she was *the* reason why he wanted to forget that episode of his past. Simple. But here she was, and here he was, because she had extended an invitation to him. At the very least he owed it to her to be congenial and supportive. Curiosity also played a part, he had to admit. Why had she invited him? Even if others were here to see and be seen. And he wondered how it was that they had received invitations if they were not here primarily for the artwork.

Teddy returned his gaze, but it gave nothing away. He turned to Melanie. He knew what her expression was saying. The smouldering look she returned was not the 'come with me if you know what is good for you' invitation full of promise that he so loved, but more a threat that if he didn't follow her, then there was no promising what she would or wouldn't do in revenge. His life had always been one of doing what he had been told, or suffer the consequences to his detriment. Teddy was testament to that. He looked again at Teddy and shrugged his shoulders.

Teddy had not had the opportunity to ask Charlie the status of who had come with him, but even so she could feel the return of the unwanted sympathy that she'd experienced whenever Charlie was caught out in yet another down-under *faux pas*. Back then, when she was still a child she had quashed that sentiment under a barrage of sarcasm and derisive laughter. She wasn't about to do that now.

She stepped forward, thrust out her hand and announced herself. "I'm Theodora Delany. I am so pleased that you and," she looked briefly at Monty, "and Monty could come tonight."

Melanie mechanically shook Teddy's hand limply and let go. "You'll excuse us, won't you?" Melanie said as she slipped her hand around Monty's arm. Her smile was syrupy saccharine as she led Monty away.

Monty looked back over his shoulder and gave a cursory shrug as he let himself be led to the group that Melanie had just left.

"Melanie," Monty's whisper was almost a hiss. "Wasn't that a bit rude? That woman is the artist. It is her work that we have come to see."

Melanie tossed her head. "Then, like I said, she and her work will be here, while this might be your only chance to meet those to whom I want to introduce. And I would be very upset for you to miss out on this networking opportunity. From the little I have seen of her work they will not be waiting around for long. The artwork is nothing to get excited about." She linked her arm through his and looked up at him with eyes that he could not resist.

Teddy smiled to herself. If Charlie's partner, surely not his wife, thought that she, or Charlie, could impress the group of businessmen and their wives she could see through in the anteroom who were standing nearest to what she considered to be her best piece, then the woman would be surprisingly disappointed.

They were a mixed bag of people, from different walks of life, but they all had one thing in common. They had all, at one time or another, visited or lived in Australia. And they all had an appreciation for Teddy's work, and a love for life that matched her own. They were all successful in their own field, but they were not "big players" to the impairment of living. They were not your run-of-the-mill stuffed shirts that it was obvious Charlie had returned to being, and that his partner was apparently used to.

Teddy smiled again in their direction, and uncharacteristically wondered if the woman was a blonde under the dyed hair, before turning to meet some of her newly arrived guests.

SEVEN

"Monty," said Mel, clinging to his arm as though it were an extension of her body, "I'd like you to meet James Romano-Woodfield, and this is his wife Penelope. James, Penelope, this is Monty Chinthurst the third."

Melanie was grinning so hard that Monty was surprised that her body was able to hold up to such sycophancy. He had heard the name Romano-Woodfield, but could not place its importance. Certainly not what significance it held for Mel, but he shook hands all the same. A flurry of further introductions followed as the other members of the group were singled out, but Monty had already mentally retreated from the people around him. His eyes were riveted on the painting that was hung on the wall behind James and Penelope. He had not seen it in the anteroom before as it had been obscured by people. But he could see it now.

It was a large, unframed canvas. "Drafting at Calinda. Oil on canvas" the label read. The painting was a swirl of reds with no visible delineation between land and sky. The only relief from red were the scattered splotches of black that Monty knew would be representing the bovine heads caught in the melee of dust being kicked up by their hooves, and those of the horses being ridden by the stockmen as they endeavoured to control the herd. For Monty, looking at the sea of red, he did not need the label to know what it was. He'd have known it anywhere.

"Come on Charlie! Why do you always have to be such a slowpoke?" Teddy was jumping up and down a few feet away from him. First running towards the cacophony that was coming from the yards beyond the outbuildings, then stopping and running back to him. "Come ON!"

This time she stamped her foot on the ground, sending a pouffe of red dust up and over her bare feet. "If we don't hurry it'll be all over before we get there. P-leease Charlie, can't you <u>run</u>?"

Charlie carefully looked around to make sure no one was watching, then let the pestering girl grab his hand and pull him away from the schoolroom. There was no mistaking their destination. There was only one venue worthy of attention today, and it certainly wasn't the schoolroom.

With Teddy skipping beside him he was forced into a fast walk that almost verged on a run, and they headed towards the action. Even though Ralph, and Teddy, had told him that the stockmen would be drafting today, Charlie had no idea what to expect.

Dust was rising into the sky, obliterating just about everything else, including the sun that he was used to blazing down unremittingly from a bright blue and unblemished sky. He could feel its heat searing into his shoulders and through his shirt to his skin below, and he was glad that he had remembered his Akubra and pushed it more firmly onto his head.

The bellow of the cows and the higher timbred call of their calves fought for space in the airways with the cracking of the stockmen's whips, their yells and whistles to the barking dogs nipping at the cattle's heels and the creak of leather as the men rode their horses hard.

They stood, the two of them, Teddy and Charlie, leaning against the sturdy wooden palings of the stockyards as the lithe men, their stockwhips lashing the air, and limber horses herded the cattle into the yard. Charlie carefully folded his arms along the top rail of the old and weather-beaten timber. It was warm from the sun and rough to the touch, and he hoped that it would hold up against the weight of the cows now being herded should any of them baulk at the action.

"Ya know, this is a lot different to a campdraft." Teddy said knowledgeably.

Charlie looked down at Teddy, wondering if he was brave enough to show ignorance and ask what a campdraft was or how it differed from the drafting mentioned over breakfast. And that had left him perplexed. The only drafting he was familiar with was the drafting of essays, and that seemed a long way from what he saw happening in front of him at the moment, which was nothing short of pandemonium.

"Wait till we go to a rodeo, then you will see some action. But not like this. This is dinkie-die drafting. It's got real purpose. Not like the fun stunt stuff you see in a campdraft where every second counts towards a prize. And everyone is out to impress."

He was glad that he had held his peace, not that he was one hundred percent sure that he was any wiser, but at least he had saved himself some embarrassment.

Teddy could see from Charlie's face that he was once more out of his depth and she dropped her head down against the wooden rail of the fence and quietly laughed. Charlie really was a drongo at times. Didn't they teach anything in England?

"Campdrafting, Charlie is when a stockman rides into a small yard – that's the camp – and chooses a beast from a small mob of cattle. He then has to move the animal towards a gate kept secured by a couple of other men. After the stockman shows how good he is at controlling his chosen animal and stopping it from returning to the rest of the mob, he calls out to the men at the gate and they open it and the stockman herds the beast into a larger enclosure where they do some more fancy stuff. What is being done here is just simply separating the cows from their calves."

Charlie didn't dare ask why. He simply smiled down at Teddy then turned his attention to what was happening in the yard in front of him. What had, to his untrained eyes, initially seemed like a chaotic jumble of animals was gradually being transformed into a structured pattern. The stockmen, with deft precision were guiding the cows from the yard in front of him to an opening on the other side where, with the aid of a swivel gate, another stockman separated the cows into one yard and the calves into an adjacent one.

Proud of her explanation, Teddy looked up at Charlie with a smile on her face, and saw that he was not satisfied. She let out an audible sigh and continued. "The different stations all have their own way of sorting out their calves. We separate them here today so that the calves can then be drafted or sorted into bulls, which will be sold for meat and heifers which will then be branded. That used to be done by jamming a hot branding iron high up onto the animal's hind leg, but nowadays it's just earmarking – that's when you snap a plastic clip onto their ear."

Monty continued to look at the painting with its aggressive brushstrokes and he could almost smell the dust and feel the heat as the memories of the frenetic excitement of the day flooded back, surprising him with emotion.

Monty also remembered lying in the comfort of his bed that night and hearing the plaintive cries of the cows and calves as they ceaselessly called out to each other. No matter what he had done to block the mournful noise – fingers in his ears, head under the pillow – he had not been able to sleep. He hadn't known which he felt the sorrier for – the cows or the calves. All he knew was that he empathised with the animals, knowing what it felt like to be forcibly separated from all that was familiar.

As the emotions from that night surfaced and swirled, he found his thoughts further transporting him back to his time on Calinda and a part of him thawed, just a bit. He silently moved away a few feet away from the group to immerse himself in the painting.

"Monty?"

He brought his attention back to the present.

"I was just telling James here that it would be a good idea if you and he got together one day. I'm sure that you'd be able to help him." Melanie said.

He glanced again at the painting before responding, "Yes, that sounds like a good idea. Why don't you set it up Mel?"

He put his hand on hers that was clasping his lower arm, lifted it up and extricated himself. He smiled at James and his cronies, "Will you excuse me for a minute?" And with that he moved off to the adjacent room, anxious to see what else Teddy had to offer, wondering if they would induce equally vivid memories. Memories that no doubt would be a kaleidoscope of both pleasure and misery, but hopefully not guilt.

He shuddered, not only because the feelings of guilt had rarely left him since the day that Melanie had handed him the envelope that had brought them here tonight, but also remembering how gauche he had been – pretty much the whole time he was in The Outback. It was a real marvel that Teddy wanted to have anything to do with him now.

"That wasn't very polite." Melanie broke into his reverie as he stood in front of a framed pastel and linked her arm through his again.

"What?" Monty looked down at her hand and wondered what he had done wrong.

"Walking away like that." It was almost a hiss. She was so irritated. She'd been dragged to this art exhibition, and now that she had seen what an opportunity it was to beneficially network, Monty had dismissed her socialising, preferring to peruse the ridiculous splotches and messes of red that adorned the walls.

"What do you mean?"

Melanie stared at Monty, her mouth a goldfish as she tried to control the words of vitriol that were so desperately trying to erupt.

This was neither the time nor the place for her irritation to be let loose.

"Well, what will James think of you?"

Monty, having his attention averted from the pastel in front of him, turned to face Melanie. He was startled and intrigued by the anger that was sparking in her eyes. He took a moment to look for the words which he hoped would extinguish the flames. But the truth was all that he could come up with, so, taking a silent breath, he replied.

"Mel, I'm here to look at these paintings, not to do business."

"You call these paintings? These can't be called paintings. Paintings are masterpieces of art. These are just red paint, or whatever, on canvas. You can't see anything in them, there's no movement, no replication of anything recognisable. Even the people, if that is what they are, are just blobs of nothingness. I mean, look at this one," she said, pointing to the pastel in front of them. "What could you call that? It's nothing. Just a strip of blue above a strip of red. Any child could create that, but it wouldn't be called *art* or thought worthy enough to be hung on a wall and exhibited."

EIGHT

Monty looked back at the medium-sized pastel that Melanie was scathingly gesticulating to. It was, indeed, predominantly blue and red. But being in pastel, it evoked a benign tranquillity which ironically was not how he remembered his introduction to the event that Teddy had so poignantly portrayed here.

"That, my dear Melanie, depicts a Walkabout." He looked at the four figures walking away from the artist. They were, to the uninitiated eye, almost stick-like black blobs of nothingness as Melanie said. But to him they were figures, people. People who had names. People that he knew.

Ralph Delany was in a right mood when Charlie entered the kitchen. He was stomping around the room, banging plates onto the table and rattling in the cutlery drawer for spoons and knives. He swung the fridge door open and started pulling bits and pieces out.

"Good morning, Ralph," Charlie tentatively offered.

"What's good about it?" Ralph muttered and with arms full of bacon, eggs, tomatoes, bread and butter, he backed out of the opening and kicked the door shut. It slammed closed with a juddering thud that set the motor rumbling. "The damn Abos have gone walkabout, again."

Charlie had no idea what Ralph was saying, but he shuddered at what was obviously a locally accepted racial slur. It certainly didn't sit well with him, but decided it wasn't his place to take Ralph to task. Instead he simply asked "Walkabout?"

"Yeah, bloody walkabout! Take a look," he gesticulated in the general direction of the window. "Betty and her mob have taken off. Who knows where to. Or for how long."

Charlie walked over to the window and looked out. It was a clear blue sky and in the distance, he could make out the silhouettes of a group of people.

"No by your leave," Ralph continued ranting, as he went about cooking up breakfast. "There never is. Never any warning. They just up and go, and I don't find out about it till I need them and look around and they aren't here."

Charlie watched as the figures grew so small that he could no longer make them out beyond a smudge on the horizon. Betty and her mob. Presumably by that Ralph meant the homestead cook Betty, hence the shambles breakfast was today, and her family. No doubt that meant that her husband Johnnie would be missing, along with their sons and their wives and their families. That could constitute a fair depletion of the work force.

"Teddy!" Ralph tilted the pan he was holding and let the mess of food spill out onto the plates set out on the table. "Get yourself in here. Breakfast's getting cold."

Teddy. Charlie felt his stomach tighten then flutter as he realised that once again he would have to admit his ignorance and ask her what a Walkabout was, and why it would have put her father in such a foul mood.

"Jeepers Charlie, don't you know anything?" It was becoming a catch phrase, along with the rolling eyes, the hands on hips and belly laugh. "Walkabout is when the Aboriginals just up-stakes and take off. They go 'walkabout'. They leave where they are, and what they are doing and take off bush."

"Why would they do that? Charlie looked over to where the Aboriginal workers lived. So their accommodation was not as modern or commodious as the homestead where he and the Delany's lived, nor the stockmen's quarters, but they wanted for nothing. "They leave all this for what? The bush? What bush?" He raised his hand to shade his eyes and stared out at the emptiness where he had earlier watched Betty

and her family heading. "Where's the bush? I haven't seen any trees, or forest out there. There's nothing!"

"Maybe not to us, but to them there is plenty out there. They will live off the land like they used to do before us white folk came here."

"But why?"

Teddy shrugged her shoulders, bored with the topic. "Who knows? Who cares?" The Aboriginals going walkabout was nothing new to her. All she cared about was that when they went walkabout it was a gross inconvenience to her father, and the running of the station. And it meant that she had to muck in and help around the house. Cook, and clean, and wash, and even make her bed. Not that making her bed entailed much more than straightening the sheets and folding the blanket at the end of the bed.

"I think in the olden days, you know, way back before the white man, like when you were a boy. It might have had something to do with initiation, you know," she looked up at Charlie, almost daring him to react somehow. "When boys become men."

He just nodded his head, as if he understood, everything. "A bit more than a bank holiday trip to Brighton then?"

"What's a bank holiday then?" Teddy looked up at him and stomped the dust off her boots as they walked into the school room for the morning's lessons.

"A-ha! Got you there, haven't I?" Charlie laughed and made an attempt at sashaying his hips. "For once I know something that you don't Miss Teddy."

"Don't call me that!" She sat down at the table and turned the computer on. "And, you haven't answered me."

Charlie, sitting the other side of the table, raised his eyebrows in query, struggling to keep a smile at bay.

"What's a bank holiday?"

"An inconvenient holiday that occurs several times a year. Now get your work out. What is it today?" He turned to look at the board across the room on which a chart was displayed, setting out the daily routine.

Teddy shook her head in exasperation and wondered why he did that. He did it every day. Were all Englishmen that stupid, or was it just him? How long did he need to realise that each day started the same way? Teddy fiddled with the microphone and waited for her classmates and teacher to come online. She looked across to the peddle radio gathering dust in the corner, and wondered, not for the first time, what it must have been like for her father and grandfather when they were young and had to use that for school. Interactive Distant Learning was so much easier.

She looked up at the clock above the board. There was still time. "How can a holiday be inconvenient?"

Charlie wasn't too sure how to answer that one, but was saved when he heard Teddy's teacher welcoming her distant pupils and outlining the Math problem for the day.

Monty smiled as he remembered Betty and her family, and wondered how they were. He looked around to ask Teddy, but she was already moving through the next doorway and into the reception room no doubt in preparation for the official opening.

"I still say that it is nothing but a couple of strips of colour and a few black blotches added in to break the monotony. How anyone can call that art is beyond me." Melanie tossed her head in disgust and noticed that the others present were slowly making their way through the room and on into the next. She linked her arm once more through Monty's and gently pulled him away.

Monty looked back at the pastel. He would have to remember to ask Teddy about everyone back at Calinda, the stockmen, jackaroos, jillaroos, Ralph, Betty and her mob. Fifteen years was a long time.

He didn't expect any of those he had known to still be there. From what he had gathered, most of the workers on the station belonged to a nomadic race, a bit like the indigenous workers, or itinerants like he had been. Did they still go, what was it, walkabout? He shook his head, remembering how different life had been on Calinda, and how easily he had acclimatised to the strangeness of it all. The items in this exhibition of Teddy's was bringing it all back to him, and he found that a part of him was missing the lifestyle.

Melanie, a strained smile on her face for the benefit of those nearby muttered through clenched teeth. "Neither that small example, nor any of the other pieces in this exhibit reflect art." She inclined her head in greeting to another couple that were entering the reception room beside them.

"What *is* art to you Melanie?"

As she had never taken an interest in any of the Arts, she had no idea what Art was to her, and had to think before answering. "Art is masterpieces that reflect their price tags," she said with a toss of her head, hoping that such a response would suffice.

But Monty was not satisfied. He shook his head in dismay. Here he was with the most beautiful woman in the gallery and she had not one jot of appreciation or understanding.

"Art, good art, evokes emotion. It makes you see something, feel something, just by looking at it," Monty said, then wistfully added, "the way that little pastel does."

Would he never let up about the ridiculous examples of childish mish-mash posing as art? Melanie wondered. The tinkling of a spoon against a raised glass saved her from commenting and an exaggerated sigh was all she uttered before a hush enveloped the room as conversations were cut off and all eyes were transferred to the spotlit point at the end of the room.

There stood Teddy. At a distance, Monty could stand back and observe, something that he had not been able to do earlier, when she had so unexpectedly approached him. Gone was the plain, freckled, Outback girl that he remembered with guilt. Here, standing in front of an albeit small crowd of people, was a confident, groomed young woman. Filigreed tendrils of contorted skin laced across her neck and lower face. He was astounded that she was comfortable enough with the evidence of his guilt to display it so openly. If it had been him, he felt sure that shame would have had him hiding it beneath high necked collars or scarves even. But here she was, in public, wearing the scars almost like a "red badge of courage". And he supposed that in fact, it could well be considered that.

She certainly had shown immense courage. Whereas, for him, it had been a moment of intense humiliation, and then guilt. Guilt that had followed him ever since and he had not allowed it to be assuaged, even though he tried to ignore it.

Watching Teddy as she delivered her speech with bright animation, he fell further into the morass of guilt, and marvelled that she had, even now, the courage to face him. Invite him to be here tonight. Was this her way of further rubbing salt? Or was she looking for an apology? If it was the latter then he would willingly ask for forgiveness. Anything to remove the remorse and burden that had festered all these years.

He refocused on Teddy as a muted applause broke into his reverie. She stood beaming at her invited guests. Her eyes scanning the faces in front of her, zeroing in on him only when the spotlight dimmed and the room's lighting returned to normal. The people started to once more mingle and gravitate to the refreshments table or to perusing the paintings.

Monty stood, mesmerised, as Teddy started to walk towards him, but she was waylaid before reaching him. He sighed, knowing that an opportunity would arise before the evening came to a close.

NINE

"Oh look, Monty," Melanie pulled on his arm demanding his attention. "There's Lucinda. I wonder what she is doing here? You remember Lucinda, don't you? Lucinda Peckenham?"

Monty frowned. He had no idea who Lucinda Peckenham was, and quite honestly he really wasn't interested.

"Oh, we must go and speak with her. Come on Monty."

Monty turned to follow Melanie but stopped when he saw another large red and raw canvas. This time there was no swirling dust dominating the painting. Just a swathe of a bright blue cloudless sky arcing above an expanse of barren red, dotted with small slightly darker splotches that resembled mole hills and could only be the rough little rocks and pebbles that were a feature scattered across the dry earth. The silent scene was broken by a smudge of activity below a stark and solitary windmill set slightly off centre. He knew that the smudge represented cattle milling around. He reasoned that no one but he and Teddy would know that in the middle of the smudge there would be a water trough from which the cattle would be thirstily drinking. He raised his hand to his nose as he remembered the smell of slightly brackish water, and how thirst quenching it was on a hot day.

"Go on Charlie, take a drink. It won't bite you. It won't even kill you. Look, see? I've been drinking it for years and I'm not dead yet."

That would be the day, Charlie thought ruefully. He could not imagine a day that could bring harm to Teddy. She was invincible. But he found her claim about the potability of the water to be suspect to say the least. He could smell the minerals in it from where he sat in the ute several feet away. No matter how thirsty he was, he couldn't see himself drinking from that trough.

"Come on, have a drink. Before the cattle get here and muddy it all up. No good then."

She had a point. He looked beyond the long grey, almost black concrete trough that ran out at an angle a short distance from the windmill, to the restless dust cloud he could see approaching. The stockmen would have the cattle here in next to no time. Not that the cattle would need any encouragement, once they caught the scent of the water. He opened the ute door and took a step forward to the trough, placing his feet carefully, trying to avoid getting his highly polished shoes even more dusted with what was obviously pulverised cow pats. Teddy was already there with an enamel pannikin that she had unhitched from a spar on the windmill.

"Here," she said, thrusting the pannikin into the water then handing the dripping white and blue enamel mug to him. Hurry, the cattle will smell the water soon and there'll be no stopping them. Come ON!"

He raised the mug to his lips, grimacing at the odour, but loath to let Teddy see his displeasure, but he couldn't stop himself from spluttering. She dropped over at the waist, gripped her legs and laughed. He felt the irritation that her laughter created in him, rise. She was really, totally, incorrigible. And he let himself be played by her every time.

He took another swig from the mug. Just to show Teddy that he was a man after all, and was surprised by how pleasant the water was, once you got over the metallic flavour. It was cool and refreshing, and he realised that he was thirsty after all. Then again, who wouldn't be thirsty with the sun creating a furnace. He finished the water in the mug and leant over the edge of the trough, the wet concrete rough under his hand, and made to dip the pannikin into the water for a refill. But Teddy grabbed his arm.

"You don't want to do that." She said, dragging him away from the trough and toward the windmill. "Get up there." And with that she let go of him and scampered up the metal framework to perch on a wooden platform about 8 feet above. "Come ON, Charlie!"

He looked up at her, then beyond her. Next thing he was up beside her looking down at a moving sea of cattle. "If you'd stayed down there, that is where you'd have stayed an' we'd be picking up pieces of poor Charlie all night." Teddy laughed again. And this time he had the wisdom to agree with her and smile. The thought of being trampled by the cattle anxious to get to the water was enough to make him pleased to have Teddy with him. Even if she did always manage to make him aware how badly he was wanting.

They had stayed up on the platform while the mob of cattle tussled with each other and circled the water trough and had their fill. Charlie was mesmerised by the seething carpet of red and white hides moving to the music of slurping water, shuffling hooves and beefy sides rubbing together with a backdrop of the creaking leather and metallic jangle of the escorting mounted stockmen. Slowly, with the encouragement of the stockmen the cattle moved away, foraging for feed. Charlie felt a fool, stuck up a windmill with the boss' daughter. But the stockmen didn't seem to notice anything unusual, simply waving a cheery hand and shouting a "gidday" as they allowed their horses and dogs to drink before following the cattle.

"Oh Monty, come on," Melanie gave his arm another tug, and looked anxiously over towards Lucinda. "We must speak with her before she leaves."

"Melanie, we came here to appreciate the artwork, not to socialise." Well, not really. He had come because he wanted to see Teddy again, and what was that other than socialising? The word 'curiosity' nudged its way into his thoughts, and begrudgingly he accepted that curiosity in all truth was a better turn of phrase.

He was curious – to see Teddy. Curious to see her artwork. And curious as to the real intent behind the invitation. The invitation had come with an 'as promised' but he remembered no such promise, and was surprised that she had. But he had certainly not come all this way to be dragged into socialising with people he did not know.

"Really Monty. Sometimes I simply do not understand you," Melanie pulled him away from the painting. "That is nothing but a splodge of paint."

He looked back at the painting. "How can you say it's nothing Mel? That painting has feeling. It has emotion. Can't you feel it?" He looked at her and realised that she did not share his emotion. "Or at least see or sense the movement?"

"All I can see is that unless we circulate and socialise with the guests this will have been a totally wasted visit to London. I honestly cannot see anything in this exhibit and the only emotion is, well claustrophobia – in that I cannot wait till we leave. Lucinda!" Melanie proclaimed as she came up beside the woman so named.

Monty watched the interchange with interest as the two women greeted each other with air-kisses and exclamations of feigned delight. He readily admitted that the 'arty-farty' set really had no place in his circle of friends and was surprised that Melanie, who claimed no interest in the art world, should appear to be as comfortable and at home with, if not the pieces on exhibit, at least the other invitees as she appeared to be this evening. He looked about him again, this time at the others in attendance, and wondered how it was that Teddy knew them enough to invite them to her opening night. That was another thing which he would try to remember to ask.

TEN

Monty was standing in front of another of Teddy's paintings when Melanie came and stood beside him, slipping her arm though his and cozying up to him.

He was perplexed by the irritation that he felt from her displays of possessiveness. Since that first evening at The Willow Tree, they had been on a number of dates, and each time he had relished the ease with which she had claimed him. He couldn't understand why this evening would be so different.

"Now that is more in keeping with what art ought to be. Though compared to Constable it is still rather primitive."

Monty tilted his head to the side. The exhibit that Melanie was talking about was more like a 2D diorama of a day he remembered well transported him back to the moment that had clearly inspired this piece of art. It had been an uphill battle to introduce Teddy to poetry, and the oppressive weather had not helped. Ralph had warned them that morning that it was going to be a nasty day of waiting for the promised rain to come, so Teddy was constantly looking out the window, hoping to see a build-up of grey clouds in the still, blue sky.

"Yes, it is different to the others in the exhibition. This one tells a complete story, leaving nothing for the viewer to think about, other than the actual event."

Melanie looked again at the painting then up at Monty. "You sound as though you know the story."

"You could say that. I look at it and feel as though I am there," he said as he thought how easily it could have been him there, caught in the flash flood, and how grateful he was to Ralph for alerting him to the dangers inherent in frequenting the dry creek beds. How, even with no indication of rain in the immediate extended area, a downpour miles away could present a torrent of water appearing as if out of nowhere and wash away everything in its path.

"Come on now Teddy, your teacher has asked you to write a poem. A poem that has meaning for you. One that reflects the emotions of the moment."

Teddy sat at the desk and looked glumly at Charlie. "Are you for real?"

"Not me, your teacher. Now come on, I know that you can do this."

"I don't like poetry. It's all gobbledygook."

Charlie was inclined to agree. It had never been a favourite pastime for him, and he could never understand the reason for studying it when he was at school, but he was not about to let Teddy know that. Then again, it had been when he was at high school that he'd had to study poetry, Teddy was still in primary school, where learning was meant to be fun. He tried to remember poems that he had liked when he was a young boy. Most of them had a sing-song rhythm as well as a tale to tell. The Highwayman by Alfred Noyes had been a favourite of his. He could still remember the beginning and how the rhythm had inspired him to reenact the poem. And he wondered if it could do the same for Teddy. He'd have to give it a try tomorrow.

The next day he recited the first verse of The Highwayman *to Teddy*

The wind was a torrent of darkness among the gusty trees.
The moon was a ghostly galleon tossed upon cloudy seas.
The road was a ribbon of moonlight over the purple moor,
And the highwayman came riding—Riding—riding—
The highwayman came riding, up to the old inn-door.

As he had hoped, Teddy was captivated.

"There you go then Teddy. Think of some incident that you can write about and then try to copy the style."

Charlie sat back and watched as Teddy slowly slid down in her chair and chewed on the end of the biro. He chuckled as he remembered a time when he'd ended up with a mouth full of ink and wondered if he ought to suggest that she be careful about chewing the biro. Teddy looked up at the interruption and smiled.

"I know what I can write about!"

"Great. Do you want to tell me?"

Teddy laughed. "You might not like it."

"Try me."

"Okay, just remember that you asked."

Charlie solemnly nodded his head, wondering what he was letting himself in for.

"I'm going to write a poem about how I had to get dad to tell you why it is not wise to camp in dry creek beds."

Charlie felt himself start to colour at the memory of once more being a naïve Pom and hoped that his ignorance would not be portrayed too humiliatingly. He took a silent breath and reminded himself that she was just a young girl, and while full of mischief at his expense she was not vindictive. Besides, he hadn't camped in the dry creek bed, he'd only said that it looked like a good place to camp.

"That should be interesting. Now you need to start thinking about how you can make that into a poem. But don't forget that you will need a rhythm as well as rhyming."

Monty was not aware that Teddy had approached until he felt her playfully bump her hip into his free side.

"I can see that you are enjoying that poem," she laughed.

Melanie leant forward and looked across Monty to Teddy. "You mean that painting is a poem?"

Teddy nodded her head. "Well, it is a story, but it came about from a poem that I wrote many years ago." She looked up at Monty.

"It appeared in the annual school magazine, you know. I was very proud, and so was my father."

Monty looked down at her and put his arm across her shoulders and pulled her in to him. "You both deserve to be proud. That was a terrific poem, for a first attempt, and it told the tale very well, as does this painting."

"Oh, for goodness' sake," Melanie muttered the other side of Monty. "It's a painting, that's all. So okay, it's more realistic than the other splotches of masquerading colour. Where's the story?"

"I guess you need to know the poem to fully understand the story," Monty said.

"And I suppose you know the poem then?"

Monty removed his arm from across Teddy's shoulders, and pointed to the painting in front of them. The predominant colour was red, darker as the eye moved from left to right, then fading back to lighter on the right. To the left a mangy dog, one front paw held up, looked out from the canvas in the middle of a desolated street.

> "The air hung heavy over the little town;
> There was sand and sky for miles around.
> Nothing stirred in the oppressive heat,
> But one dog limping on three tired feet."

Teddy smiled. Pleased to realise that he did remember. She then took hold of Monty's hand and moved it slightly to the right where, beyond the dog and street there was a man on a horse droving some cattle. She took a breath and quietly recited.

> "Out in the desert red, dry and bare;
> The stockman rode in the sun's glare
> With dog and bullocks he rode his horse
> Along the red dry river course."

Monty let her move his finger further to the right where the atmosphere was darkening. He started to whistle as Teddy continued with the poem.

> "The stockman whistled little tunes
> As they crossed sand and dunes
> Back in town no one was aware
> Of what this stockman would have to bear.
>
> "The riverbed was red and dried;
> Suddenly a bullock cried.
> The stockman cursed, and turning around
> Saw a wall of water roaring down."

Even Melanie could see the wall of water in the centre of the painting. A jumble of branches, animals and streaks of red. She shivered with emotion, hoping that Monty would respond and comfort her as he had Teddy.

But Monty was marvelling at how Teddy had managed to capture the frenzy of the cattle and the stockman as they battled the unexpected elements, and remembering the graphic description Ralph had shared with him of personal experiences of flash floods and how the unwary were easily caught. He had understood that it was a gentle rebuke directed at him, and had been suitably chastened and not gone near the creek, alone, again. Quietly he recited the next verses from memory filled with imagery.

> "He spurred on his horse towards the head:
> 'Those bullocks must leave that riverbed.'
> A wall of water was closing in,
> The terror was soon to begin.
>
> "The bullocks stumbled in their haste;

The stockman was quick in the chase.
Already the water had caught a few,
Soon it would catch the remainder too.

"Those caught in the wall of debris,
Were juggled around from tree to tree.
The torrent of water with its load
Obeyed no human-made code.

"The wall of debris with its broken trees
Passed by the horse, now on its knees.
The stockman cursed and whipped it up:
'There's work to be done now giddy-up!'

Silence reigned as Monty stopped reciting. While Teddy was marvelling that he could remember the poem so well, he was congratulating himself for having taken, and kept, a copy of it. Hoping that he could distract the women either side of him from asking how he knew the poem, he took a step forward and pointed to the next section of the painting.

The dark and destructive centre section of the painting slowly faded back to reflect the calmer and quieter ambiance that was to be found at the beginning. The last section showed the stockman and his dog being lauded in the no longer deserted street.

Monty turned back and looked at Teddy. She gave a small nod and took up the next stanzas:

"He could not save those that were caught;
Those with which the water fought.
Where once there was a dry riverbed
Now there ran a deep river red.

"The stockman surveyed what was left;

His stock had been in half, cleft.
He knew at once that he was beat
And turned around with dragging feet.

"The sky was blue above his head;
What was it his mate had once said?
"Try as you might you never win
That's why I left and won't come ag'in."

"It was a sad party that entered the town;
The stockman's head and the dog's tail were down.
Never before had he had such luck,
When things had run, like that, amok.

"The little town, now alive
Was very glad he had survived
All the people came out to greet,
(Even the dog, now on four feet)
The stockman who'd braved defeat."

Melanie did not know what to make of either the painting, or the poem. But of greater concern was the realisation that for Monty to know the poem there had to be a history between this woman, and her Monty. Their camaraderie was blatantly obvious when you knew to look for it.

She took a step back to observe them better and to try and assemble her thoughts into some sort of order. She was missing something.

If Monty and this artist woman knew each other well enough for Monty to know the poem, then why had he not been invited to the opening when Charlie Hirst, the man that no one even mentioned, had been? She tried to remember what Monty had actually said about the invitation. It had been while they were at The Willow Tree had come up in conversation, along with the envelope addressed to Charlie Hirst. She frowned in concentration. Monty had not exactly admitted that he had opened the envelope addressed to this Mr Hirst, only that he had an invitation. What was Monty playing at?

Her thoughts were jumbling like the lotto balls before they settled and she was convinced that Charlie Hirst was at the heart of the conundrum. She really would have to get Monty to divulge what he knew about the man. Was he dead? Was he the person that Monty's wife had run off with? How was he connected to this woman standing on the other side of Monty? Who had she invited to this exhibit? Why were she and Monty here?

The two, Monty and ... Melanie tried to remember what the woman's name was – something old fashioned and almost masculine, but the woman standing so close to her Monty that their arms looked almost melded together was nowhere near anything masculine. Melanie felt her stomach pitch and clunk and she wilfully quashed the embryonic tendrils of jealousy. There-Was-Nothing to be jealous of. This woman was not a threat. How could she be? Her dress sense was most definitely wanting and even without all that horrid scarring she had no redeeming features. And as for her voice! Nothing cultured ever came out of a colonial antipodean mouth. But still ...

She looked around to see who else was in attendance that she could curry favour with and drag Monty to meet.

ELEVEN

"Monty, come with me." Melanie grasped his arm and yanked him away from Teddy and the painting. "I really need to say hello to the Manninghams."

Monty looked across the room to where a well-dressed couple were standing in front of another mass of reds, and cringed.

"Fiona darling," Melanie gushed as she stood at the woman's elbow. "Fancy seeing you here. Hello George." The latter greeting was more in passing as she leant across Fiona to smile at her companion. "I didn't know that you took an interest in modern primitive art. Do you know Monty Chinthurst?" she asked as she pulled Monty to face the couple.

"Chinthurst?" George stepped forward and faced Monty. "Is that you Monty? Haven't seen you since ..."

Monty coughed and stuck his hand out towards George, hoping to cut him off before he revealed anything which could be mortifyingly embarrassing. "Yes, it's been a while. What are you up to these days?" He hadn't seen George since his exile. He disentangled himself from Melanie and took a step back to meet George separate from the women who were busy going through the customary air-kissing ritual.

"Oh, you know, a bit of this and a bit of that. Mostly following the old man into business, and the usual family stuff." George indicated the woman busy chatting with Melanie. "Been hitched for, oh, seems like forever, and a couple of kids thrown in." He laughed and nodded towards Melanie, "And you? You got a looker there," he said as he thumped Monty on the shoulder.

Monty looked at Melanie and smiled. Yes, she was a looker, but he was beginning to wonder if that was all she was. A looker.

"Yes. No, Mel's just my PA." He stopped and blinked. Why had he said that she was 'just'? He glanced around the room seeking out

Teddy, but she was no longer there, and he wondered where she had gone. This gallery was a veritable maze, with all the rooms. No doubt he would see her again, certainly before they left the exhibition.

"What do you make of the art here tonight?" George asked, but not waiting for an answer, continued. "Quite a good artist at capturing emotion, don't you think? Take this one for instance." He pointed back to the picture he and his wife had been inspecting before they were interrupted. "You could almost imagine yourself being there. But then, I guess you would know all about that, or were you in one of the big cities? The artist, Theodora Delany, you know she's from Australia?" He gave a discrete cough and laughed. "I guess you do, you being here and all. Be a bit of a laugh if you had met her while you were Down Under. Did you? Meet her?"

Monty felt himself prickle at how anyone he met in England assumed that Australia was a place where everyone knew each other. That rankled, until he remembered that he too had been ignorant of how large Australia was, and the vast distances between the built-up areas. But having lived there he felt a certain proprietorial connection with the place and its people. And, for some reason, he did not feel any inclination to enlighten George, and certainly not of how he had, in fact, not only met the artist, but had spent his entire time Down Under in her company. He wondered what George's reaction would be, or in fact how anyone present would react if they knew of his Teddy's connection and history. Somehow he did not think it would go down well. Or then again, it might work conversely, but that would put him in the limelight, and he did not want the evening to turn into an interrogation of his time in Australia. That would not be fair on Teddy, and besides, he was not interested in generating attention. Instead Monty simply smiled at George and nodded his head. Not that George noticed. He was too busy nattering on like a fishwife to allow anyone space to turn the monologue into a viable conversation.

Monty let George's words wash over him and turned his attention to the painting in question. Rather than the usual oils and acrylics on show which displayed one flat image, this picture was vertically bisected, creating a perspective. The left side of the canvas was the expected predominantly red abstract. And Monty could feel himself being drawn back to the day of the camel races. Those not as privileged as himself would only see puffs of dust mingled with dabs of dark grey and the odd slash of colour, suspended like UFOs above the red path. But he could not only see the feet of stampeding camels pock-marking the red dirt, but he could smell the dung, sand, adrenalin ...

It was the right-hand side that made this painting stand out from all the others in the exhibition. It was the only one that deviated from Teddy's usual regulation palette of blue sky, reds and black. Admittedly the bright colours were simply splotches decreasing in size as they marched away from the viewer. But with the parade of colour he could see and hear those who had travelled many miles and hours to attend fill the air with encouraging screams and yells as the camels' jockeys urged their mounts forward.

Monty smiled at the memories.

"Come ON Charlie. Geez, you're as slow as a wet week. Dad's ready and champing at the bit, and so am I."

Her father shook his head, much the same as what Charlie was doing as he stumbled down the steps of the veranda, losing the battle he was having with his boots. Finally he kicked the one in front of him and picked the other up in one hand, and his Akubra in the other, then hobbled towards the ute.

Ralph laughed as Charlie opened the door of the ute, threw his boots in then swung up into the front seat, pushing Teddy against the gear stick and across closer to her father. "Can't see much evidence of your success at making this one into my princess."

Teddy dug her elbow into her father's side then turned and scowled at Charlie. He ignored her, stuck his hat on his head and struggled to tug on his boot while Ralph fumbled to get the handbrake off and the ute into gear.

Charlie was still bent over in the front well of the vehicle when Ralph missed avoiding the pothole that heralded the beginning of the corrugations. He put a restraining arm across Teddy and looked over at Charlie who was muttering and rubbing his head.

"Blast it! Thought Ben had filled that one in. Sorry about the noggin."

Teddy, bouncing up and down more than the corrugations warranted, smirked at Charlie "Seat belt Charlie."

Charlie looked past Teddy to her father who nodded his head. "After you."

"Ain't got one in the middle."

Ralph sighed, then took his left hand off the steering wheel and fiddled around the space between the seats. Charlie did likewise. Then both men held up their side of her seatbelt. "Belt up," both men said in unison, handing her the two ends of the seatbelt.

The hour that it took for them to drive to where the camel races were being held was filled with Teddy's inconsequential chatter which did not provide for adult conversation, nor for any real input on the part of the two men between whom she was sandwiched. Ralph concentrated on his driving which left Charlie ample time to stare out the side window at the seemingly unchanging vista. He was perpetually surprised at how diverse a desert could be. He had always supposed that deserts were monotonous expanses of sand. But here the red dirt, while ever present, was also smattered with things of interest. Mirages aside there were the sporadic appearances of anthills, mulga trees, spinifex grass, the occasional kangaroo, willy-willys and tumble weed.

Teddy's thumping him on his arm broke into his mental musings. "Look! Look Charlie! See?" She was gesticulating crazily towards the windscreen. "We're almost there."

Charlie turned his attention to what was in front of them, but all he could see was a screen of red dust being churned up by the vehicles travelling ahead and converging from a road coming in on the right.

"When's the first race, dad?"

Ralph twisted his arm to read his watch. "Couple of hours yet. Time to find us a parking space and grab some tucker. D'you put the Esky in the back?"

"I put both of them in dad. One with the tucker and the other with the drinks."

"Good girl."

Ralph drove into the designated parking ground and looked for a place to park. Ralph had hardly pulled the handbrake on before Teddy was pushing at Charlie.

"Steady on there,"

"But I want to get out dad, I don't want to miss anything."

The three piled out to the sound of camels *grunting and the chatter of the excited locals. Amid the animated exchange of greetings among the others setting up foldout chairs and picnic rugs it hadn't taken Ralph, Teddy and Charlie long to enjoy their picnic lunch on the tray of the ute.*

Charlie, more used to race meetings held at long-established and well-maintained venues, frequented by immaculately attired punters, had no idea what to expect at an Outback camel race meeting. No amount of imagination could have prepared him for what followed their lunch.

The two men followed Teddy as she skipped along in front of them. Charlie looked about him. There was no manicured green turf, no grandstand; instead the spectators, who had driven or flown in from the surrounding stations, were lined up beside and around the roped off area which constituted the racetrack.

The heat of the sun, as usual, beat down on his back, while the ever present and persistent flies fought for space in the shade around his face from the protection of his Akubra. As he looked around he saw that a number of people had fly-veils attached over the brim of their hat, and he could see the wisdom in these, even if they were certainly not a fashion feature.

There was none of the expected finery adorning the punters, though to be realistic he was feeling more comfortable in what he was wearing than if he had been fitted out in his usual race-going wardrobe of full-length trousers and jacket with a collared shirt and tie. The clean moleskin trousers and checked shirts everyone was wearing made more sense under the burning sun, and polished R.M. Williams boots suited the dusty ground better than dress shoes. Similarly, the Akubra was more sensible than a top hat. He looked over to Ralph and laughed at the contrast to the image of his father ready for the Royal Enclosure at Ascot. No. He had to hand it to the Australians, they knew how to dress for the occasion. They may not have been in formal attire, but the array of colour was as spectacular and refreshing as anything that could be seen on the established and revered racetracks elsewhere.

The jockeys had a similar disregard for formal decorum, the dress code was as relaxed as that for the spectators – there was not a silk to be seen.

As the time came for the races to start the jockeys approached the camels which had been relaxing in an area beyond the track which had been roped off. The camels' long necks swayed side to side as the jockeys climbed onto their backs. It was mesmerising watching as they perched on the majestic animals, first lurched back and then were thrust forward as the animals rose onto their feet.

Despite the discrepancies in location and presentation the buzz and excitement could not be faulted, and he realised that the thrill of *anticipation as the camels and their riders lined up at the start was as palpable as any he had experienced at Ascot or Cheltenham.*

As the race began, the camels set off at a surprisingly quick pace, their cushion-like padded feet kicking up puffs of dust at each foot fall, which when churned up multiple times made it hard to see who was in the lead until the jockeys guided their mounts around the last bend of the track. Charlie's ears rang with the babble of the excited spectators as they all leaned forward to catch a better view of the animals stampeding towards them in an ungainly and totally random fashion. He could only laugh at the overall sense of disorder.

"What are those?" Melanie asked, flapping her hand in front of her as she moved towards Monty and George. "Surely they are not horses?"

"Are you admitting that you can see what this painting is of?" Monty asked her.

She stopped gesticulating and turned to look at him, trying to determine if he was laughing at her.

"Well, I am guessing that it is *supposed* to be a race of some sort as there is that long flat bit lined by a row of, oh, I don't know, people?" She flapped her hand towards the right side of the painting.

This time Monty did laugh, but mainly because he did not want to create a scene in the presence of others. What he really wanted to do was either scream or cry. He turned and looked at Melanie, frustrated. How could she, his PA, the woman that he thought he was falling in love with, be so unappreciative of the talent that he could see in Teddy's paintings? Granted they were more impressionist than realistic, but there was so much movement and emotion in them.

"Melanie, if you took the time to read the label, you would see that yes, it is a race, and yes there are people. They are enjoying a day at the camel races."

"They race camels? That's totally ridiculous." She moved towards the painting and peered closely at it before stepping back and shaking her head. "No, can't see it myself. I've never heard of anything so absurd. Just goes to show you how ridiculous this exhibition is. None of the paintings look anything like what they are meant to be. None of it can be called 'art'. And as for coming all this way to see it. Ridiculous. The only good thing about this evening is talking and being seen with the other guests, and you are not interested in that at all. If only we had driven down, I would go and sit in the car. If you want me, I'll be in the other room with the refreshments. Would you like to keep me company George?"

George looked to Monty, shrugged his shoulders and followed Melanie.

Stunned, Monty watched her walk away. Then he shook his head and turned to look at the painting again. To him this one was so very realistic that he had no problem recalling the euphoric atmosphere of the day that Ralph had taken he and Teddy to the camel races.

He sighed. Why could she not see the beauty in the paintings that he could? Or at least take an interest in what he found interesting? He looked to where Melanie and George had gone. George was nowhere in sight, but he could see Melanie through the doorway, champagne glass held captive in her hand as she animatedly gesticulated to some people whom he vaguely recalled her introducing him to earlier.

Suddenly his reverie was interrupted.

TWELVE

"Do you remember that day?" Teddy laughed, and slipped her arm through his.

Monty frowned. He recognised her laugh. It could only mean that something had happened that day. Something which, in his ignorance, he had succeeded in making a fool of himself, again, He had no recollection so had obviously conveniently forgotten. He looked at Teddy. She clearly had not forgotten. She was grinning fit to burst.

"Oh Chr... Sorry, Monty. You *have* forgotten." She pulled her arm free and took up an exaggerated pose from her childhood. One that Monty knew only too well, and he burst out laughing. In no time they were both bent over, hands on knees laughing.

Monty heard footsteps approaching and quickly tried to catch his breath. "Someone's coming," he said between gulps of air, hoping that it was not Melanie. She would be mortified to find him behaving frivolously; then he wondered why he should be concerned about that, after all he was enjoying himself. "And this is not the most becoming of positions for either of us, here, let me help you stand." He leant forward and placed a hand on Teddy's shoulder, their heads touching.

She nodded and levered herself up using his arm, then once standing upright again she smoothed down her dress. "You're quite right, as usual. But still, you don't remember what happened after the races, do you?"

The humorous lilt in her voice reflected the mirth that Monty remembered from his time on *Calinda* when Teddy would take the mickey out of him on his many faux pas, and he inwardly squirmed trying to remember how he had embarrassed himself after the races.

"Come on, see if this reminds you," Teddy said as she grabbed his hand and led him through into another room, smaller than the others he had been in.

Monty stood in the doorway and looked around. Each of the walls held a pair of black and white sketches, and he recognised the subject of each one: boiling the billy; the flying doctor; yabbying; the rodeo, and others that were obviously the first drafts for the oils and acrylics featured in the other rooms. But none of them represented a moment of embarrassment.

He turned to Teddy and shrugged his shoulders. "What am I meant to be seeing?"

Teddy laughed and pulled him further into the room. "Now turn around."

Monty did as he was told.

Either side of the door were two larger charcoal, contrasting sketches. The primitive almost stick-like figures in the sketch to the left of the door Monty could see represented the corroboree[1] that he had watched when one of the station hands was getting married. He remembered being mesmerised by the rich, resonant continuous drone of the didgeridoo that sounded like the rumbling of distant thunder. It had been captivating and almost mystical, and he could now hear it again in his mind, and see the decorated bodies of the dancers. Monty smiled and felt at peace.

He then looked to the sketch to the right of the door and slowly turned red. Oh, now he remembered. Not so much the actual event, but the aftermath of the marathon drinking and dancing that had been captured in a photograph. He creased his brow, wondering how, or when, Teddy had come in possession of the photograph. He thought he'd succeeded in retrieving all the ones that had been printed. Yet here it was, not the photograph per se, but as plain as anything, a charcoal rendition of it. A naked stick figure cavorting on

---

1.   https://en.wikipedia.org/wiki/Corroboree

top of a table, surrounded by an audience, glasses and jugs held high in salute.

"How could you?"

"Don't worry, no one, other than you, would understand what the swirls and markings mean."

"What do you mean no one else? *Every*one was there, and they will all know, and remember."

"Only if they see it. And who is likely to do that? It's only on show here. No one has seen it."

"But what if they are visiting London, and happen upon the exhibition? And you. You weren't even there, you were asleep in the ute. How'd you get hold of the photograph?"

"Oh really Char ..." Teddy stopped, not only because she noticed Monty's scowl at her use of what he considered his obsolete Australian name, but because she could see Melanie approaching.

"There you are!"

Melanie was standing in the doorway, and Monty could almost feel the air frost over.

"I've been looking for you." Her glare was enough to make Monty cringe.

He involuntarily moved to create some distance between himself and Teddy, and his heart sank, surely Melanie hadn't found more people to introduce him to.

Melanie sashayed menacingly towards Monty.

Teddy, well aware of the vitriolic vibes emanating from Monty's partner quickly let go of his hand and took a step away from him. "Never mind, no need for you to worry. I'll get a sold sticker put on it." She smiled up at him and walked out of the room, sharing the vestige of the smile with Melanie as they passed.

"What was that all about? Surely you are not buying one of these atrocities?"

Monty hardly heard what Melanie was asking, being too busy watching Teddy walk away without a backward glance and finding it a trifle perturbing that his mind was making a comparison between the two women who had walked away from him. Melanie exuding pretentious class in her High Street wannabe couture and stiletto sandals. He frowned. Surely sandals did not go with the heavy velvet of her dress? But what did he know about women's fashion? Teddy on the other hand had simply walked away, much the way he remembered from when she was a precocious pre-teen. Except the clothes were different. And he marvelled again at how comfortable she was with her scars, so much so that she could wear lace next to them. It was almost as if she was proud of them. He shook his head.

"Did you hear me?"

"Sorry, what did you say?"

"Really Monty! What has got into you tonight?"

"Tonight? I'm enjoying a night out, with you."

"With me? I'm starting to think that you don't care if I am here or not. Ever since we arrived all you've done is moon over these excuses for art, leaving me to circulate alone. I've been trying to make connections for you, but you don't appear to be interested.

"Well, that is what we came here for, the art."

"And you are intending to bring some of them home?"

"What?"

"When I came in to this room, you and that woman were talking about buying something. Don't tell me that it is one of these things?" She waved her hand around and slowly turned, taking in the sketches on the walls. "These? God, you can't be serious? Any kid in preschool could do better than these stick figures."

She turned back to stand beside Monty, who was still looking at the contentious sketch in front him.

"What is that one meant to represent?" She pointed to where Charlie was cavorting on the table, and Monty blanched, then mentally cursed Teddy. Obviously she did not realise how realistic and suggestive her stick-figure representation of him was.

Melanie grabbed hold of Monty's arm and leant closer to the sketch. "Is that meant to be a man?"

Monty wilted and once again cursed Teddy. If Melanie could determine the subject, then so could others. His life was ruined.

"Oh, no, it can't be a man. It's not a person," he said, mentally crossing his fingers as he led Melanie out of the room and back into the main display area.

THIRTEEN

He looked around the room lined with Teddy's artwork – pastels, watercolours, sketches, oils and acrylics, all sizes, and all evoking memories. He wondered if the future with Melanie could be destined to be as blissful as he imagined. He disengaged himself from Melanie's arm and wandered over to another pastel that had caught his eye.

An island of green rose up out of the sea of red, the cloudless blue sky home to a couple of birds circling, caught in an updraft. Just as he was now caught up in another memory, and he smiled.

He smiled and could feel the beginnings of something inside of him letting go, just as it had back when he had first seen the smudge of grey-green on the horizon.

"It looks like it could be a good day," Ralph commented as he came into the kitchen where Teddy and Charlie were finishing breakfast. "Weather-wise that is. Could be the right kind of day to take off from work. What do you reckon?" He tousled Teddy's hair as he passed.

"Da-ad," she sighed, patting her hair down. "Of course it's a day off from work, it's Saturday."

"And that makes what kind of difference to my life?" Ralph laughed as he felt the teapot and pulled a face that it was cold. "You got any plans Charles?"

Teddy spluttered and looked up at her father. Charles? Was he still calling him Charles? She then turned to Charlie. "Yes Charlie, what have you got mapped out for the day, seeing as how there is no school today? Do you want to go for another ride?" The corners of her mouth twitched in merriment.

Charlie chose to ignore the implied dig at his first Outback outing on horseback. Would the kid never let him forget that? He looked at Ralph standing in front of the stove. "Thought I'd get Teddy to take me to Spud's Billabong today. She keeps harping on about the place, and laughing that I don't know what a billabong is. Have a picnic out there – bit of a reward for the improvement in her table manners."

Ralph raised his eyebrows in silent query, thinking that he hadn't noticed much of a change. His daughter was still rough and ready and would raise a mention in the boarding school's staff dining room. But he smiled indulgently all the same.

Teddy sat forward in her chair and looked first at Charlie, just to make sure that he was serious, then to her father. "Can I dad? Take Charlie out to Spud's?" She then looked back at Charlie before asking "Can I take the ute out there? You know what Charlie's like on a horse."

"Sounds like a good idea, just make sure that you bring back plenty of yabbies, and maybe even a fish or two. Best take the ute, Spud's is a bit of a ways, but Charlie drives."

"Da-ad!"

"You'll have to direct him, and be in charge of the gates, that last one is a bit tricky. And best take some tucker with you, If you are thinking about a picnic. Teddy, you think you can organise that with Betty?"

"And don't forget to bring something to drink this time. No bore water for me thank you very much," Charlie muttered under his breath.

"Teddy, you didn't …" Ralph looked at his daughter reprovingly.

"Charlie has to learn."

"But bore water? Really?" He shook his head, "Go see Betty. Come on Charlie, I'll introduce you to the ute, she can be a bit cantankerous if you don't know how to pander to her inner workings."

They spent a couple of hours of bouncing across the vast expanses of red isolation, over rough tracks and skirting around termite mounds, boulders and clumps of mulga—the small, heath-like low shrubs that grew scattered across the station – and conversation had been inconsequential until a smudge of grey-green started to rise above the horizon.

"So, is that our destination?" Charlie waved his hand towards the half-moon of cleared glass on his side of the otherwise dust-smeared windscreen.

"Spud's Billabong? Yes."

"Tell me now, what is Spud's Billabong?"

"Do you want me to tell you about Spud? Or about billabongs?"

"Both."

"Well, you're going to have to wait."

Teddy laughed as Charlie eased the ute to a stop and she jumped out to open the final gate before their destination. Charlie drove through and waited for Teddy to clamber back on board, bouncing on the cracked vinyl bench seat.

"Okay. So Spud," she said. "This is many years ago when there were still plenty of sundowners about."

Charlie turned and looked at her, an eyebrow raised in question.

"Knew that'd throw you!" Teddy laughed.

Teddy sat up straighter, inwardly preening with pride. "Okay, so you know what a swagman is, don't you?" She looked over at Charlie but did not wait for him to answer. "Well, a sundowner is a swagman who is lazy. He only turns up at the door when the sun is going down and it is too late to do any work for his keep for the night, and then he is off again at first light."

Charlie harrumphed, but didn't interrupt.

"So, Spud was a sundowner, only he'd miscalculated and when he turned up there was still an hour before sunset, and there was meant to be a full moon. So he was told to see Betty for some tucker and then he

could go and take a sack of potatoes out to the billabong and keep the bunyip there company for the night."

She paused and looked across to Charlie again. He knew better than to look at her, so, without taking his eyes off the track ahead he took the bait.

"Bunyip?"

"Jeepers Charlie. You don't know anything, do you?"

"Guess not. Not out here I don't." This was certainly his day for learning. "You'd better tell me, hadn't you?"

"A bunyip is something like a bogeyman. You do know what one of those is don't you? Something that goes bump in the night and frightens little children."

"Bogeyman. Right. And your ... sundowner, he didn't know ...?"

Teddy shrugged her shoulders. "Like I was telling you, the sundowner had to be a bit thick, turning up early enough to be given work. Anyway, he goes on down to the billabong, carrying this heavy bag of what he's been told were potatoes. By the time he gets there the sun has set, and the moon hasn't yet come up. So it's dark, see? And he decides to wait for the moon before he feeds the bunyip. He waits three nights and the bunyip stills doesn't appear, and the sundowner is getting pretty hungry, so he decides that he'll eat the potatoes. He opens up the sack and there is not one potato there to be eaten." She looked at Charlie.

"Okay, so what was in the sack?"

"It was full of eyes," she burst out laughing. "Eyes! You get it?"

Charlie, imagining human, or at least animal eyes and wondering where they had come from, and why this sundowner hadn't smelt them rotting looked at Teddy blankly. She shook her head in disbelief.

"Really Charlie? Eyes. You know, eyes. The potatoes had been in the sack so long they'd all sprouted eyes."

Charlie shook his head and muttered to himself before stopping the ute at the top of a slight rise. Below was what he could only describe as paradise. Spud's Billabong. An oxbow lake that had formed eons ago when a nearby river had changed its course. The river was now no more than a dry creek bed, but the billabong was an oasis. A mass of trees ringed the banks except at one end where there was a beach of sorts and reeds gathered in the shallows. There were several clouds of insects hovering over the brackish water surface and an occasional 'plop' could be heard with an accompanying swell of circles denoting that Ralph's request for them to return with fish was likely to be prophetic.

"And what happened to Spud?" Charlie asked, waiting for the rest of the story.

Teddy opened the ute door and jumped out, then turned to face Charlie and shrugged her shoulders. "Don't know."

"What do you mean, you don't know?"

"No one ever told me."

FOURTEEN

"Careful the bunyip doesn't get you." A familiar laugh from the distant past rippled beside him and he knew that Teddy was at his side before she slipped her arm through his and gave it a gentle squeeze.

Monty turned and looked down at her, a smile spreading across his face at the memory of his introduction to bunyips and billabongs. "Do you still call it Spud's Billabong?

"Of course, what else would it be called?"

"And nothing's come to light about what happened to him, Spud?"

She shook her head and laughed again. It was still the same mocking laugh, but this time it was tempered with maturity and not marked by the brashness of a young tom-boy struggling to keep a hold of the girl whose body was intent on becoming a woman. "That's probably because no one really knows. But you must admit the story I told you was pretty convincing."

"Not sure about that. I think I chose to humour you by accepting it as gospel." Monty smiled down at her upturned face, noting that she no longer sported the freckles that he remembered teasing her about. Then a frown accompanied the wince of guilt as he again noted the scarring down the side of her face.

She leant her head against his shoulder and again squeezed his arm. "I'm pleased you could come. Tonight, I mean."

"I'm jolly glad you invited me." It was a whisper charged with emotion. He *was* glad. Genuinely glad. Even though when he had first read the invitation he had been somewhat puzzled that Teddy would want to have anything to do with him after all the intervening years. And he had been unsure about accepting. Still, he would have been devastated if he had learned afterwards that she had been in the country and not made contact.

Teddy pulled away from him and took a step back. "How could I not invite you? I promised that I'd do so."

"When was that?" He remembered the promise he had made to himself. That was to leave Australia as soon as he could and forget about his time there. And, until Melanie had handed him the envelope the other week he had, in the main, been successful. But in all honesty, he could not remember any exchange between Teddy and himself that involved any promise.

"When you gave me the painting set. That was what got me started. Now if you will excuse me, I need to spend time with the others."

Monty felt uncomfortable at that memory. It was not right that she should sound so buoyant about that time of her life. Not when he had been so unsuccessful in erasing it from his mind. And he wondered if that episode was also on display. He was sure that he had walked through all the rooms and had not seen anything resembling that event. Then again, nothing would surprise him when it came to Teddy. Should he ask her, or take another walk around the gallery?

He turned to ask her, but she had already released his arm and was walking away. He looked around the room where he stood. Many of the guests were preparing to round up the evening and leave. He wasn't sure if that would be to his advantage or not to take another walk around the rooms to see if he had missed another potentially incriminating image that would further fuel his guilt. The stick-figure charcoal had been enough. Maybe he could simply ask Teddy, if he could find her. He looked around the room again. He could see Melanie, still at the refreshment table, animatedly doing what she had been doing all evening. Talking. Teddy was hovering near the entrance, occupied farewelling her guests.

Monty looked at his watch and decided that to err on the side of ignorance would bring bliss so with a mental shrug he walked over to join Melanie.

"Monty, darling. Where have you been? I've just been telling George and Fiona here that they should come around for dinner next week. What do you think? They tell me that it has been ages since they have visited Cambridge, and I know that George would love to catch up with you. Wouldn't you?" she gushed.

George was busy nodding his head. "Sure, I'd love to catch up. Lots to share." He gave a laugh which hinted at shared escapades that did not fit the image that he currently portrayed. "Here," George fumbled for his wallet. "Take my card."

Fiona smiled demurely, joining in with the head nodding, while Monty quailed in his shoes and feigned a smile. Coming here and meeting Teddy was a hurdle that he had actively prepared himself for, but coming face to face with George had been totally unexpected and was something he would normally and knowingly have avoided like the plague. They may have known each other, been friends even, in the past. And that was where Monty would have preferred the acquaintanceship stay.

Monty took a closer look at the man whom he had once been friends with, and wondered how he, along with so many others that Melanie had felt honour bound to ingratiate herself with, had come to be invited tonight. His curiosity was such that he knew he had to meet with Teddy again. There were too many anomalies and questions bouncing around for him to be able to leave without further reconnecting.

"Monty?" Melanie tugged at his arm, bringing him out of his thoughts and back to the task at hand. Melanie's invitation to the Mannighams. He appreciated her commandeering ways in the office. But really?

He turned to Melanie, and said with a smile that did not quite reach his eyes, "I'm sorry, but next week would not be suitable. Maybe another time?" Like never, Monty thought as he let his smile take in Fiona and her husband. There was no way he wanted to have

George, or anyone, introduce Melanie to the liturgy of past antics that George would mercilessly elaborate. That was a period of his life that he was even more disinclined to recall than his antipodean sojourn.

He put an arm around Melanie's waist, "Ready to move on?" he asked, gently urging her away from the Manninghams. "Nice to have met you Fiona, George," he said as he gave a nod of his head and ushered Melanie towards the entrance where Teddy stood waiting to say goodbye.

She stretched her hands out to Monty as he and Melanie approached.

"Monty! I'm so glad that you could make it." She released his hands and turned to Melanie. "And lovely to meet you. I do hope you both enjoyed the evening."

"Thank you for the invitation, Te..." Monty paused briefly before he corrected himself and continued, "Miss Delany. It was a most insightful exhibition."

Melanie sniffed and hoped her noncommittal smile would suffice for acknowledgement of the evening. She could not, even if decorum called for it, fudge any appreciation of the exhibits, or the artist. She did, however, congratulate herself for the successful networking she had conducted. If only Monty had picked up on it and shown more enthusiasm. So many high-powered names to rub shoulders with, and Monty not moved by their presence. She could feel herself glow with triumph and hoped that once they were back in Cambridge Monty would realise and acknowledge all that she had achieved on his behalf.

Monty was not immune to the calibre of the other invitees, but he was more interested in how they fitted into the social circle of the young woman from the Australian Outback. It must have been a prestigious boarding school that Ralph Delany had sent her to, and she must have taken full advantage of the connections made there.

Whatever the reason for the invitee list, he could only feel immense pride in what she had accomplished. And he admired the flair and vibrance she brought to her artwork.

The two of them walked to the nearest Tube, lost in their own thoughts.

FIFTEEN

The next morning Monty silently cursed himself for neglecting to find out where Teddy was staying. He didn't even know if she was visiting or living here. All the time he had spent with her the previous evening, and he had asked her nothing. He still didn't know why he'd been invited, or how she knew where to find him. He had wasted the time reminiscing about the time he had spent on the station with her and her father. Until last night he had not thought about the good times he'd experienced in those few months. And now they consumed him.

He needed to find Teddy. She was a part of his life, no matter how hard he had worked at blotting those months out. And now that the memories had been so gloriously resurrected he realised that he wanted to find her. To spend time with her. He realised that until he did he would not be able to settle to the demanding work that would be piling up on his desk.

Monty arrived at the office determined to track down where Teddy was staying. It was something, he realised, that he could not ask Melanie to do for him. He would have to do it himself. And he had no idea how he would go about it. Hiring a private detective seemed a bit drastic, but it was all he could think of. Either that or put an ad in the Personal's Column of the paper, but which paper? And what guarantee did he have that Teddy would see it?

His dilemma was resolved shortly after he had settled down at his desk. Melanie all but bounced into the room. Monty sighed. That was why office romances were not ideal – so often the lines became blurred. He'd have to have another polite talk with Melanie.

"Good morning, Melanie. You have a good night's sleep?" It certainly appeared to have been better than his.

Melanie came closer, her face lit up as radiantly as the sun breaking through the clouds after a storm. She was waving the morning's paper above her head in a victor's salute.

"Look at this!" she said as she reached the desk and dropped the newspaper in front of him.

"Yes?" he asked. curious as to what it was that he was meant to be looking at.

Melanie took a deep breath, and held it for a couple of seconds waiting for her pulse to settle down. She opened the paper up and smoothed the pages down.

Monty looked down to where she was framing an article and a couple of photographs. He looked up at Melanie. "That was quick. Did you see any press there last night?"

She shook her head. "If I had, I would have made sure that they had taken my good side, and that you had your arm round me rather than stuffed in your pocket. A smile would have looked good. Still, it is a nice group photo. See, there's ..."

But Monty was not listening as Melanie pointed out and named the people standing in a semicircle, champagne flutes held captive in front of stuffed shirts. His eyes were rivetted on the small, obviously press photo, of Teddy that was superimposed over a corner of the larger group photo that Melanie was fawning over. He looked up at Melanie and grinned. The newspaper could be his answer to finding Teddy.

"Will you listen to this!" Melanie was now running her finger along the lines of print. "The newspaper must have been desperate to report the opening. I wonder if Miss ..." She peered closer and read what her finger was adjacent to, "Miss Delany paid to have this printed. Whoever was there last night representing the media must never have visited The Tate. They are claiming that she is a virtuoso and a savant. I bet they don't even know what those words mean."

It was Monty's turn to run a finger over the newspaper. He was marvelling that even in a press photograph Teddy had done nothing to hide her scars.

The following week Melanie once more excitedly entered Monty's office, this time, instead of a newspaper held triumphantly above her head, she was bearing the morning's mail. She delicately placed two brown paper wrapped parcels on his desk, then stepped back expectantly.

Monty looked up from the files he was reading. Melanie, he could see, was almost itching to see what was inside. She really was overstepping the line. And he was getting tired of it. Couldn't she understand that she had to be two personas, and to know the place for each?

As though reading his thoughts, Melanie's face took on a slight pout. "Mr Chinthurst."

Monty smiled, at least she remembered that part of his last talk-to with her.

"These have come to the office, and therefore, as your PA I am entitled to know what the packages contain. I mean, if they are pertinent to the business then you shall be requiring me to respond to them, and therefore I will, at some point, know their contents. So why not now?"

Monty picked up first one, then the other, turning them over to see who had sent them. One was from a newspaper, and he wrinkled his brow. That one posed a puzzle. The other had no return address, but he smiled as he recognised the writing. But it too was a puzzle – why would Teddy be sending him a parcel?

"And, with you standing there, if one of them is a parcel bomb it would be goodbye to both of us. Are you prepared to take that risk?" He put the two parcels face to face and tapped their shorter ends on the file in front of him, smiling as Melanie's face paled and she involuntarily took a step back.

"Why would anyone want to be sending you parcel bombs? Besides, I know where one is from, and I also know what it contains." She reached across the desk and tapped the parcel that she could see was obviously from the newspaper she had contacted. "This one is quite safe to open. Go on, open it. Here." She handed him a pair of scissors that he had not seen her holding, then, almost leaping in anticipation she waited impatiently for him to open the parcel.

Monty bent his head down in an attempt to hide the amused smile that he could not otherwise hide, and deliberately slowly unwrapped the parcel of lesser interest to him. Melanie gave a little squeal and stopped herself from reaching for the framed photograph that Monty released from its covering and bubble wrap protection.

He tried to match her enthusiasm for the framed photograph of the group at Teddy's exhibition. Why she thought that he might want a copy was beyond him.

"Here, let me take that and hang it up for you. I think behind your desk, or maybe over near the sofa. Just imagine how impressed your visitors will be to see you mixing with the likes of the Romano-Woodfields, Peckenhams and Mannighams."

Monty stared at her. She was like a giddy child on Christmas morning, faced with a filled stocking dangling from the mantlepiece. He shook his head, almost in dismay to realise that he was contemplating taking their relationship to the next step. Did he really want that? He had no idea how she knew these people, or expected him to know them. None of them held any history in common with him, other than George Manningham. And he very much doubted that any of his clients would know them, or be impressed.

His fingers itched to open the remaining parcel. Maybe if he allowed Melanie to occupy herself with hanging the wretched

photograph he could open the parcel from Teddy. From its similarity
to the one he had just opened he suspected that this second parcel
also contained something framed and worthy to be hung. Then his
anticipation took a nose dive as he remembered Teddy and the sold
sticker. Surely she wouldn't have? But what if she had? Suddenly he
wasn't sure if he was up to opening it in the presence of another, just
in case.

Monty's silence had tempered Melanie, so she was more subdued
when she next spoke, and she remembered her place.

"Where would you like me to hang this, Mr Chinthurst?" she
asked as she held the photograph in her two hands, trying hard not
to run her finger over the faces.

"Why don't you go and ask someone for the bits and pieces you
will need to hang it, and then I'll let you choose where you think
would be best."

Melanie beamed, then put the photograph almost reverently
down on the desk. "Right. I'll be back directly."

Monty impatiently waited until Melanie had closed the door
behind her before he ripped open the second parcel. There was not
one, but two frames, wrapped individually and packed facing each
other. But he was yet to turn them over to see what they held.
Knowing Teddy and the perverse humour she exhibited when she
was a preteen, he steeled himself for the inevitable. He took a breath
and slowly separated the frames, holding one in each hand. He put
one down when he saw, through the bubble wrap, the other had a red
'sold' sticker strategically placed.

Typical Teddy.

He was now the rightful owner of a charcoal original from
Theodora Delany.

Thank God the two of them were the only ones to know what
it represented. He was still laughing when Melanie returned. He put
the frames back on to the desk then turned the offending picture

over and slid it, and the wrapping, into a drawer before Melanie had made it to the desk, where she picked up the photograph and walked towards the window. He watched as she carefully and almost reverently hung the photo on the wall near the sofa. Then stepped back to admire her positioning of it. He smiled to himself imagining Melanie's response when she later saw the charcoal beside the photograph, as that was where he mischievously intended to hang it.

"What's in the other parcel?" Melanie asked as she walked back to Monty's desk, swinging a small claw hammer between her hands.

Monty looked up and smiled.

Melanie took the smile as an invitation and put the hammer gently down on top of some files, then she put her hands on the desk and leant across, her head not far from his and her breasts tantalisingly close. Her perfume wafted towards him.

Monty found it interesting how sometimes he could smell her perfume, and other times not. And when he did, he found that somehow it would elusively remind him of something, or some place, or someone, yet he could never place what it was. He wrinkled his nose. Today he could detect it. Had she applied more than usual, or had she taken the opportunity, when gathering the picture hanging paraphernalia, to reapply? Whatever it was, he was still not sure if he liked it. He shook his head slightly to clear his thoughts and the air.

"About to find out," he said as he smiled and pulled the second wrapped frame towards him. He wasn't sure why, but he took deliberate care in unwrapping this second frame. He could not detect any tell-tale embellishments, but he still did not want to be ambushed by Teddy. Slowly the bubble wrap was released and fell back onto the desk. Monty took a silent, deep breath then turned the frame over.

He let out an audible breath of relief.

"Whatever is *that?*" Melanie asked, standing upright, staring at the picture resting on its packaging.

Monty stared at the pastel drawing in front of him. To Monty, the subject appeared almost 3D it was so lifelike. It was reaching out to him, but in a benign way, not as he remembered.

"It's a kangaroo, and its joey," he whispered almost reverently.

"That's a kangaroo?" Melanie asked scathingly, and pointed at the collection of orange, red and ochre that stared up at her. She looked at Monty. "And what's a joey?"

Monty looked up at Melanie, amazed that she had to ask. Didn't everyone know that a juvenile kangaroo was called a joey?

"A joey is what you call a juvenile kangaroo."

"I didn't know that kangaroos gave their babies names. And why do Australians always diminutise their names? They are all called Tommy, Timmy, Bobbie ...: She looked at Monty. "It's a wonder that this artist woman here," Melanie peered closer to the picture to read the signature. "This Theodora doesn't call herself Teddy. I guess if you were an Australian you'd be called Charlie," she laughed.

Monty, head down idolising the picture on the desk was glad that Melanie couldn't see him blanch. Little did she know, he mused and hoped that she never found out. That was a name that he could only tolerate Teddy calling him.

He needed time to recover.

"While you're standing there with those things beside you, would you mind hanging this up beside the photo you've just put up."

"You want to put this beside the photograph?" Melanie wanted to add 'are you mad', but one look at Monty's face and she keep the words firmly behind her stiffly sealed lips. Instead, she picked up the hammer, then put it back down. "I need to get another nail," she threw over her shoulder as she walked to the office door.

Monty watched her sashay away and shook his head. He could not believe that she had to ask what the picture was. Couldn't Melanie see? And then she had to be disparaging about things she knew little about. Then again, he reminded himself, it stood to reason that Melanie could be gauche at times, after all she had not travelled or had such a privileged education and upbringing as he had.

He picked up the frame again, staring at the image that Teddy had so beautifully captured. If she had sent this to him to reinforce a guilt trip, then it was a success.

SIXTEEN

Monty didn't want to, but he could not help himself. As he looked further into the picture he could almost see the doe saying she was sorry, that she was also only doing what came naturally and he ought to have known that.

Teddy was anxious to leave the classroom. She'd repeatedly said that there was something special that she wanted to show him and no amount of his cajoling or attempts at bribery had worked in getting her to reveal what it was. She had refused to be more forthcoming, and had simply shaken her head, refusing to wipe the smug smirk off her face. He could almost hear the words that she was not uttering 'Nah, ngh, na, na, ngh'. In the end he had given up making suggestions as to what it could be, and had, in retaliation, endeavoured to make the time spent in the classroom as boring as possible.

When the lessons for the day could not be drawn out any longer Charlie had conceded defeat, and had called it a day. Teddy had skipped and jumped the whole way back to the homestead. Charlie had followed, not exactly fuming, but still mildly irate, and perplexed. In all the time that he had been at Calinda *he had never known Teddy to maintain such control over keeping a surprise secret and it was eating at him.*

Teddy bounced up the path in front of him, her plaits flying in time. "Hey Charlie, better get your station clobber on!"

Puzzled, Charlie looked down at his cleanly washed moleskins and pale blue shirt. Wasn't he already wearing what was expected of him on the station? "Now what's wrong with what I'm wearing?"

"Jeepers, Charlie. That's not farming clobber. That's your school teacher gear. No, you gotta go get into some old clothes, stuff that won't matter if you get grubby," she giggled.

Charlie, wondering what she was up to this time, sighed and ambled towards his bedroom.

"Get your skates on!" Teddy yelled after him, and frowned. She wondered, as she did each time she heard the phrase being used, if she would ever get to wear skates and experience how they would make her go faster than her bare feet.

Once in his room Charlie stood looking at the meagre array of clothes hanging in the wardrobe. He presumed when Teddy said 'old' clothes, she was not meaning the clothes that he had arrived with. They were what he thought of as his old clothes. But that still left little for him to choose from, everything else was 'new' even if they were essentially cast-offs, except for the moleskins. He had to admit that he did rather like wearing those. They made him feel less 'foreign'.

Finally, at the bottom of the wardrobe he managed to unearth a pair of well-worn Levis. He grabbed them, and a checked shirt that had seen better days and hoped that Teddy would approve.

Teddy was sitting on the wooden table that dominated the kitchen swinging her legs in a random pattern which no doubt matched a song swirling around in her head, when Charlie entered the room.

"Great! Finally you're here. Let's go," she said as she picked up a hessian bag from beside her, slung it over her shoulder and jumped down from the table. and made for the door leading out to the veranda. Once there she looked at the line of boots.

"Guess we'd better tog-up and put some boots on today." She slipped the bag from off her shoulder and shuffled her feet into the smallest pair of boots in the line.

"Where're we off to?" Charlie asked as he struggled to pull on a pair of elastic sided boots. If he was going to be staying here much longer he'd need to get into town and buy a pair for himself. Sloughing around

in any old pair that lay about was not his idea of orthotically fitting footwear. Neither did it make for a good image, though that apparently was not important. Out here beyond the black stump there was no one to impress, except maybe Teddy, but she was more interested in laughing at his dress sense than appreciating his ability to be sartorially elegant.

"You'll see soon enough. Just follow me." And with that Teddy hefted the bag over her shoulder once more and swaggered down the path towards the woolshed.

Charlie demurely followed.

"Isn't she beautiful?" Teddy asked as she squatted down in the only bit of shade this side of the woolshed.

"Hm-muh." Charlie nodded as he crouched down beside Teddy. It was the first time he had come this close to a live kangaroo. Not that anyone could call the distance between them and the red kangaroo 'close'. The animal was on the far side of the holding paddock behind the woolshed, and was bent over, its shorter front limbs scratching in the soft red dust that filled the paddock. He presumed it was trying to find something nutritious. And Charlie wished it luck. There was not a blade of grass to be seen.

"Is this what you wanted to show me?" He asked, looking at Teddy and not knowing what she expected him to say. It was his first kangaroo, and it was beautiful, in an odd kind of way.

"I've got a bottle here," Teddy said, tapping the bag over her shoulder. "I thought she might like something more than dirt."

"How'd you know it was here?" Charlie's knees, not used to the locals' penchant of squatting for long periods of time, were cramping, so he stood up.

"It's not an 'it' it's a 'she'," Teddy replied, as she also stood up, grinning at him. "I saw her last night when I came back from collecting the eggs."

Charlie, knowing that the hen house was nowhere in the vicinity of the woolshed, simply raised an eyebrow. He wasn't about to enter into an argument that he knew he'd lose.

"Ah-huh. Were they the eggs we ate at breakfast then?"

Teddy gave a quiet harrumph and kicked at the dirt at the base of the tree they were under. "Come on. Let's give this 'roo a feed."

"What are we feeding her? What'd you put in the bottle, water?

"Why water when there's a perfectly good trough with water for her over there?" Teddy pointed to the far end of the paddock, and Charlie shrugged his shoulders.

"I've put milk in the bottle dummy. You coming, or what?" Teddy started to walk slowly towards the kangaroo. Charlie hesitantly followed her.

"Do you think that milk is best?"

She stopped walking and looked back at Charlie, waiting for him to catch up to her. "Kangaroos are animals and all animals drink milk."

There was a challenge in Teddy's tone and so he knew that she was baiting him.

Not wanting to engage in an argument he was unlikely to win, he simply shrugged.

"What?" demanded Teddy. She'd been expecting a reprimand or something and was put out that none had been forthcoming.

Two can play at that game, thought Charlie, and tried not to smile as he responded. "I didn't say anything."

Teddy sniffed. "That's what I mean. When you don't say something I know that you are stewing inside." She set off again towards the kangaroo. "You're human and humans are animals, and you drink milk. So why not kangaroos, they're animals too."

Charlie wasn't too sure about the validity of Teddy's statement when it came to the adults of the marsupial population but knowing next to nothing about the dietary habits of Australian wildlife, he kept silent, and followed.

"We need to be careful now that we are closer," Teddy said when they were a short distance from the kangaroo. She crouched down and slowly pulled the bag around to her front.

Charlie crouched down beside her. So okay, close up the animal did look a bit flea-bitten, but still, so did the lions he had seen in zoos where there were keepers to care for them. Out here the wildlife were on their own.

The doe lifted her head at Teddy's voice and looked towards them, her over-large ears twitching as they zeroed in on their locality. She then bent down and stretched both short front feet forward, the claws splayed. Simultaneously, her tail moved forward between her hind legs, serving to balance her weight as the hind legs came forward and extended beyond her front paws. Slowly she padded towards them.

Charlie stretched his hand out. He wanted to touch the kangaroo.

"Don't do that!' Teddy shouted.

The kangaroo stopped moving towards them and stood up on her hind legs, her thick tail acting as a support and reminding Charlie of a back-to-front tricycle. She was almost eye-to-eye with him, and as she puffed out her chest Charlie's attention was distracted from admiring her majesty to watch, fascinated, as a small head rapidly pull back into the doe's pouch.

Before Charlie knew what was happening the kangaroo, balancing on her sturdy tail, with astonishing speed and force both hind legs struck out towards him.

He instinctively pulled back, and, losing his footing, fell heavily onto his backside. He could feel his heart racing like it hadn't since the pub punch-up that had brought him here. Only this was a far worse situation – those claws looked lethal. Breathing heavily and with only his safety on his mind he tried frantically to back-peddle, kicking up dust as the kangaroo lowered her legs and ominously bounced towards him before once more taking up the fighting pose. But before Charlie was able *to scrabble back up onto his feet and move out of range of the menacing long-clawed toes Teddy was barrelling between them.*

"Noooo!" she cried out as Charlie watched the kangaroo once more lash out. Only for Teddy to take the brunt of her claws.

Charlie, momentarily frozen in a mixture of anguish for Teddy and relief that he was not the victim, watched as Teddy tried frantically to grab the kangaroo's legs. It did not take the animal long to pull away from Teddy and lunge forward scoring her claws down Teddy's face and neck.

Teddy screamed, as much in anger as in pain before collapsing onto her knees, her hands clutching at raw flesh as blood dribbled over her hands and down the front of her shirt. The screams, which Charlie knew would haunt him for life, continued for what seemed like ages before subsiding into silence, and he panicked.

Forgetting the threatening presence of the kangaroo, Charlie's only focus was on Teddy, and he didn't see the kangaroo bound speedily away from the screams and confusion as he quickly crawled over to Teddy.

"Teddy! Teddy? Can you hear me?" Charlie was the one now yelling, but Teddy had already lost consciousness. He could feel himself break out into a sweat as panic set in. Teddy needed medical attention, but the hospital was hundreds of miles away. He cursed the arrogance with which he had refused to attend First Aid training, thinking that he would never be in a position to not have other people to take responsibility. Hell, he didn't even know what to do to stem the bleeding from the gaping wounds. He felt the bile in his throat and turned away as he felt his stomach heave. Charlie wiped his sleeve across his mouth and took a deep breath. He needed to get Teddy to the homestead, and medical attention, quickly.

Gingerly, and what he hoped was gently, he scooped the limp girl up in his arms before struggling to his feet wishing he was not alone. He looked around. There was no one in sight. He had no idea where Raph was but knew that he had to get help for Teddy. In almost a run, and as well as he could while carrying Teddy, he raced back to the homestead, calling out for anyone, as loud as he could.

Betty was the first to respond to his alarm. She raced out from the kitchen and down the path towards him.

"I need help. No, Teddy needs help, urgently. She's been attacked by a kangaroo!"

This kangaroo, the one that was depicted in front of him, was *that* kangaroo, along with the joey that she had been protecting. Monty traced his finger over the glass and felt the beginning of tears. She was only doing what comes naturally to all mothers. He could not blame her. But he blamed himself for what had happened.

SEVENTEEN

Monty leant forward, his elbows on the desk, cupped his head in his hands and briefly closed his eyes in the vain hope that he could relegate the associated memories to the back of his mind.

It was a relief to hear the office door open. He looked up and watched as Melanie walked in.

She pointed to the framed pastel on the desk. "Are you sure that you really want me to hang that beside the photograph?" She shook her head in disbelief that Monty would adulterate such a terrifically promotional opportunity. Didn't he realise that by placing the stupid and primitive picture so prominently he would be distracting from the importance of the photograph portraying the calibre of people that Monty mixed with?

"Yes, please," he said, and watched, amused, as Melanie picked up the frame as though it was contaminated then walked to where she had earlier mounted the photograph that held no meaning for him.

It was, he realised, silly really to put the kangaroo on display seeing as how he had spent the last 15 years putting that day, and the days that followed, behind him. Plastering over the pain, anguish, and guilt with as much Englishness as he could. And here he was, asking Melanie to mount it on the wall where he would see it every day. Was that the rationale behind Teddy sending it to him? To ensure that he would never forget the anxious wait for the Flying Doctor to arrive, and watching as a distraught Ralph followed the stretcher bearing her onto the plane. Once the plane and its precious cargo was airborne he had gone to his room and packed his bag. He had to escape. He had no idea the extent of her injuries. He didn't want to know. To know would indelibly etch his guilt into his psyche – something that he knew he would never be able to live with. But, knowing her panache for creativity and remembering her interest in painting, there was one thing he could do for Teddy before he left Australia behind him. Back on British soil and in his own, privileged, environment he had worked hard to forget his sojourn in 'the colonies'.

Now Teddy had cracked open the time capsule that he thought he had destroyed. Each day he was unsure which persona it was that entered his office – was it Monty, or Charlie?

Whichever it was, he found himself spending more and more of his time in the office standing and looking out the window, thinking how different the scenery of Cambridge and its environs, or anywhere else that he had experienced in his travels, was to the stark and harsh environment that abounded around *Carlinda*. Then, when he was at his desk, he would often open the drawer containing the charcoal sketch and muse over how much he missed the station, and the life that he had experienced there.

Melanie was doing her best to distract him from his musings. When her persona was that of a girlfriend their relationship was progressing in the direction that she was manipulating. In the office, however, despite doing her best to distract him, her efforts were unsuccessful, as Monty could still feel the pull of the artist behind the charcoal picture in his desk drawer. And he was no nearer to locating Teddy. Which was not surprising considering that he had yet to initiate any effort in that direction.

In the end, he did not need to expend the energy.

"You will be coming, won't you?" Melanie asked. She was once more provocatively leaning towards him across his desk, and Monty had to smile to himself. They both knew what effect that pose had on him, and he was glad to be seated where his interest was hidden.

He pulled his desk diary closer to him, but could see nothing scheduled for the day. "Coming?" he asked curiously, as that was the only response he could think of, having no idea what engagement Melanie was referring to.

Melanie sighed. Monty had been like this, distracted, for weeks now. Ever since that stupid gallery opening. Mind you, that had not turned out to be the fiasco that she had been dreading. She had been astonishingly surprised at the calibre of people who were in attendance. And as a consequence she had had the opportunity to make herself known to many people whom she only recognised from various media sources. And had then made a number of potentially good connections, for herself, if not for Monty. She had never figured out why he was so enraptured by the so-called artwork. And then he had even had the audacity to get her to hang one of the stupid pictures.

"The cocktail party."

"Cocktail party?" Monty, drawing a blank, and hoping to gain some time, thumbed over some of the pages in the diary, didn't miss the sigh that escaped from Melanie. He looked up at her and wondered if she had meant for him to hear.

"Yes, *my* cocktail party," she said, with a forced smile. How could he forget? It was to mark her birthday. But, more than that, it would also provide her with an opportunity to reintroduce Monty to her newer social circle. The one that she had been nurturing since the art exhibition.

"You're having a cocktail party? I thought those things were no longer in vogue. What's the occasion?"

"Cocktail parties are always in vogue if you know the right people. Don't tell me that you've forgotten."

"Sorry Mel, my mind has been taken up with other things of late," he said, stating the obvious.

"Well? You are coming, aren't you?"

"When is it again?" He flipped some more pages before shutting the diary. Of course it would not be in his work diary; cocktail parties were never work-related. So that could only mean it would be in the evening, and he wondered what evening, and if he could fabricate a reason not to attend. Normally he was not averse to socialising, but with his head in such a turmoil it was the last thing he wanted to do – mindless chatter.

"It is this Friday, and it is at my place because I am hosting it. You did say that you would come." Melanie allowed a pout to appear as she tilted her head and leaned in even closer.

Monty sighed, yes, now he did remember. Of course, it was Melanie's birthday. She would most certainly want him to be there. Maybe an evening of senseless prattle in such an environment might dull his mind sufficiently to erase the current quandary occupying his thoughts.

Averting his eyes from the inviting cleavage confronting him across the desk he looked at Melanie and orchestrated a beguiling smile. "Of course I'll be there. How could I not?" He smiled weakly. "Can't wait, looking forward to it." And hoped she was not a mind reader and could see his mental crossed fingers.

EIGHTEEN

Friday arrived too quickly for Monty, but after a couple of strong, stiff drinks he was about as ready as he could be. Or so he thought.

Normally he had no problems dressing for any occasion. The mandatory tails, tuxedos, and black-and-white tie ensembles filled a dedicated wardrobe. In the everyday wardrobe hung a selection of shirts in a rainbow of hues to be matched with any of his charcoal or black suits. Cravats and ties adorned the back of the wardrobe doors. He had deliberated over how formal to go for the evening. Knowing Melanie, she would have gone all out to dazzle her guests and would be expecting him to do the same so he took his time deciding what was best to wear. He walked to where an oval freestanding full length mirror stood, expecting to see an impeccably dressed reflection.

Monty gasped, and his reflection frowned back at him. Puzzled, he looked down at himself. Yes, he was wearing the chosen suit, shirt and cravat. He looked back at the mirror and saw a suntanned man in moleskins, checked shirt, elastic sided boots and an Akubra on his head. He shook his head. Enough! He then laughed as he quelled the juvenile impulse to stick his tongue out at his reflection. He ran his hands over his suit, straightened the cravat and walked out of the room.

"Monty! You made it!" Melanie gushed when she opened the door and saw him standing there. She fought hard to keep her irritation under lock and key. She'd asked him to come early but obviously he had forgotten, like so many things since that gallery opening.

Monty, totally oblivious to the underlying emotions, had to restrain the desire to emit a wolf-whistle as he gazed up and down. As he had predicted, she was dressed to kill – the lacy burgundy off the shoulder dress left nothing to his imagination as it clung to her figure.

"Did you think that I wasn't going to?" he asked as he looked into her eyes and smiled.

"Well," Melanie put a hand on her hip and pouted. "I was expecting you to come early and help me set up. And now you are the last one here." She wasn't about to admit that she had been anxiously waiting for him to arrive.

Her cocktail party had been nose-diving from the arrival of the first guests – the Manninghams. She had included them in the invitations to ensure that Monty would have someone with someone to converse – she knew from past experience that he was not always the most comfortable in her friends' company. The only trouble was that George had arrived with that artist woman and not Fiona.

Apparently, when their children had complained about feeling sick, Fiona had suggested that she stay at home with them, and for George to ask the artist to accompany him. After all, Monty would be there and he evidently knew them both. Besides, she, Fiona, didn't want to upset any seating plans. As if. Didn't the woman realise that it was a cocktail party, not a sit-down dinner? Kids. Who in their right mind would have them?

If Melanie had not been to the beautician and had nail extensions applied, she would have already bitten her own nails down to the quick. Instead, as soon as her next guests arrived she had made introductions and left them. She then channelled her vitriol to mingling with her other friends as they arrived, and fortifying herself with cocktails.

Monty smiled again, and slipped himself out of his coat, hanging it on the coatrack in the entrance hall before leaning in to kiss her cheek He wrinkled his nose at the citrusy aroma of margarita. And frowned. It looked like it was going to be a long evening, and he would probably have to stay and play nursemaid.

"You mean that I will be making a noticeable entrance?" He hoped that there was enough levity in his voice to placate Melanie.

She merely shrugged, grabbed his arm and propelled him into the living room. She hoped that the two of them would, indeed, make an entrance, and establish her ownership of Monty. Unfortunately, her guests were comfortably engaged in their own conversations, which did nothing to improve Melanie's mood.

She made her way towards the makeshift cocktail bar on the breakfast island, dragging Monty with her. "What can I get you?" she asked, her hand hovering over a display of opened bottles of spirits.

Monty sighed. He looked at what was on offer. Cocktails had never been high on his priorities of beverage. "Do you have something light? I drove here, and it's still early."

"Early? You call this early? Do I have to remind you, you are the last one here."

Monty looked at his watch and shrugged. He'd hardly call 'late'. "Then, what about a Sparkling Rosé?"

Armed with the requisite glass Monty turned around to see who else was present. It appeared to be only a few of the usual collection of Melanie's friends and mainly the people he'd been introduced in London. All people who liked to be seen rubbing shoulders with those who they hoped might benefit their rise up the social ladder. Then he spied George Manningham and he felt his gut clench. Monty looked around to see where George's wife was, but couldn't see her. Instead he found himself linking eyes with Teddy. That was even more confusing. Teddy was the last person he would ever imagine Melanie inviting, and he wondered why she had.

Teddy, occupied in a group of people whom he recognised, shrugged her shoulders and gave a small smile.

Monty felt Melanie, beside him, stiffen, but wasn't sure if it was the effect of him seeing Teddy, or George's approach. He took a sip of his drink, hoping that it would help validate the smile that he shaped his mouth into.

"Monty my boy! What a treat to see you again. Twice in a matter of weeks after years of silence. Where've you been?"

Monty braced himself for the back-slap which had been George's trademark greeting, and he wasn't disappointed.

Melanie, wanting as little as possible to do with George without Fiona, disengaged herself from Monty and returned to the bar.

Monty took another sip of his drink before responding. "Good to see you too, George," he lied. "Where's your wife? Fiona isn't it? I can't see her."

"Fee? Oh, she's back home with the kids. They're not well, though," George leant in to Monty, and gave him a light elbow dig in the side. "I think that was just an excuse to get out of this shindig."

"But you still came?"

"Wouldn't have missed the opportunity to spend some solo time with the luscious Miss Theodora." Another dig in the ribs accompanied a lecherous grin. "Isn't she something to get the blood racing? We met her a few years back, when we were on a cruise around the Pacific."

Monty raised his eyebrows in query.

"Oh yes, she was part of the entertainment. Well, not entertainment exactly." George laughed. "She was running art classes. Didn't help either Fee or myself, so you're saved from seeing any exhibitions from us. But we fell in love with her art. Bought a couple of seascapes that she did while we were on the cruise. She and Fee hit it off and kept in touch. Email's great."

"So, The ... er, Miss Theodora ... she wasn't invited?"

"No. Not at all. Fee thought it might be a bit of a laugh for me to bring her seeing as how Mel doesn't think much of her artistic talent, if her attitude at the gallery is anything to go by. Oh, sorry, she went to that opening with you didn't she. Are you, you know ...?" Another dig in the ribs accompanied the question.

Monty rubbed his side and sidled a bit away from George. He really was a bit of a bore. Is that how others saw them? Were they an item? He looked across the room to where Melanie was talking with some woman by the bar.

"Melanie? We work together, she's my PA."

"PA huh?" George punched the space that Monty had created. "You sly dog you. She's a looker isn't she? Mind you, take it from me, never marry your secretary." George laughed. "That's how Fee and Mel know each other – they trained together. Can I get you fill up?" He tilted his empty glass to clink with Monty's nearly full one.

"Thank you, but I'll sit on this one for a bit longer. Nice to catch up." Monty took a further step away and looked for Teddy. She was still engaged in conversation, but he didn't care, he needed to speak with her. Find out how he could contact her afterwards.

"Yeah, we must do it some more. You'll have to come over for dinner one day," George said as he turned around. "And bring Melanie," he said with a wink over his shoulder as he made his way towards her.

Monty stood as though magnetised to the white tiles on Melanie's living room floor. He knew that he had fallen short of her expectations, but for the time being he was not interested in approaching her, not even to rescue her from the lascivious advances being made by George. Nor did he feel inclined to interrupt the animated conversation that was holding Teddy enthralled.

He stifled a yawn before taking another sip of his Rosé, and wondered why he had even bothered to come this evening when he knew that it would feature Melanie's friends and that the evening would be taken up making meaningless conversation to colourless people with whom he had little in common. He looked from Melanie, leaning suggestively against George, twirling her glass enticingly in front of him, across to where Teddy stood in a simple demure waisted dress, and engaged in what appeared to be an animated and engaging conversation. The contrast was so blatantly obvious. Melanie who so wanted to be one of the 'in' crowd, and Teddy who didn't have to try.

What had he been thinking?

He put his glass down on a nearby side table and walked over to Teddy and whispered in her ear while he smiled at the others in the group. He then walked over to the bar.

"Sorry Mel, but I've got to leave. I'll see you on Monday."

"But Monty, you have only just got here. I thought you were going to help me."

"Maybe George here will help you. Won't you?" Monty slapped George on the shoulder, smiled, and walked out the front door.

Melanie watched Monty leave, shrugged her shoulders and turned her attention back to George who was beaming at her.

"It will be my pleasure to help you, in whatever way you desire."

It was only a couple of minutes before Teddy made her excuses to a relieved Melanie and a confused George who was torn between his promise to his wife to look after Theodora, and his attraction to Melanie.

Teddy met Monty outside beside his car.

NINETEEN

"Phew," Teddy uttered in relief as she almost fell into the front passenger seat of Monty's silver BMW 5 Series. "Thanks for rescuing me. Nice set of wheels by the way," she added, strapping herself in.

"Thanks. Didn't think you needed rescuing. I was about to apologise for dragging you away from your admirers." Monty clipped his seatbelt into the anchor point and turned the key in the ignition.

Teddy laughed. "Not a problem, I can only take so much fawning. And it gets rather tiresome having to explain away these," she said as she traced her finger down the scars along her neck. "You Brits and your stiff-upper-lip syndrome, always too polite to ask, but at the same time they can't avert their eyes from staring. It's all rather tedious once the novelty wears off."

Monty raised his eyes in silent reply, not sure what to say. "Where to?" he asked as he indicated to enter the flow of traffic. "Do you want to go somewhere for a coffee, or shall I take you home?"

Teddy snapped her head to look at him, mouth, and eyes, wide open. "Home? Isn't that being a bit forward of you? I mean, we may know each other, but that was years ago."

Monty gave an embarrassed laugh. "You still trying to correct me when I put my foot in my mouth? I meant, would you like me to drop you off wherever you are staying?"

Teddy shook her head. "Best we have a coffee or maybe something to eat. A girl can't survive for long on cocktails and nibbles. Then if you could drop me off at the station, that would be great, thanks."

Monty momentarily frowned, but it made sense that she would be staying in London, after all, that was where the exhibition was, and where George lived. "So be it. Let's go find us a café."

While they waited to be served Monty looked briefly at Teddy, then at his shoes. He could feel a flush start to make itself known. For goodness' sake, what was the matter with him? He was no longer the naïve man dumped into a foreign culture. Fifteen years had passed and he was on his own turf now. But the guilt would never die. And here was Teddy unashamedly almost flaunting her injuries and expecting him to be happy to open the mental hatch that he had spent those years trying to keep securely down and buried.

"Are you married?" Teddy asked forthrightly, which took Monty by surprise till he remembered who was asking, and he was taken back to *Calinda*, and he smiled.

"You haven't changed, have you? No beating around the bush with you is there?"

Teddy shrugged her shoulders. "I might be out of Australia, but that doesn't mean that Australia is out of me." She smiled up at him, her eyes twinkling like he remembered they did when she was taking the mickey out of him, and he couldn't help but smile back. It felt good to banter again. It had been a while.

"Well, are you?"

"Why do you ask?"

"Only I thought it might have been your wife that was with you at the opening. But it couldn't have been if tonight didn't involve you. I kinda felt sorry for you that evening," she laughed. "Sorry, but she wasn't what I imagined your wife would be like. So ...?"

"I'm divorced."

Teddy nodded and gave him a gentle push forward. It was their turn to order.

"Children?"

"What?" Monty turned from talking with the young man behind the counter and looked down at his feet to see them shuffling, much as they had on numerous occasions back on *Calinda* whenever Teddy had taken delight in showing up his ignorance of life in The Outback.

"Children. Do you have any?"

"Two," he said as he paid for their order, picked up the table number stand and led the way to a vacant table near the window.

Teddy sat down. "Do they have names?"

"Chas and Lottie," Monty replied as he set the table number stand down on the table and sat down opposite her.

"Good grief Charlie Hirst. You have subjected your son to be a fourth?" With hands joined in reverence and a slight bow she imitated subservience, "Charles Montgomery Chinthurst IV," she laughed.

"It's a family tradition. My father expected it."

"Your father expected it?" she asked. "How many more generations, are going to have to endure a number after their name?"

"Chas will be the last,"

"What? You already know that he will have no son?"

It was Monty's turn to laugh. "No, it will revert to what it was before my grandfather."

"And what monstrosity of a name was that?"

He wanted to ask her if his name was so offensive, then what did she think about her own name, but decided against it.

"Montgomery Charles. And before you ask, there were four of them before my grandfather." He watched the incredulity filling her face, and felt embarrassed. It did seem rather pompous.

"What about you? Are you married?"

"Me? Married? Really? You think anyone would want to be married to me with all this?" She waved her hand in front of her face. "These scars might be a source of conversation, but no man wants to be seen with me as his wife."

Monty was surprised this was said with no hint of maliciousness, and he gave an embarrassed cough.

"Then those men are not worth the air they breathe. They ought to be honoured to be seen with someone as courageous as you".

Teddy laughed.

"How do you do that?"

"Do what?" Teddy asked, totally perplexed by Monty's reaction.

"Laugh about that day, and ... and that." Monty used his head to point in the general direction of the scarring that, to him, was all too obvious.

Teddy raised her right hand and ran it across her lower face and down her neck. "You mean this?" Teddy laughed again.

"Er, about that. I'm still mortified. I try to forget that day."

"Yes, I guess that would be about right for you."

Monty, startled by the levity in Teddy's voice, wondered if once again she was making fun of him, and was surprised that he didn't mind. He looked at her and shook his head. How could she laugh?

To Monty the trilling seemed to echo around the room, and he looked about him to see who was there to witness his discomfort. But the few patrons that were sharing their space were too engrossed in their own worlds to notice.

He could only nod his head as the tendrils of vivid memory started to once more leach out of their stronghold.

Monty watched, almost hypnotised, as, sitting across from him, she let her fingers play across the scars as though they were the keys of a piano. "This is my badge of honour."

"Badge of Honour?"

"Oh, of course, in hospital with all the attention and treatment I was too doped up to be embarrassed or mortified. It hurt like hell, you know? But I guess you wouldn't have known. You didn't hang around long enough for me to yell at you! Naturally all the locals were very solicitous, and telling me how brave I was. Not just for what I had done, but for how I had survived all the treatment and convalescence. I was the local hero – even got my picture in the newspapers. 'Young Girl Survives Kangaroo Attack.'"

Teddy noticed that Monty had started to blush and was trying to hide his fidgeting. "I caused you so much pain," he mumbled.

"You didn't hang around to find out. Or to see the recovery. Oh, don't worry, I didn't drop you in it. Well, not too much. Couldn't make you out to be the total loser you were in The Outback." She laughed again. "Anyway, I went away to school and the girls could not hide their curiosity, so I hammed it up and soon I was almost a poster-girl, some of the girls even kinda hero-worshipped me. By then it was too late for me to become a 'woe-is-me' sympathy seeker, and so, here I am."

Monty watched as she lay her forearms over the top of the table, and smiled at him. It was done in such a natural and unpremeditated way that he found himself comparing the woman with him to Melanie. If it had been Melanie sitting opposite him he would have suspected that it was an invitation for him to reach out and hold her hands. And strangely, it was all he could do to restrain himself from doing so. This was Teddy with him. Teddy. The little girl who had delighted in lambasting him at every opportunity. What was he thinking? He swallowed, "Yes. Here you are. But what are you doing here?"

"Here-here in Cambridge, or here as in, in the UK?" Teddy laughed, her head tilted to the side so that the scars on her neck stood out like knotted cables, and she slid her arms from the table and placed them in her lap as the waitress placed their order on the table.

"Here in the UK. George has already explained the here-in-Cambridge bit, and how you know each other. Which begs the question – who were all those people at the gallery that night?"

"So which question do you want me to answer?"

"Both, I guess. Order doesn't matter."

"Actually, they go hand-in-hand. At boarding school I realised that with my brothers well entrenched helping dad back on *Calinda* there was no room for me back there. I did contemplate Ag College, but I was encouraged to pursue art as a career, so I became an art teacher to sustain me while I painted. Stood me in pretty good stead as it turned out," she laughed.

"Who would have known some daubs of red could produce clammerings verging on the chaotic? A bit like Picasso, I went through different styles and techniques before settling on what you saw at the gallery in London. I've stuck with that one as it was the style that seemed to attract the most public interest. Certainly with you Brits who really are a fickle lot. Personally I like things which are a bit more realistic. But these seem to evoke more emotion in the public. They tell me that they 'feel' things in what I portray. Anyway, those who I invited to the opening are they who have been the most vocal in encouraging me to come over here. Not sure if they think I can evoke the same 'feelings' into paintings in this cold climate, but here I am anyway. I know that I like to create images from personal experiences. Just hope that I can acquire some while I'm here."

"How long have you been here in the UK, and when are you returning to Australia?"

"You trying to get rid of me?" Teddy laughed.

Monty winced he didn't think his question had warranted a laugh. Still, he enjoyed hearing Teddy's laugh. He didn't know why, but it sounded so much more genuine than the laughter he rarely heard from his colleagues and friends. He wondered if it had something to do with one's background. His and Teddy's certainly were different.

"No, just curious." What he was curious about was the time difference between her arrival in England, and her contacting him.

"Well," Teddy sat back and placed laced fingers on the edge of the table. "I arrived in London in time to finalise the exhibition and send out the invitations. How long I'm here for is anyone's guess.

No plans. But seeing as how I've come *all* this way, I may as well see something of the land of my ancestors."

"Then allow me to repay your hospitality from years past, and show you something of *my* land."

Teddy laughed again, and Monty felt his pulse ping. "You mean it's payback time? I'll have you know that I am probably better prepared to experience life in England compared to the floundering you displayed on your arrival in 'the colonies'. My goodness but you were such a buffoon!"

"Yes, well, that was then, when we were both much younger. This is now and the world has become smaller. I would expect you to have a better knowledge of what to expect. After all Australia originally came from Britain, so you would have a certain innate understanding of what to expect once you put your feet on British soil."

"You mean the concreted streets of London? Not much soil to be seen there."

"You want to experience British soil then? I know just the place." Monty smiled. "I'll pick you up next Saturday. Now I believe you have a train to catch. Don't want you arriving back in London in the dark." He stood up and put his hand out to help Teddy.

Later that evening Monty re-ran the conversation with Teddy. He marvelled that she could be so cavalier about the scarring that his idiocy had caused and thought that he might have felt exonerated. But to his dismay he realised that acknowledging his role and admitting his remorse were not enough to feel free from the guilt. What he needed was to hear Teddy accept his apology and forgive him.

TWENTY

Melanie frowned as she came into Monty's office with the morning's mail. There he was, as had been his wont of late. Standing in front of the two framed pictures which he had had her fix onto the wall, while the previous days' mail, along with the accumulated files that needed attention were in competing piles vying to imitate the tower of Pisa. It was so unlike him to not be collected and functional.

She sighed quietly. Nothing had changed. For days she had been tactfully trying to coerce him back to his desk and away from either the window or the frames. Yet the more she needled him to get his work done, the harder it was to dodge and his oscillating moods. It was so very out of character, and she could not place what could have brought on the cloud that Monty seemed to be hugging. She quietly walked over to the desk, deposited the mail beside the tottering tower, and quietly walked over to join him.

"Hmm, that's a rather attractive couple there, don't you think?" she said flippantly, making to lean her head against his shoulder.

But Monty turned aside and stared at her.

"I have no idea why you even bothered to get a print, far less have it enlarged and then framed," he spat.

Melanie took a step back and gaped at him.

"I did it for you! It enhances your profile."

"There's nothing wrong with my profile. My profile is an excellent example of my bloodline I'll have you know." Monty turned side on to her and ran his finger down his face from his hairline to chin. "See, I have a chiselled profile, aquiline nose, and a strong jawline."

"I don't mean that kind of profile, and you know it. You need to display to your clients the circles that you move in. It is most important in business, you know."

"Oh, and you know, do you?" He allowed himself to smile at her discomfort.

Melanie bit her tongue and felt like stamping her foot and thumping him.

"You know what I mean," she almost wined, exasperated to think that Monty was making fun of her. Either that, or he was a total dullard when it came to networking. Which, as she thought about it, possibly he was. Besides, the firm was so established that it probably didn't need the publicity.

"I was only thinking of you, M... Mr Chinthurst. Of enhancing your standing among your clients.

"Total waste of money if you ask me," Monty said as he turned to walk over to look out the window.

"Well, it's a good thing I didn't ask you then, isn't it? At least it is better than that monstrosity," she said, pointing to the kangaroo hanging beside the black and white group photo.

Monty stopped and turned back to face Melanie.

"I mean," she continued, looking at the picture and not at Monty who was clenching his jaws. "What impression does a dumb kangaroo present?"

Monty looked at the kangaroo and joey, and unconsciously ran his finger around the collar of his shirt. It, and the charcoal sketch hidden in his desk drawer, were his very own albatross.

He needed to talk to Teddy.

It was as though the envelope was the Pandora's Box he thought he had firmly sat on when he boarded the plane back to England. Teddy knowing the address to send the invitation to had been the beginning of what was becoming an unwelcome and unsettling bother. He worked his jaw and ground his teeth. How was he expected to concentrate on work, or his blossoming relationship with Melanie while the guilt, so long buried had resurfaced and still hung over him with a regret that was now deeper than it ever had been? And all because Teddy had found it necessary to reintroduce him to her world, which he had never wanted to enter.

Oh, there were so many things he found he was yearning to know. For starters, would Teddy find it possible to forgive him? Then there was the question of how had Teddy come by his address? If she had his address, why had it taken her till now to contact him? Not that he would have welcomed an earlier intrusion. But now that she had forced open the suppressed memories he wanted to know more – how Ralph was, and if Betty was still alive.

"I'll have you know," Monty was struggling to keep his tone under control, "that piece of art means more to me than any media generated kudos could ever do."

Melanie stared at Monty. She had been perturbed by the cloud that had hung around Monty of late. But now, if he had some attachment to the proclaimed artistic ability in the picture that he was fixated on, she had major concerns that maybe there was something seriously afflicting him.

"I have no idea how anyone can ever suggest that that Australian woman could be considered an artist. And those ghastly scars. How she can parade them so openly and without embarrassment. Has she no decorum or decency?" Melanie felt, rather than saw, Monty stiffen, and she quickly recognised that she had probably overstepped some line. "Though," she quickly added, hoping to recover from her faux pas, "I am quite sure that many might find it in their heart to consider her attractive. Certainly if she had plastic surgery to remove them. Not that that would improve her artistic ability."

It was Monty's turn to stare at his PA. He had acknowledged that their tastes in art differed, but he had not expected her to be so unfeeling towards a person who wore disfigurement as openly and proudly as Teddy.

Monty watched as Melanie put her hand out to touch his arm, then, when she did touch him, he covered her hand with his. He had no cause to blame her for her unkind words. Melanie did not know that the scars were Teddy's talisman. And exposing them the way she did said more about her bravery than any amount of heroics in his lifetime could his. No, he admired Teddy's unflinching courage. Not only in openly wearing her scars, but also in the act from which she acquired them.

"Would you like me to fetch you a drink? Tea, maybe? Or ..." Melanie looked towards the drink's cabinet further along the wall.

Monty disengaged himself, turned and walked back to his desk. "No thanks Mel, I'd better keep a clear head and tackle some of these files. A tea would be nice, though."

Though he doubted that he would manage to achieve much, not while where he was to take Teddy on Saturday still occupied his mind. He was still no closer to deciding on a destination.

Monty had spent more time thinking about where he could take Teddy than concentrating on the work Melanie kept depositing on his desk. He had told Teddy that he knew just the place, but in all honesty he had no idea where would be the most exciting place for Teddy to visit. He had no idea what she had seen or where she had been. Or even what she might be interested in seeing that would inspire her artistic talent.

By Thursday he was still no closer to deciding on a destination. He had entertained the notion of asking Melanie or his father for suggestions, but then thought better of it. Melanie would immediately think he was intending to take her someplace, and his father simply had no imagination. This was something he had to do on his own. He had promised Teddy that she would experience putting her feet on English soil. And he had less than two days to come up with where that was.

"Mr Chinthurst." Melanie sounded exasperated, and when Monty looked up at her standing in front of his desk, she looked more peeved than she usually did when he hadn't been concentrating and keeping up to date with his work.

"Yes Melanie, what is it this time?" This time. That is all he seemed to recall saying to her. This time. Was he really falling that far behind in his work?

"You really do need to sign these papers," she said, flapping a handful of papers across the desk and in front of him. "And Mr Whelps is here for the 3 o'clock meeting with you and your father."

Monty looked at his watch, and quietly cursed.

"Right. I'll be right there. Show him in ... er, where's the meeting to be, did my father say? Oh, and leave the papers here, I'll get to signing them after seeing Mr Whelps. Do you have his file handy?"

Melanie sighed, put the papers she held in her hand onto the desk, then moved around to squat down beside Monty's chair. She put her hand on his arm. "Monty, you really need to pull yourself together and get back to work. Why don't you come round to my place after the meeting? I'll fetch in an Indian and we can talk."

Monty stared at her hand, then at her and smiled, in what he hoped was a manner which she would interpret as compassionate and not reflecting the irritation that he felt – she knew the protocol of no first names at work. Slowly he lifted her hand off his arm, pushed the chair back and stood up.

"Mr Whelps' file please, and where is my father?"

Chagrined, Melanie levered herself to her feet with the help of Monty's desk and, smoothing her skirt down with her hands, she walked back to the front of the desk.

"Your father has the file. He and Mr Whelps are waiting in the smaller meeting room," she said as she tossed her head, and with a sniff she walked out of the office. She was inwardly fuming that Monty would fob her off like that, and not even have the decency to acknowledge, far less accept her invitation. He'd hardly spoken to her beyond business all week. He hadn't even apologised for not only his late arrival to her party, but also his premature departure. Not that, in the end, it really mattered. George Manningham had filled the role that she had mentally prepared for Monty, and she could smile at the memory. But still, it was her boss who was in her sights, after all he was a bigger catch, and he wasn't married. Yes, she could forgive Monty. But she would not let him off lightly.

TWENTYONE

It was a hard decision, but in the end, having already arranged for Teddy to catch the train out to Cambridge, Monty decided that a drive out to Anglesey Abbey might work. He hadn't been there for years, but remembered being impressed with the grandeur of the place and its extensive gardens.

As he patiently paced the concourse waiting for Teddy's train to arrive, Monty just hoped that she might be similarly enthralled. He was excited to see what art such a visit might inspire. He laughed for a fleeting moment wondering what Melanie would make of English life and landscapes rendered at Teddy's hands. There would be little, or no, opportunity for splashes of red to offend Melanie.

"I thought you said you were going to let me stand on soil today," Teddy exclaimed as Monty skillfully negotiated his way out of the carpark and threaded his way through streets of terraced houses. "I mean, this is all very English, and I suppose quaint, but it is still concrete and stone."

"There'll be grass and trees coming up, and plenty to be found where we are headed."

Teddy looked across at Monty, puzzled. He almost sounded excited, and that was not an emotion that she expected from him. Country? Excited? And dressed like that? She was starting to get nervous and looked down at her dress ensemble, and wondered if she had made a fashion faux pas.

When Charlie had said a day out in the country, she had dressed in what she thought was appropriate – jeans, jumper and sturdy sneakers. Then there was her sturdy shoulder bag that went everywhere with her. Quite the contrast to Charlie who had met her at the station, turning the head of every female in sight, in a fashionably cut charcoal suit with, she had to smile, a muted pink shirt. She noted that at least he had not bothered with a tie or his

123

usual cravat, though he was wearing cufflinks and had a deeper pink pocket square visible.

"So, where are we headed?" Teddy asked, looking out at the mix of industrial and residential buildings that lined the road. Still no suggestion of 'country'.

"Ah, wait and see. Otherwise it won't be a surprise." Monty grinned. He was liking the opportunity to turn the tables on Teddy, even though he felt deflated that what he had in store to share with her was definitely lacking on the comparison scale to the surprises she had exposed him to. His mind started to once more veer towards the memories he'd locked away, but Teddy conveniently interrupted. The recollections that had resurfaced when he'd viewed her artwork at the gallery were still vividly bouncing around, nudging his thoughts into places he still wanted kept buried.

"Who said I wanted a surprise?"

"I thought you liked surprises. I recall that you were always anxious to go out of your way to create them for me."

Teddy laughed. "Of course I did. You were so gullible and such an easy target. Didn't you think to do some homework before you arrived in Australia? You must have known that things would be different. Didn't you?" She looked across at him and he briefly took his eyes off the road to flash her a quick glance.

"Did you bring a camera with you?"

"Always," she laughed, pulling her phone out of her bag and waggling it in the air. "Don't you?"

Monty looked across at her incredulously. "You mean I could've phoned you? Why didn't you give me your number? It would have saved me wondering how to contact you." And saved me having to resort to asking George, he thought dolefully shaking his head.

"You mean you have a mobile?" she laughed sarcastically. "Who'd have thought?"

"I try not to use mine, certainly not for photos."

"Same. Well not exactly. I try not to use my phone as a phone either," she laughed. "I use mine mainly for taking photos. I don't like people knowing how to contact me when I'm at work, or on holiday."

"Then why bother with a phone at all. You can get small cameras you know."

"Oh, I know that silly. No, I like knowing that I have a means of communication if I need it. You know, emergencies and the like. But no, not for people bothering me."

Monty, marvelling at their mutual dislike of this aspect of modern technology, didn't respond immediately.

"I only asked as I couldn't see any arty paraphernalia, nor photographic equipment. Thought a camera would be easier and quicker than carting around all your painting gear. Or do you work totally from memory? Can't say I recall your memory being all that good when it came to remembering details when we were in the classroom back on Calinda."

"Huh! That might have had something to do with how ineffectual the tutor was. Or, that I simply wasn't interested."

"Yes, I do recall that the opportunities to humiliate me outside held greater appeal."

"Are you going to have a go at reversing the roles now that I am here on your home turf?"

"I wouldn't dare," he laughed, and hoped that the lie couldn't be read. He had never been good at covering his lies, but there was no way that he was going to allow Teddy to learn that such was what he wanted to do. If she found out, there'd be no knowing how she would retaliate. Easier to fib and hope.

"Don't tell me that we're going to be flying somewhere?" Teddy asked, seeing the signpost to the airport.

"What makes you think ... oh, the airport. No, don't think I ever want to see you inside a plane again. Besides, being airborne, or even getting into a plane, you don't have your feet on British soil, and I thought that was the whole point of today's outing."

"So why is it all a surprise?"

Well, there goes the subterfuge and lie, Monty thought. It had to come out, better now than later. He took a deep breath before answering. "Because I wanted to have the opportunity to get my own back and have you wondering and guessing and not knowing what to expect."

"Huh! You are trying to better me then!" Teddy laughed again.

"To better you would be a real challenge, one that I'm not up to. No, the difference here is, that today it will be nothing as earth-shattering, unusual or nerve-raking as anything you put me through. All we have here in the UK that is not to be found in Australia, is history. And, before you jump down my throat, I'm not knocking your indigenous First Nations history, I'm talking about European history. You know the Romans and the Normans, and the Saxons, kings, and wars and all that sort of history."

Monty slowed the car down as he approached their destination.

"You've brought me to an abbey?" Teddy, reading the signage, sounded incredulous as Monty turned off the road and into a carpark. "An abbey is still not soil. And I bet the surrounds are concrete, or pebbles, or something that isn't grass. You're a fraud!" she laughed.

"Come on, you'll soon see why I've brought you here," Monty said as he undid his seatbelt, got out of the car and went around to open the door for Teddy. Then mentally chastised himself – of course Teddy wouldn't wait and was already out of the car by the time he arrived at her door.

Together they walked to the Visitor's Centre to buy their entry tickets, Teddy's head swivelling faster than a table fan.

TWENTYTWO

Teddy stood at the entrance to the grounds and turned to Monty. "Hey Charlie, which path do we take?"

Monty gave a mental sigh, and wondered whether he should tell her, again, that his name was Monty. Still, he did rather like the way she called him Charlie, so decided to give it a miss. Besides, he didn't want to get on her bad side before broaching the elephant that he was desperate to be rid of. He hoped to find the opportunity today, and then he could get on with his life.

He smiled, and inclined his head to the right. "This way."

"Right," she said and, not waiting for him, headed off down the path that gracefully curved its way between a colourful array of shrubs.

Monty followed her as she set off, almost bouncing down the Winter Walk, her feet softly scrunching on the pea gravel path. And he found himself comparing her enthusiasm to the last time he had come here and almost laughed at the difference. That occasion had been an office picnic – his father had thought it might be a good bonding session, and Melanie, new to the firm, had been a leech, all but clinging to him as the party walked sedately to the Lode Mill before then making their way to where a picnic was being set up for them.

Teddy was now well ahead of him, almost skipping before she turned around to face him, walking backwards, her smile broad enough that it almost matched her wide-spread arms.

"This really is something. And such a different palette to what I am used to seeing in Australia. Will you look at that!" she said as she waved her hands in a huge circle. "So much colour, and everything is so green. I never knew there could be so many different greens. Did you? It's so much nicer than the almost universal dull grey-green of the vegetation back home."

Monty caught up to her and looked about. He'd never really noticed, but yes, there were many shades of green on display, from dark to light, and every imaginable variation in between. Nothing at all like drab monotony of those few trees he'd come across around *Calinda*. He smiled at the memory, one which was not fraught with embarrassment, and could almost bring to mind the heady almost overpowering fragrance of their leaves when scrunched in the palm of his hand.

"Oh, this is so wonderful," Teddy exclaimed as she twirled around in a 360, her face beaming.

Monty looked up at the sky and sent a silent prayer of thanks for the blue, cloudless canopy above them. He felt sure that his companion would not have been so enraptured if it had been one of the dreary grey and dull days that frequently plagued his outings. He felt sure that any experience he shared with Teddy would pale compared to the world that she had opened up to him all those years ago. But for some primeval reason he was desperately wanting to impress her. The limited time he had spent in her company was refreshing

"Come on, there is plenty more for you to see," Monty said as he took her elbow and encouraged her to continue down the Winter Walk. If she was as enthusiastic about these plantings, he couldn't wait for her to see what was coming up next.

He didn't have long to wait, and he was not disappointed.

"Oh, Charlie! Will you look at this?" Teddy exclaimed, pointing down a short path to where a statue of a man stood on a square plinth with a plaque. "Does he remind you of anyone?" She grinned at Monty and stuck her signature pose.

Monty knew both what she was looking at, and what she was referring to, and he felt himself start to blush at the memory. Not only of the night in question, but of the framed picture residing in its bubble wrap bed in his desk.

Teddy then burst out laughing. "You do remember. But of course you do, I sent you your own personal reminder. Come on, let me read what it says." She grabbed hold of his hand and pulled him into a quiet garden filled with lavender and wooden slatted seats.

She bent down to read the inscription before standing back up, disappointed. "It's in Latin. You must know what it says. You must have learned Latin."

She looked up at him enquiringly with just the hint of humour and Monty wondered if she was once again baiting him, like she used to do back in the classroom on *Calinda*. She had been a imp back then, and he was beginning to realize that she hadn't changed. For a moment he wondered how best to respond. Then, remembering that he had brought her to experience England, and not to engage in childish verbal one-up-manship decided to keep things neutral, and he took a look for himself.

"You must remember, that it has been quite some years since I was exposed to the Latin language. Not sure that my schoolboy Latin is up to the task, but I'll give it my best try."

Monty took his time reading the inscription before turning to see that Teddy was slowly walking around the garden. He caught up to her.

"You got it sussed then, have you?" she asked.

"Well, it was put here in 1996 ..."

Teddy laughed. "Even I could have told you that. Roman numerals are easy. What does the rest of it say?"

"Let's say that the statue is dedicated to the memory of Huttleston Broughton."

"And who's he when he's at home?" Teddy had moved to sit on one of the benches, hands clasped in her lap and swinging her feet like a child.

Monty felt pleased that he had taken the time to 'bone-up' on the place. He may not have been able to translate the plaque verbatim, but he *could* share what he knew about Anglesey Abbey. "He died in 1966. He owned this property, and was instrumental in establishing the gardens that you are now enjoying. At least I hope you are enjoying them."

"Very much so. It's beautiful here."

Monty was enjoying watching her delight, but he was also anxious to find an opportunity to broach the subject that had been plaguing him since, well, since seeing her lying in the dust, crying and bloodied as the kangaroo hopped away; then comatosed as she was lifted into the Flying Doctor plane.

"Come on, there's more to see."

"Can't we just sit here for a bit longer?"

"Plenty time to sit when we've finished looking at what else the place has to offer. There are lots of interesting things. Come on," he said, reaching out his hand to her to walk back to the main path they had been following.

"That, is certainly interesting," Teddy said, pointing across from where they were exiting the quiet garden. "What is it?"

Monty had to admit that it did look interesting, and enticing, but it was not what he had in mind as the 'interesting' item.

"Oh, that is covering the porphyry bowl in the garden pavilion," he said, leading the way further along the Winter Walk. But Teddy was not finished, and stood looking at the square dome peeping above the high hedge, trying, and failing, to imagine a bowl sitting under it.

"The what bowl?" she asked, hurrying to catch up to Monty.

"Porphyry. It's a type of igneous rock, you know, rock that's formed through the cooling and solidification of lava."

"I'll take your word for it. Are we going to take a look at it?"

"Not right now." Monty really was wanting to rid himself of the guilt. "I think you will find the next thing, er, more interesting." In all honesty, he had no idea if she would find the statue of the man and his dogs interesting or not. But he liked looking at it, imagining that the man was himself, all set out to go hunting with his two dogs. Besides, he hoped the vague similarity of the subject, hunting, might provide the right atmosphere for his confession. But he did not get the chance.

"This really is something," Teddy exclaimed as she ran ahead, by-passing the path that led to the Huntsman and dogs statue by Alfred Jacquemart. "I don't think I've ever been on a path heralded with so many trees. It's not like walking in the bush back home. Gotta watch for snakes and all. And the trees are all higgledy-piggledy. Not like these regimental ones. What are they?"

"Birches." Monty tried not to sound thwarted as he looked down towards the statue. "Not sure what sort." There went his opportunity, which was probably for the best. He had no right to disrupt the enjoyment Teddy was exhibiting. So different to the indifference shown by Melanie. He shook his head, whatever had she been thinking, wearing heels to the office picnic?

Monty caught up to Teddy as she walked under the arch and stopped.

"Oh Charlie, will you look at that. What is it?" Teddy asked as she slipped her arm through his.

Monty looked first at the white building and watercourse appearing before them then down at her hand on his arm and smiled. Her touch felt so light and not at all proprietorial compared to Melanie's. He placed his hand over hers and smiled. It felt good, which surprised him. In a good way, and he decided to chicken-out and leave his confession to another day. Tomorrow maybe. He didn't want to leave it for too long, his courage might dissipate and he would be left with the guilt festering, and there was no way that he would be able to submerge it again.

When Monty didn't respond immediately Teddy dug her elbow into his side, interrupting his musings. He looked down at her, and, still caught up in his thoughts answered in an offhand manner.

"That's the Lode," he stated.

Teddy removed her arm and stepped away from Monty before turning to face him.

"Load? As in load of what?" she asked, her head tilted to one side.

Monty wasn't too sure if Teddy was asking a serious question or if she was up to her usual tricks when it came to interacting with him. Either way, he found it somewhat endearing – it was nice to be reminded that not everything in his life was dictated by the socially accepted constraints demanded of his station.

"It's a load of water," Monty replied, surprised at how easy it was to lapse into frivolity and decided to take a leap and join in with some levity, hoping that it would cover all potential variables of her query.

"No kidding? I'd never have guessed."

"Well, how am I to know, what with you coming from a drought-ridden country, that you would know what a river of water looked like?"

Teddy harrumphed and chose not to dignify him with an answer. "And the white building?"

"That's the Mill."

"Looks different to the water mills back on *Calinda* doesn't it?"

This time there was no doubting the sincerity of her question.

"Most definitely, and it serves a different purpose as well," Monty said, remembering the first water mill he encountered, and then the one which Teddy had him experience intimately. "If you'd had more water running back on *Calinda* you would not have needed any water mills," he laughed, and felt a warmth spread through him as Teddy's trilling laugh joined his.

"No, this water mill, is now used to grind grain to produce wheat and oat flour that is sold in the mill shop."

"You say 'now', does that mean that it wasn't always a flour mill?"

Remembering the enquiring mind that Teddy had displayed as a young girl, Monty had read up on what the Estate had to offer. Now he realised that he wasn't as well versed as he thought.

He scratched his head, hoping to buy some time, but Teddy wasn't fooled.

"Ha! You don't know do you?" The laugh was more of a giggle this time, and he felt prickles of sweat in his armpits and across his hairline. He should have known better. He looked down at her triumphant upturned face and could see the restraint – she wanted to jiggle in delight at his discomfort.

He laughed. Surprised that it felt good to do so.

"In all honesty, no. I don't know. Unlike you, I was happy to accept what I was told. But I will find out, if you like." He smiled to himself and looked at her. "You haven't changed, have you?"

"Me? Not likely," she laughed again.

But I have, many times, Monty thought. I'm no longer the reprobate sent away to a far-flung land where I learned what it was to be a carefree larakin, only to return home to the mould that I'd been fashioned to fill. Now, having Teddy re-enter his life he could feel the rigid corners of his existence under threat of being eroded. And he was beginning to like the notion. He shivered to think what Melanie, and his father would have to say about the pending metamorphosis.

Thoughts of Melanie and his father brought with them the memory that the only comment she had made at this same place, had been to do with her ruined shoes, and to ask how much further, before the champagne picnic lunch.

"It is getting a bit chilly isn't it?" Teddy asked after seeing Monty shudder. "I don't think I would ever get used to this climate. Give me the wide, open spaces, blue skies and sun, plenty of sun, any day. Even if we do get rotten weather, at times."

There was Teddy's laugh again. He couldn't remember the last time he heard Melanie laugh. Then he wondered if he'd ever heard her laugh. Did she even laugh?

Monty looked up and was surprised to see a skyful of clouds gathering and he shivered for real.

"Yes, let's get moving. We may have to skip some of the features. Don't suppose you are in the market to visit the plant shop, but there is bookshop. That's in the house proper, are you interested in taking a tour of the main house? Or we could have some lunch then head home." With the change in weather bringing a potential dampener to the day there was the possibility that he could, over lunch, bare his soul to Teddy and rid himself of his guilt.

TWENTYTHREE

Teddy and Monty were back standing not quite under the departure screens in the main station hall, at the railway station in Cambridge. Teddy held a bag of flour and pot of tulips in her arms and straddled a carry-bag filled with second-hand books between her legs. Monty stood with his hands stuck in his trouser pockets, safe from getting physical.

"It's been a beaut day out, thanks Charlie. I've enjoyed every minute of having my feet on English soil. Makes me feel almost at home. Not that it looks anything like home, but it was good to get away from the bustle and concrete of London," Teddy laughed.

Monty didn't feel like laughing. He was still fuming.

"Are you positive that I can't drive you back to London?" Monty eyed the bag of flour jiggling in her arms. It reminded him of a squirming child looking to escape, and he frowned.

"Absolutely. I've told you. I already have my return ticket. Besides, even I know that London is a bit out of your way," she laughed again. And Monty wished that she wouldn't. He could get drunk on her trilling laugh, and he needed to stay sober if he was to maintain his English decorum in such a public space as the station concourse.

"And how do you anticipate being able to control your purchases?" It was the only thing that he could think of to help persuade her to let him drive her home. Yes, she was right, a drive to London was most definitely out of his way – he lived only a couple of miles away from where they were now standing – but it might just provide him with the time to ask for her forgiveness.

"For goodness' sake Charlie, I'm a big girl now, I'm sure I can manage. And if I find that I can't, then, I'll simply play the 'damsel in distress' card, someone will come to my rescue. They always do."

Monty stared at her. Did she realise what she had said? Fifteen years ago he had not come to her rescue, she had come to his, and was marked for life because of it. He felt a right cad.

"I imagine they would. Who would be able to resist coming to the aid of such a beauty as you?"

"Are you joshing me?" Teddy assumed, as best she could, 'the pose'. It was almost comical as her shoulder bag slipped down to her elbow, jostling the pot she held in the crook of her arm, and nearly dropping it in the attempt.

Rather than laugh, Monty leapt forward and grabbed the pot before it could nosedive.

"Me? Jest with you? I thought joshing was solely in your domain," he said, holding fast to the plant in one hand, Teddy's elbow in the other and surreptitiously distributing the spilt soil with his foot.

"Oh, for goodness' sake Charlie, give it here," Teddy said, shaking herself from his grasp and foisting her shoulder bag back up, before opening it with her now free hand. "Stick that in here, will you."

Just then the grating tones from the PA system announced the pending departure of Teddy's train to London.

"Once again, Charlie, thank you for the outing. I not only had great fun, but feel fully inspired to try my hand at recreating it in paint. It's just a pity that you didn't indulge in any dancing, or nefarious activities that I could record for posterity."

"I should hope not. I've already given you my full repertoire. But I look forward to seeing your renditions of today. I'm imagining that there will be a lot less red and more green."

"I think you can rest assured on that score Charlie." Teddy fumbled with the bag of flour then reached down to pick up the carry-bag of books.

"Now's your last chance," Monty said as he relieved Teddy of the books. "I can carry these to the car and drive you home?"

Teddy laughed again as she stretched out her hand. "Give them here Charlie."

Monty held his hand out of her reach, his mind racing for a solution.

"Come on, or I'll miss my train," Teddy said, a mix of mirth and annoyance in her voice.

"Tell you what. How about, instead of driving you home today, I'll let you use your precious return ticket, but I'll take all your precious purchases and drive them up to London tomorrow."

"Why'd you do that?"

"Because it would save you falling prey to some stranger smitten by your fumblings with all this lot." He lifted up the carry bag of books and nodded at the bag of flour in her arms. "Besides, today you saw some of the English countryside, I thought tomorrow I could take you to see the sea. The English Channel, from the ground, rather than the air."

The final call came for the train's departure and Teddy looked at the carry bag of books already in Monty's hand.

"Sound's great. Here you go," she said as she hefted the bag of flour at Monty. "Thanks again for today, see you tomorrow. Whenever you get there, I'll be ready."

TWENTYFOUR

It wasn't until he had parked his car in his driveway that he realised that he did not know Teddy's address, nor her phone number, or if she even had one.

"You idiot!" he said and banged his forehead on the top of the steering wheel in frustration. He sat there trying to think how he could go about tracking her down. It was Saturday. The gallery was probably still open and might know, but would they pass that information over to a voice on the phone? He doubted it.

Who would know Teddy's contact details?

Melanie's name came to his mind, but he soon dismissed her. She had been circulating the evening of the gallery opening, no doubt collecting contacts, but she also had shown no interest in Teddy.

He sat back up and thumped the steering wheel in satisfaction, before slumping down in the seat.

George. He would know, but Monty didn't relish the idea of contacting him. He looked at the pile of Teddy's things in the footwell beside him, and shook his head. He had not imagined that she would get so excited over the Plant Centre, and then the Book Shop. She'd been like a young child in a sweet shop. It was all he could do to get her out of either of them. It was only after his stomach audibly made itself known that he'd been able to encourage her to show an interest in the visiting the Redwood Restaurant back at the Visitor's Centre.

Still, he had promised Teddy another day's outing, and to deliver her purchases. He couldn't let her down. Not again. He would have to phone George. And that meant, unless he could find his phone number somewhere, he'd have to phone Melanie. He flung his head back against the head rest and groaned.

Melanie. She would have been expecting him today. To either phone, or visit, like he usually did. And, not only had he not done either, to make things worse, he hadn't even thought about doing so. Oh, he'd thought about her during the day, but that had been in contrast to Teddy. To contact her now felt as though he would be pulling the plug and letting the euphoria of the day gurgle away like water from the bath.

Why did life have to suddenly become so difficult for him?

Once inside, and after fixing himself a stiff drink and a sandwich, he went looking for George's phone number.

Without looking at the business card that George had given him, Monty flipped the card through his fingers, hoping that the action would boost his courage sufficiently to make the phone call. The card suddenly spun out of his hand and fell facedown onto the floor. He sighed.

Monty reached down to pick it up and saw that there was what looked like a lipsticked mouth on the card, along with some writing. He frowned, puzzled that he hadn't noticed it before. Then gave a short laugh. Of course he wouldn't have seen it. Back when George had thrust it at him, he'd simply slipped it into his pocket. He hadn't been interested in Geroge's card, till now. Straightening up he looked more closely at what was written, then turned the card over to make sure that it was George's and not some gigolo's.

Monty had no difficulty in seeing that it was George's card. His embossed name, in a bold and flourishing font, dominated the limited glossy space, leaving little room for his contact details, and even less for the nature of the business he was representing. He turned the card back over to have a closer look at what was there.

He ran his thumb over the lips. His eyes snapped wide open in alarm. The lipstick had been applied by living lips, his thumb having smudged the lipstick over the numbers and name 'Samantha', that were written between the lips, almost like an inviting tongue. Monty caught his breath and dropped the card in disgust. The dirty dog. It had not been Fiona who had kissed George's card.

He looked at the card on the floor, and gave it a swipe with his foot. Luckily it did not scoot under any of the furniture, and he bent down and picked it up. It was none of his business what George got up to, and with a smirk he wondered if George realised that he had given him an incriminating business card. He bent down and picked the card up, squinted at the fine print denoting George's phone numbers – work and home.

Monty rang George's home number and let his mind wander while the ringing tone droned in his ear. What was George doing handing out business cards to random women with lipstick to spare? Was Samantha a random woman, or something else? He then remembered how cozy George and Melanie had been the night of her party.

His ruminations were interrupted.

"Manningham's answering service, please identify yourself," accosted Monty's eardrum, followed by a rasping giggle, then a cough.

"Grow up George," Monty muttered. He was remembering why he had never really liked the man when they were students. Back then he had been a prankster and habitual party animal bordering on becoming an utterly incorrigible infantile excuse for a man. Time, apparently, had done nothing to curb the swell of immaturity. Monty tried to recall from the brief meeting at the gallery, what his wife was like. It was obvious that she had had no success in curbing his excesses. Then again, maybe she liked him this way.

"Monty? Is that you? I can't believe it! You've rung me. It is me that you are wanting to talk with, isn't it? Not Fee? I can't believe it!"

"George! What are you on?"

"Me? On? Nothing that ought not be enjoyed on a Saturday night. What can I do for you? Wait a minute, can you hang on for a bit? I gotta fill up this glass."

Monty sighed as he heard the phone put down on a hard surface and fall off as George's footfall faded. He could hear mumbling in the distance. It sounded like there was a gathering of sorts happening at the Manninghams, he wondered how long he'd have to wait. But it proved not too long.

"I'm back," yelled George.

"Look, sorry to interrupt your evening, but I'm hoping you can help me."

"No trouble, you're not interrupting anything special. Fee's got a few friends over. You know, a hen's party or something. Great opportunity to see what's on offer," George laughed, then belched. "Oops! Sorry about that. The bubbles do it all the time, don't they? Now, what was it you wanted?"

"I need to contact ..." Monty stopped himself. No need to feed George more information than necessary. "Miss Delany. Thought you might know how I can get in touch with her."

"Miss Delany?" George's voice spluttered through the phone into Monty's ear and he instinctively held the phone further away, then laughed to himself.

"Come on, you mean Theodora? She's a piece, isn't she?"

Monty sighed, he could feel a long monologue being born.

"Yes, that's the one. You brought her to Melanie's party the other day, can you tell me her address?"

"Tut-tut. You are a wily one, after the delectable and talented Theodora while you have that luscious PA? What do they say about two birds in the hand?"

"Wrong proverb there George," Monty said, then regretted interrupting.

"No, no, you know what I mean. You're dangling two birds to your bow. Doesn't that Melanie satisfy you? No, no, take it from me. One should never mix work and pleasure. It doesn't pay to bed the staff. Look where it got me." George hiccupped, then barked a laugh.

"George! Miss Delany's address, please."

"Now there's a piece worth getting to know. Shame about all that scarring. She'd be a real looker without them. Wonder what caused it. Fire, maybe? What do you think?"

"The address!" Monty almost screamed into the phone.

"Oh, right. Give me a minute. I'll be back."

Monty heard the phone land on the floor as George once more left him hanging, the murmur from the gathering in the background preferable to the usual canned 'hold-on' music, at least there would be no repeating to mark the time while George did whatever he was doing to bring him Teddy's address. For goodness' sake, could he not have simply told him the street name and number? Surely he would know that if he'd picked her up from there.

Monty sighed again. It had been a wonderfully refreshing day spent in Teddy's company, but the effect of the memory was being eroded by the interchange with George. If only he'd thought to get the information from Teddy before she boarded the train, he could have been spared this unpleasant interlude.

"Got it!" George yelled down the phone, "Now you go get it, if you can," he laughed, and Monty could feel himself start to colour at the callous inuendo as he jotted down the address.

"Thanks, George. Go back to your harem and enjoy the evening."

Monty disconnected to the sound of ribald laughter.

Hackney. He had no idea where he thought Teddy would be staying, but even if he had thought about it, Hackney would never have featured in the possibilities. Still, he shrugged his shoulders, with Teddy there had never been any knowing predictability.

TWENTYFIVE

Monty woke up the next morning wondering if he had once more fallen prey to Teddy's mischievous conniving. He would not put it past her to have made the outrageous purchases yesterday, knowing or even thinking or hoping that he would step up and be her rescuing angel so that she could spend another day with him. Then again, she was not like Melanie and he could not see her being so obvious. Still. Was she snuggly comfortable in her digs, as she called the flat where she was staying, while he was doing his best to quell the beginnings of annoyance as he carefully negotiated the narrow streets leading in to where he hoped he'd find her?

Looking around him as he drove the unfamiliar streets, he was starting to understand why she had been vague about where she was living, and insistent that he not drive her home. There were plenty of suburbs more congenial to healthy living, and with upright citizens for neighbours. And he wondered what her father would think of her living in such surroundings. But, as she had put it, she wasn't *living* in Hackney as much as *staying* there while in London.

After a couple of wrong turns down dubious streets he arrived at the address, and found a park close by, right under the sign saying 'Permit Holders Only'. Too bad, he thought, as he got out of the car and locked it behind him. He was only going to be a few minutes. Still, he hoped that it would still be there when he returned

Monty quickly strode across the street and walked along the row of cream brick terraced houses with their white painted window frames and front doors recessed behind tall and ornate columns. The only thing that distinguished one abode from the next was the subdued colour of the doors, and the mostly brick front fences. But he was looking for one that had a metal fence and concrete yard.

It didn't take Monty long to arrive at the number George had given him. He carefully picked his way across the litter strewn patch of concrete and mounted the five steps to the front door. He looked at the array of names on the entryphone panel and selected the one that George had told him to press. He stepped back down and looked up at the building, wondering which window was hers – the bay window beside the front door, the large one on the floor above, or the smaller two on the top floor. Or was it the basement one?

He shuddered to think of her living behind any of them. While he was used to the dichotomy between inner London and rural Cambridgeshire he wondered how Teddy was coping with how diametrically opposed this terraced house was to *Calinda*. He'd have to remember to ask her why she chose here of all places. The thought that, as an artist, she might not have been able to afford anywhere else never occurred to him.

He was pleased when the front door opened and interrupted his musings.

Teddy stood at the top of the steps. She was dressed as she had been yesterday, with the straps of her shoulder bag clasped in one hand and what he recognised as a beach bag in the other.

"Great day, hey Charlie?"

Monty watched as though in slow motion as she launched herself from the top step. He mentally shook his head and reached out to grab her, but she landed almost beside him, the two bags swinging with abandon.

"Wouldn't have been if you'd twisted your ankle, or worse."

"Tosh! As if that'd happen," she laughed, grabbed Monty's elbow and spun him round. "Where's the car? Oh, there it is. Come on, don't want to miss the crabs biting."

Monty blinked, and allowed himself to be led to his car, which was still where he'd parked it, and in one piece. Though, to be fair, he did take a surreptitious reconnoitre, before unlocking the car, relieving Teddy of her bundles, and helping her into the front passenger seat.

Teddy was as excited as his preschool daughter, almost bouncing in the seat in anticipation. Restrained by the seat belt, she twisted in her seat as best she could, to face Monty. "So Charlie, man of mystery, where are you taking me today?"

"I told you, Teddy, my name is Monty."

"Nah, you'll always be Charlie to me so you'd best get used to it. Again," she laughed, then twisted back to look out the windscreen. "I have no idea how people can live like this, squashed up all together. And why don't they have grass and gardens? Do you also live like this?"

"Not everyone lives like this. These are the older parts of London. Been around for decades, centuries." Monty had no idea, and wondered if he should have spent some time last night boning up on ... he laughed. Who knew what questions Teddy would come up with? He'd just have to hope he could wing it.

"Do you live in a place like this? I know that Melanie almost does."

Monty was pleased that there were two questions, so he could avoid the one that would cause him embarrassment. Not that he was ashamed of the house he had shared with Lyndall, but the home that he grew up in ... well, that was in a different league altogether.

"What do you mean 'Melanie almost does'?"

"Well, she lives in an apartment, doesn't she? So that means that she's living cheek-by-jowl with other people in very close proximity, and doesn't have space around her. And it's a modern one, so it doesn't have the character that some of these places exude."

"What about you then? You didn't always live at *Calinda*."

"True, but I still had space, and a lawn, and a garden. Oh, and a pool," she laughed. Monty squirmed. If having a pool was the benchmark for acceptable accommodation then his Georgian house, and the monstrosity he grew up in, were both dismal failures. Mind you, this being England, pools didn't count for as much as they did in Australia.

The remainder of the trip to the coast continued in friendly banter interspersed with the occasional burst of comfortable silence and Teddy's exclamations of delight as the landscape changed.

Monty thought that travelling on the Motorways was anything but inspiring. If he'd thought more about it, and there had been more time, he probably would have tried to take A23 or even the B roads. Then again, with the hedges, Teddy probably would not have seen much anyway. Better to get to their destination as quickly as they could. That way there was more time to explore all that the coast, and Brighton, had to offer. And, he still needed time to actually *talk* to Teddy, about what was so weighty on his mind, and he couldn't do that whilst driving. It needed to be face-to-face, with no distractions.

TWENTYSIX

"You have got to be kidding me!" Teddy exclaimed, leaning on the seafront promenade railing and staring down at the beach.

"What?" Monty, preoccupied with running, yet again, through his prepared speech, looked out to the English Channel. For once the sea was devoid of any activity. Not even a distant tanker, and he wondered what it was that had caught Teddy's incredulous attention.

"Where's the sand?" she asked, waving her arms out in front of her before turning to face him.

"There isn't any." She expected sand? Hadn't she had enough of that back on *Calinda*?

Teddy turned to lean back against the railing, and defiantly folded her arms across her chest. "Then how can you call it a beach?"

"Beaches don't have to always be sand. A beach is whatever strip of land there is before the water starts. It can be anything."

"Then how can people enjoy lying out sunbathing? Those stones can't be anywhere as relaxing as hot rock massages. Must be worse than having stampeding calves running over you." She laughed at the thought.

"Ah! That's what deck chairs are for. See." He nodded his head towards where a few early hopefuls were lounging further down the beach.

Teddy looked to where he was indicating, and shuddered. "Look at them will you. They must have goosepimples as high as Everest sitting out there in this weather. No, no can do. How can you get a proper suntan sitting in a chair? A beach has to have sand. Sand that is hot to walk on. Bet those pebbles never get hot. And even if they did, you'd break your ankle trying to hop and skip across them like you do on the sand back home. I tell you, Noël Coward had it all wrong, the English and their dogs don't need midday sun to be mad," she laughed.

"Do you always have to make comparisons? This is England. Accept it for what it is."

Monty wanted to sound miffed, and defensive of his countrymen, but somehow he couldn't quite bring it off, instead his comments were infected with a hint of humour.

"Oh, don't get me wrong, I'm loving being in England, and seeing for myself all the differences. It was you who first awakened my curiosity for what England has to offer. Thanks to you it is not such a foreign place as it might have been. It's just that I didn't expect there to be quite so many differences." Her laugh trilled out across the beach and Monty felt his heart thrill at the sound.

But he was here to get something off his chest, not to have the day flounder off on a different course. And one which he didn't want his heart to go down. For Pete's sake ... No, he couldn't allow his thoughts to go down that route. Least ways not till he was rid of the guilt which had only surfaced since Teddy's return to his life. he He turned away from the railing. "Come on, let's walk down and visit the Pier. You must be getting hungry."

Monty was feeling decidedly uncomfortable. They had just finished a lunch of

iconically British fish and chips and mushy peas. How could he possibly even entertain the idea of disturbing Teddy's enjoyment? He coughed, and Teddy looked at him.

"I've been wondering, how is it that you knew where to send that invitation, and the pictures? And why address it to Charlie Hirst?"

Teddy laughed. "Thought you might enjoy that little dig. Actually I did that so that I could be pretty confident that you alone would receive it. Didn't want just anyone turning up on the night. Did it set the gossip mongers going, wondering who this person was? Oh, I hope it did." She laughed again, and looked at him enquiringly, almost baiting him.

And Monty knew that if she had been standing then she would have adopted her trademark pose that used to annoy him. "Okay, but how did you know the address to send it to? And after all this time, too. When I saw the name, I knew it was from you, and wondered what it could be. I knew that if it had something bad to do with Ralph then you would have used my proper name."

"Nah, sorry, but you could never be anything but Charlie. Charles sounds so pompous, and as for Monty – well, that's the kind of name you would give an animal, a horse, or a dog maybe. And you are neither, so Charlie it is."

"Then I'll start calling you Theodora."

"I wouldn't advise it. You do that and I'll broadcast to all and sundry some of the antipodean antics of yours that I've immortalised on my canvases."

"Are you purposely avoiding my question?"

She laughed again. God, how he enjoyed listening to her laugh, it did something to his innards that Mel's he-haw laugh never did and he was startled to realise that Melanie had entered his thoughts.

"Dad? No, he's all good. Meant to be retired, now that the boys are home and pretty much running the place. You know ... well, no, I guess you wouldn't know, would you? You never met my brothers. I've got three, all older. But then, you'd know that. Two are married, and living in cottages that Dad built for them as wedding presents."

Monty glared at her and started to drum the table with his fingers.

"Ah, yes. Your address." She smiled and Monty solemnly nodded.

"My address. Yes."

"Well, after I got home from hospital, I wanted to write to you, but Dad refused to tell me your address. Then, on the numerous later times I'd ask, he would still refuse. I think he was afraid that I wanted to use paper to scream and yell at you, and abuse you for what you caused to happen to me. Not that I would have. Only he never believed me. Probably because my brothers were all ~~to do and~~ anxious that legal action be taken against you."

Monty's finger drumming increased in intensity.

"Well, yes. So I never did write to you. Then, before I was heading over here for this exhibition, Dad asked me to get something for him from the office. Guess it was the exhibition that prompted me to take a thorough look through the drawers and papers for the address. Piece of cake to find it. Don't know why I'd not thought to take a look for his address book. So, there you have it. Next question mine inquisitor."

She leant her elbows on the tabletop, cupped her chin in her hands, and grinned like the picture of the cat in his childhood book *Alice's Adventures in Wonderland.*

Now was his opportunity.

"Teddy, there is something that you really need to hear."

Monty felt his palms go clammy and he rubbed them against his trousers. It was stupid for a grown man to feel sick at the prospect of apologising. Whenever his suppressed memories had surfaced and he had felt the need to apologise, he had always imagined that he would be doing so to an embittered woman so self-conscious of her disfigurement that her life was in ruins. He cleared his throat, and while he had been wanting and waiting to make his apology to her face, he could not bring himself to look at her. Instead he observed his hands twisting in his lap and out of her sight.

"I must apologise to you for being such an arrogant prick all those years ago. I thought I had the world at my disposal, and then after just one night I found that my father was casting me as a total miscreant and the only way to reform me was to send me as far away as he could, so that I could not be an embarrassment to him and the family. And I ended up, very resentfully, at *Calinda*, only to become the butt of all your ribald antics at my expense. And I am truly, and humbly, sorry for acting in such a foolish manner that when you once again came to my rescue you ended up in hospital. Then, when I saw you in that hospital bed, well I acted most uncharitably. Instead of standing up and facing the consequences of my appalling stupidity, i lily-livered ran. Can you possibly forgive the cowardly me?"

After what seemed like hours of silence he looked up and Teddy laughed. Startled, Monty immediately averted his eyes and felt himself colour. Of the possible responses she could have given him, he had never conjectured that Teddy, upon hearing his heartfelt apology, would counter with her usual trilling laugh.

"Oh, for goodness' sake Charlie, that was years ago. And I ought to have known better than to get in the way of a doe and her joey. Yes, you were foolish, and so was I. Besides, as it turned out, rather than you apologising to me, I ought to be thanking you. As I said back at Melanie's. If it hadn't been for the paints you gave me in hospital, I would never have become the person, the artist, that I am today.

TWENTYSEVEN

Melanie had been perturbed by the cloud that had hung around Monty. She had never seen him display such inefficiency. She had spent the past week juggling trying to placate him and needling him to get his work done, all the while dodging his oscillating moods. She had hoped that the arrival of the weekend, and time shared outside the office, would bring him back to normality.

She forewent the luxury of a sleep-in and was up early, ready to spend most of the morning racing around her flat ensuring that it was clean and tidy. Then, after completing all the household chores she attended to her own appearance, taking pains with her makeup and hair, before getting dressed to impress. Next she started preparing an appetising lunch, and, having forgotten to go shopping on her way home from work the previous day, she was pleased that she had all the ingredients the online recipe promised would melt her man's heart. She was more than happy with the result of her effort; till it started to wilt.

Melanie stalked past the phone willing it to ring.

Even though they had not been 'an item' all that long, Melanie had come to expect that Saturday lunches together had become a routine, and if Monty was running late, or could not make it to her place for lunch on Saturday, he always phoned. Melanie stalked past the phone once more, willing it to ring. Her fingers itched to phone him, but she knew better than to phone Monty because his children might be with him. Besides, her mother's admonition to never phone a man as that would look like she was chasing him, was well entrenched.

She was not impressed.

By lunchtime Sunday, and still not having heard from Monty, Melanie was beyond livid. She paced the length of her living room muttering all manner of expletives, and what she wouldn't do to Monty when she next saw him.

First there had been the fiasco of her birthday cocktail party. There had been something bothering him that evening. Maybe she ought to have been more understanding and not lost her cool. But it had been her *birthday*, and he had not only arrived late, not helped her, and left early, but he hadn't even given her a gift. Whatever had been upsetting him had followed into the office and a week from hell had followed.

And now this. After all the effort she had put in to ensure that they could enjoy a relaxing time, just the two of them as she purged him of his demons, Monty had the audacity to neither show up, nor let her know that he wasn't able to do so. Maybe he was bed-bound with some incurable disorder that had been fermenting all week, putting him in the bad mood.

Melanie walked past the dining table and looked at her lunch plate comprising yesterday's left-overs and wondered if she should phone him. Then again, if he was truly indisposed, he might not be able to get to the phone to answer it. Maybe she ought to visit him. Did one take flowers to sick men? Then she realised, with surprise, that she didn't have his address. All she knew was that he and his wife had shared a house in the more affluent part of town. But not the address. He probably had a garage so there was no point in her doing a drive-past through all the streets hoping to spot his car.

She paused in her pacing, and wondered why she had never been invited to his place, nor to his parents'. And what was it that had set Monty off on such a bad mood? She needed to think. She sat down at the table, picked up a fork and played it around the food on the plate in front of her. Her cocktail party, that was when things really changed when he had left in a huff, and then that stupid woman had disappeared. The evening had been a disaster, until George had consoled her. She smiled at that memory before viciously stabbing at a sliver of carrot several times.

She had come into the office to find Monty standing in front of the two framed pictures which he had had her fix onto the wall. She had taken a deep breath and quietly walked over to join him. She had made some flippant comment about what an attractive couple they made, and Monty had turned to face her and accused her of wasting money on the group photo, and then he had gone on about how much more meaningful the damn kangaroo picture was. She had then made some disparaging remark about the Australian artist. That had really set him off. It was almost like the woman meant something to him.

Melanie slammed the fork down on the table. "Come to think of it, I bet that woman is at the bottom of Monty's malaise. Her or that Charlie Hirst, whoever he is. That was what started the yo-yoing of Monty's emotions. Damn the man," Melanie exclaimed.

She sat back in the chair. "I wonder if George knows anything?" Melanie drummed her fingers over the tabletop, hoping that the thumping would get her brain working.

She wasn't too sure that she wanted to approach George again, not after his overtures at her birthday, pleasant and enticing though they were. However, there was a good chance that Fiona might know something. Did she feel up to reacquainting herself with Fiona? While it had been convenient to acknowledge her at the gallery, they had never been close as students. More like rivals on the dating scene. She supposed that she'd be cutting off her nose if she did not take advantage of the Manningham's connection to both the artist and Monty. Yes. She would contact Fiona and invite them to dinner. And she would insist that Monty come as well. Surely if the men were plied with drink and she guided the after-dinner conversation she might learn something.

Feeling relieved to have come up with a way to resolve her predicament Melanie spent the remainder of the weekend organising her dinner party which she envisioned as being the dinner party to end all dinner parties. She'd pull out all the stops to impress the Manninghams, as well as Monty, though she was not going to let his lapse go unnoticed.

TWENTYEIGHT

Monday morning saw Monty bouncing into the office, rested and ready to tackle the papers and business that had languished the previous week. Even the secretaries and lowly assistants noticed the improvement in mood as he strode through the open plan workspace to where he and his father's suites were, and they all relaxed. No one wanted a repeat of the previous week.

"Good morning, Melanie," he said as he breezed past her desk and entered his office. He walked over to the sofa by the window and dropped his briefcase on the seat, then stood and looked out at the view. It had been a good weekend, and so he was able to enjoy the panorama across Cambridge pleased that it was his hometown skyline that he was seeing and not that of the Australia that had haunted him of late.

He turned when he heard the office door open and watched as Melanie entered with some files in her hands.

"That looks like I have some work this morning," he said, walking towards his desk.

"Indeed, these files, plus all those already on your desk from last week."

"Yes, last week. I need to apologize for my lassitude and inattention. I hope that the cause is now all in the past."

He smiled and sat down at his desk, choosing to ignore the unspoken questions that Melanie could not camouflage. And he surprised himself that he felt a wave of delight course through him knowing that her questions would remain unanswered. Melanie and he might be 'an item', but that did not give her liberties to know everything that he did. Teddy and he had a shared past which no one would ever understand, and Melanie, with her animosity towards Teddy, would never comprehend.

Melanie transferred the files from her hands onto the desk. "Yes, there is a lot to catch up on, I'm afraid. But I am sure for a small consideration the girls in the office will catch you up soon enough."

"Small consideration?"

"Well, you really weren't yourself last week, so a bit of sweet bribery never fails. Maybe a special morning tea? I can go down to Gregg's and grab a tray of delights. You know, some of their donuts, or muffins. Something like that. It's just next door, so I wouldn't be long."

"If you think that'll help get me back on track with all this paperwork then go ahead, take whatever you need from petty cash and head off. Grab something for yourself while you are at it."

"And something for you?"

Monty shook his head. "Haven't time for indulgences today. Probably not for the rest of the week. A coffee would be good, before you go. Thanks."

"Very good."

"Oh, and before you go, sorry about the weekend. Something came up." He wanted to make it sound better and add that it was something he couldn't get out of, but something held him back. His conscience maybe? He coughed in an attempt to clear his thoughts. For some reason he did not want to share with Melanie how he had spent his weekend, fearing that she would not understand. But he did feel a niggle of guilt. "I know, I should have let you know, but, well, sorry, I didn't."

"I'll get you your coffee then go get morning tea for the floor," she said then turned and walked out of the office. At least Monty had apologized, even if she was none the wiser as to what had occupied his weekend. And so she was experiencing mixed emotions – she was mystified, intrigued and peeved. Retribution could wait. For now it was simply nice to have Monty in the office back the way that she considered 'normal'.

Once Melanie had closed the door behind her, he looked down at the drawer of his desk where the potentially incriminating charcoal sketch lay swathed in its bubble wrap. His hand hovered near the handle, then he remembered where he was, sighed, and moved his hand to pick up the top file on his desk and opened it. Releasing the sketch and letting it see the light of day beside the kangaroo could wait for another time. He had to make up for the time he had lost last week.

Melanie re-entered the office, this time bearing a tray with a cup of coffee and an insulated mug.

"Here's your coffee," she said as she placed the tray at the edge of Monty's desk. "Thought it better here than over by the sofa. Don't want you distracted too much from your work. And sorry, I know you said you only wanted a drink, but something sweet to go along with it would do you good, but you are going to have to wait until I return from *Greggs*. I thought about bringing you one of their fancy drinks, but it would be cold by the time I got back, so here's a second cup keeping warm for you." She smiled and indicated the mug.

"All good. Thank you. I'll wait to be surprised." he said with a grimace, and watched appreciatively as she sashayed out. Monty smiled. The two women currently in his life were different in every possible way. How was it possible to be so easily and comfortably drawn to them both, he wondered as he picked up the coffee cup and took a sip. It didn't taste anywhere near as nice as the coffee he and Teddy had shared yesterday, though that may well have been a figment of his imagination after his confession. It had been such a relief.

Monty had managed to successfully wade through several pending letters and one file before Melanie returned with the treats from *Greggs*. She handed these around the office before a quick trip to the toilet to tidy herself up. She then took the remaining two treats out of the paper bag, arranged them on a plate, along with two cups of fresh coffee. These she then put on a tray and carried them into Monty's office.

He looked up from the file he was working on. "Were the girls suitably placated or bribed?" Monty asked, checking the file, closing it and putting it on top of the other files and papers that he'd finished with.

"Yes, they were. And they all thank you profusely, and said that after they have finished eating they will be ready for the onslaught of work. So I hope you will not disappoint them." She smiled, placed the tray on the desk and walked around to stand beside Monty, her hand hovering over his shoulder. Did she dare to touch him? Then, thinking better of it, she walked back to the front of the desk.

"I made you a fresh coffee, and thought we might enjoy an eclair. Shall I take the tray over to the sofa?"

Monty shook his head. "Nice thought, but I do really need to get through these."

Melanie pouted, not that Monty was looking.

"But Mr Chinthurst," it did not harm to be formal, after all it was the office and he still preferred formality, and she was still feeling put out by his silence over the weekend. "Everyone is entitled to a coffee break." She smiled sweetly, again not noticed by Monty.

This morning really wasn't going as well as she had planned. Having seen his cheerful mood on his arrival she had hoped to be able to re-establish the cosy, almost intimate relationship. His reticence must have something to do with a lingering fragment of his disquiet from last week. She would have to try another approach.

"Did you have a busy weekend?"

"Hmm?"

"How was your weekend? Busy?"

"Oh, yes. Good thanks. You?"

"Mine could have been better."

Monty looked up as he reached across the desk for his coffee. "Sorry to hear that. Nothing too serious I hope?"

Melanie gritted her teeth, she could not afford to lose her composure. "When I hadn't heard from you, I thought you might not have been feeling the best. If I knew where you lived, I would have come around to see if you were all right."

Monty put his cup down. "Oh Mel, I'm sorry. I didn't know that I was meant to ring you. Was it something you needed?" He hoped the lie, which had slid out so easily and surprised him, sounded genuine.

"No, no. I was fine. It's just that I've started to get into the habit of us having some time together out of the office."

Monty had the decency to look abashed, but under that guise he was frantically trying to think how he could explain his way out of his neglect. Talk about being in a muddle. He was momentarily reminded of a stage play he'd seen – *One Man Two Guvnors*. Was he coursing towards being one man two women? The play turned out well for the one man, and he hoped he could fare as well.

"Yes, I guess it has become a bit of a habit for us. I'm sorry. I ought to have let you know that I'd be away for most of the weekend. I was, er, showing a friend from overseas, some of the countryside. Took them down to Brighton and we had a look around Anglesey Abbey – you remember the office all went up there for a picnic last year. Lovely place." He knew he was babbling like a star-struck girl, but he could never pull off a lie, even when it was a half-truth. He could only hope that Melanie would buy into it.

But Melanie had a knack for detecting subtle hints and hidden meanings within the truth. She was now convinced that there was something serious going on with the artist, Charlie Hirst and Monty. Thank goodness Fiona had tentatively accepted the invitation to dinner, she just needed to confirm with her husband. She really needed to get the spectre of Australia, the artist woman and Charlie

Hirst removed from Monty's life, and she was counting on the dinner with the Manninghams to be the key. Even if she had to wait a full week before that happened.

TWENTYNINE

It was the afternoon of Melanie's dinner party.

During the week, Fiona had confirmed that she and George would be coming, and they were looking forward to spending the evening at her place.

Melanie ought to have been pleased. And she would have been, if that had been all Fiona had said during their telephone conversation. But no, Fiona had to spoil the week by 'letting it slip' (and Melanie wondered how contrived the slip had been) that George had given Monty Ms Delany's address.

Melanie had spent the remainder of the week wondering why George would do that. The phone call had opened up all manner of scenarios, and they had covered nearly all the W's she remembered from her long distant school English classes – Who, Why, What, When, Where, well, maybe not so much the 'who', but the others were all featured. Why would George do that? Or had Monty asked him for her address? What was Monty doing wanting the artist's address? The questions tumbled around in her mind until she was almost paralytic with anxiety. And that was not the best way to start the evening.

Monty stood outside Melanie's door, straightened his jacket, and squared his shoulders. Tonight was a night to enjoy Melanie's company and forget about everything else. He took a deep breath, put a smile on his face and pressed the bell beside the door.

"Monty!" Melanie beamed at him and leant forward to peck his cheek before grabbing his arm and drawing him into the hallway. "I was wondering if you had forgotten where I lived." She looked meaningfully at her watch.

"Yes, well, I had something come up that I had to take care of before I could get away."

Melanie's eyes momentarily clouded over as she wondered if the 'something' had anything to do with the two shadows that seemed to dance around her boss– that dratted Australian artist, and the allusive Charlie Hirst.

"Never mind, you are here now. I'm just about to get things ready in the kitchen, come on in and join the other guests."

"There are others here tonight? I thought it was, you know, a quiet intimate tête-à-tête, just the two of us."

"Don't be silly," she said in an off-hand manner and Monty raised his eyebrows in query.

Melanie ignored his unspoken question and continued to drag him down the hall.

"You remember the Manninghams, Fiona and George? Oh, of course you do," she tutted, releasing Monty's arm and almost propelling him into the room. "George is a friend of yours," she said as she disappeared into the kitchen.

Monty stood in the doorway as Fiona glared at him from across the room where she was sitting beside her husband. The way she was feeling at the moment she could not tolerate being in the same room as he. She stood up to join and commiserate with Melanie and joined her in the kitchen.

Trying not to grimace, he sighed before stepping into the room. Well, there went the evening he had been looking forward to with Melanie. Instead, tonight there was George; and tomorrow his father.

"Monty, my man!" George bellowed as he stood up, crossed the room, clasped Monty's hand, and gave him a back-slap that nearly knocked the wind out of him. Monty barely succeeded in masking his displeasure. There went any idea that the evening was going to be enjoyable.

"I hope I didn't drop you in it," George whispered close to Monty's ear.

Monty resisted the momentum that George was exerting on his back to propel him forward and stopped. He turned to look at George.

"What do you mean?"

George clapped Monty on the back again and moved him forward across the room and almost pushed him down onto the sofa, then sat down beside him. Monty felt the sag in the sofa and tried to right himself, pushed himself back into the corner and glared at George.

"Never hurts to give some incentive for a bit of envy, if you know what I mean." George's tone of voice and face implied the silent nudge-nudge, wink-wink.

Monty had no idea what he was going on about and stared as though he was a newly arrived alien.

"Oh come on Monty, you know. Jealousy. A bit of flirting with your Melanie there." He grinned, licked his lips and nodded his head towards the kitchen. "That put a bit of zing back into the bedroom. Had the best night's sleep for many a month." He dug his elbow into Monty's side.

Monty looked at George. He had no idea what the man was going on about. He'd seen the flirting at Melanie's cocktail party, but had not thought that there was anything to be concerned about, then again, knowing George of old, he should have known better. He looked towards the kitchen and saw Melanie savagely attacking something in there, all the while skewering he and George with virtual daggers. What was going on?

"George. I've had a hard week and the old grey cells don't seem to be firing on all cylinders, you are going to have to be a bit more precise if you want me to join you in the hilarity you are starting to exhibit.

"Oh, sorry there Monty. I thought you knew."

"Knew what?"

"About you and Theodora."

"What's there to know about me and Theodora?"

"That you and she are a ... you know ... you and she have been seeing each other."

"What do you mean 'seeing each other'? For god's sake, I asked you for her address. That's all. And how does that make you dropping me in it?"

"Well, I kind of let it slip to Fee, that you had asked me."

"Let it slip?"

"Well, Fee overheard me giving out Theodora's address, and she asked me who had been asking. You know that Theodora is a very private person? She doesn't really want anyone to know where she lives, and such." George was starting to show signs of discomfort – his forehead was beading and he was playing with his fingers, intertwining them like a pimply schoolboy outside the headmaster's office.

"You still haven't told me how letting it slip is dropping me in it."

"Ah, well, you see, I think, just think mind you, I think that Fee might have shared that piece of information with your Melanie."

Monty dropped his head back, stared at the ceiling and sighed. Thinking back over the past week he thought he could name the exact time that the inflaming information had filtered down to Melanie. He had never liked George, but now he had burned any chance of kindling a friendship and was most certainly crossed off the Christmas Card list.

He stood up and glared down at George. He felt like throttling the man, but now was not the time or place. He had to think of Melanie. And Fiona, he guessed. He shook his head as George had the decency to cower. He had half expected him stand up as well so that they could have had a decent set-to on equal footing. But then remembered that as a student George had always been a philandering coward – he had always sought pleasure in fleeting affairs, but could never face up to the consequences when the attraction had worn off. Apparently he hadn't grown out of the trait, and he wondered why Fiona stayed. Maybe it was the children. He tried to remember how many George had said they had.

"Who's looking after your children?" Monty asked, unclenching his hands which he suddenly realised he'd fisted ready for a fight.

"Theodora's looking after them," Fiona called out as she came into the room, wine bottle in one hand and glass stems in the other. "She's a real whiz with them, and they love her to bits. Don't they dear?"

Monty watched the interplay between the two of them, and wondered if things in their household were as good as they could be. That thought led him to wonder how safe Teddy was. He'd have to try to remember to ask her tomorrow. She was too nice, and naïve, to be fodder in George's collection of conquests.

Melanie was also watching. Not the exchange between the Manninghams, but Monty and George. She'd been hoping that George was giving Monty the What For. After all, that had been one of the aims for the dinner – George was in Fee's bad books and could only appease her if he took Monty to task over his two-timing her friend Mel. But it appeared that it was Monty who had the upper hand. She picked up the last of the dishes and carried them through to the dining table.

"Dinner is served," she announced as cheerfully as she could, and smiled as she watched the fraught atmosphere between her guests fizzle out and clear.

The remainder of the evening progressed without further incident or revelation, no matter how hard Melanie tried to steer the conversation in the direction she hoped would generate some answers. All her efforts were redirected, unintentionally, by her guests – George regaling the table with his youthful exploits in an attempt to draw Monty out to sharing his; and Fiona introducing the various achievements of her two girls. Monty, it appeared, had mostly been in a world of his own; except when the conversation was directly addressing him. The conversations were all interesting and entertaining, but would she ever find out what the connection was between the three people who were interfering with her own plans?

Melanie sat quietly at the table and she smiled as a thought started to niggle and while talk swirled she busied her thoughts in how best to engage the support of someone with more influence in Monty's life.

Monty, unsuspecting of Melanie's plans, left the dinner party perplexed. What were the Mannighams doing at Melanie's. and why were they the only dinner guests? If he'd known they were going to be there, he might have found a reason to beg-off. He might not always fit in with Melanie's social circle, but he would have drawn the line at keeping company with the likes of George Mannigham. What were they doing there? Up until Teddy's exhibition he had never heard her mention them. What was Melanie playing at? Did she think that, after the cocktail party, flirting with George would make him jealous?

He shook his head. There might have been a time, not so long ago, that he might have. But since Teddy had re-entered his life, he was starting to doubt the depth of his feelings for Melanie. Reluctantly seeing her through Teddy's eyes fractures were appearing in her veneer.

Thinking of Teddy calmed him somewhat and when he got back to his home he was able to relax.

THIRTY

His mother had invited him to Sunday lunch. Though there was nothing unusual about the invitation, the proviso had him perplexed, as too, apparently it did his mother. She wanted to know who Ms Theodora Delany was, and why his father *insisted* that she accompany him. Monty would have liked to have asked his father the same questions. Presumably his father knew that Teddy was in the country through the contact he had with her family. But why *now*?. Did he know about the exhibition? Did he know that he had been to the opening?

He would have approached his father at work, if the summons from his mother had come during the week. But she had phoned mid-afternoon Saturday. Fortunately it had given him sufficient time to phone Teddy and pass on the invitation and try to make arrangements for picking her up. Little Miss Independent had refused to allow him to collect her from London, but had compromised and promised that he could drive her back later in the afternoon.

"Jeepers Charlie." Teddy gave a long slow whistle as Monty nudged the car through the massive stone and wrought iron entrance and gave a wave to the almost liveried man standing in the doorway of a picturesque gatehouse.

"What?" Monty asked, glancing over at her as she sat relaxed in the passenger seat.

"When you were in Australia you never let on that you were a toff. No wonder you were so posh."

Monty laughed. "I may have been naïve in many ways, but I wasn't totally stupid. If I'd told you then where I'd come from, there would have been no end of you ribbing me. It was bad enough as it was, being shown up by a mere kid."

"Too right I would have taken the mickey out of you. And you would have deserved it. And not so much of the "kid" either. I was on the cusp of becoming a woman I'll have you know."

Monty laughed. "That was where I was meant to help. Mould you that is. Fat chance I had. You were all tomboy and loved every minute of reminding me. You wanted nothing to do with ladylike decorum and femininity. Still don't see much evidence of it even now. You might be a little kid no more, but I'm still not convinced that I achieved much in the way of your father's hopes for you.

Teddy took a breath, ready to remonstrate, but she was brought up short when the drive that they had been travelling on for what seemed miles, took a turn and revealed their destination.

Monty was never sure if it was pride or embarrassment he felt each time he saw the monstrosity that was his childhood home. It had stood the passage of time well, but the perpetual additions that progressive generations had made what had once been a sedate stone mansion into a hotchpotch collection of architectural disasters. Or so he thought. Today, approaching it with Teddy's reaction beside him, it was a mixture of both.

"Oh, my goodness Charlie. Is this really your family home? It's huge." She turned to look at him, and was surprised to see a flush creeping up from his neck.

"Yes." He felt decidedly uncomfortable, and wasn't sure why. Yes, it was his home, or rather it was the place where he had been raised. But how did one define their 'home'? Home was said to be where one's heart was. But he'd always thought that phrase to be patriotic twaddle.

"And, if you'll excuse me for saying so, it's a veritable jumble. Does it have a recognisable architectural style? I mean, it seems to lend itself to a number of design eras. And with all that half-timbered black and white bit in the middle there ... How old is it?"

Monty coughed. "Um, I'm not too sure. It's been in the family for a while now. I'm the fifteenth or sixteenth generation I believe."

"You what?" Teddy laughed. "Did you say six*teenth*?"

'Something like that." Monty stopped the car a bit away from the front door and turned the ignition off. He leant his head back against the headrest and quietly sighed. This was it then. Time to face his parents. He took a deep breath and released his seatbelt.

"Come on. Let's get this over with."

Teddy looked at him as she fumbled with her seatbelt release. "Get this over? I thought you wanted to be here?"

He had had no qualms about bringing Teddy here. It was the circumstances under which he was doing so that put him on edge. *Whytecliff Manor,* which for some unknown reason was the name of the estate, had not been a permanent home for him for many years. Not since he was first farmed out to boarding school aged 8. And its appeal had certainly been soured with his exile. It was only more recently, since the conversion of the wing, that he had felt he belonged here. But to be summoned, by his father, for a formal visit, and to bring 'that Australian,' with him, because he 'wanted to meet her' made him decidedly uncomfortable.

"It's not that I do not want you bring you here, it's just that I'd have preferred it to have been on my undertaking and not at the request of my father. However, I'll put a smile on my face and run the gauntlet. Come on." Monty got out of the car and walked around to open the passenger door for Teddy.

Unfortunately, Teddy was too quick for him, and she slid out of the car, in full view of Charles Montgomery Chinthurst II standing on the top step of the mansion.

Monty could hear his father's silent judgement. Not only on his tardiness, but also on Teddy's lack of decorum, and he started to wilt. Monty quickly stepped to her side and managed to close the car door before she did. He took her by the elbow, and they made their way across paving stones to where his father waited. Once more Monty mentally heard his father's impatient foot tapping.

The two of them stood on the bottom step and looked up at the imposing man blocking their further passage.

"Father."

Teddy was surprised that Monty didn't bow, and wondered if she was expected to. Not that she would be so inclined. The man wasn't royalty.

"Monty."

Talk about stiff upper lip and all that twot, Teddy thought. She was damned that she would stand on ceremony so took a step up and thrust her right hand out.

"Theodora Delany, pleased to meet you."

Monty cringed and wondered how his father would react. Trust Teddy to be forward. He should have expected something like that from her, and he castigated himself for not priming her in the expected protocol when it came to his parents. Why hadn't he taken the opportunity in the car coming here? Stupid. Stupid, Stupid.

Monty's father stared down at the proffered hand and sniffed before extending his hand and briefly passing it over her palm.

Teddy smiled benignly. Stupid git, she thought as she furtively wiped her hand down the seat of the plaid skirt that Monty had insisted was the appropriate attire for the occasion.

"I suppose you had best come in," Monty's father said, taking a step back.

Monty and Teddy mounted the steps and walked into the cavernous entrance.

The four of them, Monty, his parents, and Teddy, had endured an enjoyable meal amid a strained atmosphere and were now sitting in one of the many rooms designated for informal relaxation. Though there was little relaxation happening. While Mrs Chinthurst had been the epitome of a congenial hostess, her husband had been anything but.

Teddy could contain herself no longer. She settled herself more comfortably in the armchair she had been directed to, and took a deep breath before turning to Monty's father, and smiled.

"So you are the one responsible for sending Charlie to the nether reaches of the globe?"

Because she had her eyes riveted on Charles Montgomery the second, she only heard Monty splutter, and could only guess at Mrs Chinthurst's reaction. Her husband, however, was showing signs of turning puce, which surprised Teddy, who imagined she could see a rolodex spinning as it searched for the appropriate comeback. Having found the required response, his normal demeanour returned and he targeted Teddy with a vindictive glare.

"Hardly. He did that all on his own. I simply facilitated his departure. Not that it did any good, him going there. He came back a different person, and not in a good way. Had to reintroduce him to all the norms again. Waste of time. Total waste of time."

He settled himself back into the sofa he was sharing with his wife, crossed his arms and glared smugly at Teddy. His pose was so 'stuff that in your pipe and smoke it.' It was all she could do to stop herself from laughing.

"Is that what you honestly think Mr Chinthurst? Then I beg to differ." Teddy looked across to Monty who was sitting looking rather uncomfortable. 'Buck up there Charlie' she felt like yelling out to him, but instead she tilted her head and looked enquiringly at his father.

"You damned colonials. No sense of civility."

"Then I am truly sorry for you." Teddy then looked to Monty's mother and smiled, wondering what she made of the interchange. The two of them had only exchanged the usual pleasantries associated with a sit-down luncheon. She was indeed a sweet lady, and she now smiled apologetically at Teddy.

"Mrs Chinthurst, it has been a pleasure to meet you, and thank you for your hospitality and lovely meal." She turned to Monty before standing up, "Charlie, I believe it is time for us to leave."

She chuckled at the reaction to her use of her childhood pet name for Monty, which she had purposely used. Mrs Chinthurst gasped, covered her mouth with her hands and looked to her husband. He was busy trying to control his jaw from tearing apart, while Monty had looked at his watch and bounced out of his chair. He now stood beside her.

"Yes, indeed. Time to get moving."

THIRTYONE

"Well, I must say that went well, don't you think?" Monty muttered as he drove back down the long driveway. "Whatever possessed you to bait the old man like that?" He wasn't angry, and hoped that it hadn't come out like that. In fact, he looked across at Teddy sitting beside him, head down and twirling her fingers in her lap, he was in awe of her, taking on his father like that. Then again, it shouldn't have surprised him. He couldn't see even years away at boarding school making any dents in Teddy's forthright approach to life that he had seen evident when she was younger. If anything the years had nutured and matured her character to what it was today. And he smiled.

"I know, I know, and I really ought to apologise to you. Might even drop your mother an apology when I send her a note of appreciation for the visit. But I'm sorry, I can't." They had come to a stop at the gatehouse, waiting for the traffic to clear, and she looked across at Monty, who stared back at her with a look of utter incomprehension. "Well, I mean, it is not my place to apologise to you for your father's behaviour towards either of us. He wasn't even civil. And besides, I didn't see you sticking up for me. What happened there? Where'd the chauvinist go?"

A break came in the traffic, saving Monty from replying immediately. She was right, of course. He'd been a right prick. He and his father, both. Neither of them had behaved in a proper manner. He shook his head. He could have done a lot better and defended Teddy, but that would have meant standing up to his father. Something which he was not willing to do. Wimp that he was.

"I'm guessing the chauvinist got lost somewhere along the way." He knew it had been a bad move on his part to take Teddy to meet his parents, but he'd seen no way out of it. He'd already agreed to the visit when his mother had then tagged on the 'oh, by the way, your father has said to bring the Australian with you.' He wondered again how the heck his father even knew that Teddy was in the country and that he had had contact with her.

The drive to London was conducted pretty much in silence as both Teddy and Monty regressed into their own thoughts. But Monty, while fuming over his father's treatment of Teddy, could not get over Teddy's quiet audacity in confronting his father. That was something which he greatly admired in her, and which he wished he had the courage to do. Then, also, he was kicking himself for exposing her to his father, knowing full well that he would not see her in a good light. A light which he himself delighted to see her in.

A light which was increased in magnitude when he pulled up outside her place in London.

Once more Teddy was out of the car before he could open the door for her, and bouncing across the concrete garden as though nothing untoward had happened earlier. He caught up to her as she inserted the key.

"You are coming up for a coffee or something aren't you? You ought to have something before driving back. I know it's only a short way compared to what I'm used to, but I realise that it is considered a distance for you Brits," she said jokingly as she held the door open for him.

Monty joined in her laughter. "Oh, don't worry, even after all these years, I still equate distance in Australian terms, so here to home is nothing. That's why I'm happy to drive you 'all this way'." He grinned as he walked past her, and stopped.

The air in the cramped and dingy entrance was musty, and as he looked around he could see evidence of damp in the peeling wallpaper.

"Come on up then," Teddy said as she closed the front door. "I'm up with the gods. Least ways, that's what I call the room I'm in. It's small compared to the rooms in *Calinda*, but then all the rooms here are."

She started to walk up the bare wooden staircase. He could see that there had once been a carpet runner, as both sides of each tread showed evidence of once being painted. But now all that embellished the stairs were cast off shoes and spent take-away wrappers.

"Yeah, I know, it's a bit of a dive," she said, noticing Monty's repulsion. "But it's cheap and handy to the tube station. So I'm not complaining. Besides, I'm not here for long."

"When do you go back to Australia?" Monty asked, stepping over a pile of clothes. "I've been meaning to ask."

"Well, you are asking now, so that's not a problem. Hiya Frank," she said, bending down to talk to what Monty thought was just another pile of clothes. "You taken your meds today? It's Sunday you know."

Monty heard Frank mumble something as he reached out a scrawny hand to Teddy. He went to swat the hand away, not wanting the filth to touch Teddy, but she was already holding his hand and helping him onto his feet.

"Come on, come up and have some coffee with us. I'll even make you a sandwich if you haven't had anything to eat."

Again Frank mumbled something as he stood up, and Monty could see that he was a young boy, maybe about 10. It was hard to tell under the grime and odd wardrobe that he was wearing.

Monty shook his head in disbelief as he watched Teddy and the boy Frank climb further up the stairs. What did Teddy think she was doing dragging an obvious derelict into her home? At least it was a young boy and she knew his name, and not some degenerate homeless stranger. He tried to hear the conversation that the two of them were engaged in, but, even being a tread behind them, he couldn't determine what was being exchanged.

When Teddy and her companion reached the top of the staircase she let go of Frank's hand and slid her hand along the lintel to dislodge a key. Monty shook his head again, and waited till the door was opened then followed Teddy and Frank into what turned out to be little more than a tiny bedsit.

"This is where you live?" Monty asked, as he looked around, hoping he didn't sound too incredulous or judgemental. The flat reminded him of Lynne Reid Banks' book *The L Shaped Room* – not the context or circumstances, but the actual flat. It was miniscule and almost bereft of anything resembling creature comforts. His spartan university accommodation was Five Star in comparison.

"Why? What's wrong with the place? There's a bed, a table, a bathroom cupboard over there," she waved her arm to a door in a corner. "I've got a microwave, an electric jug – sorry kettle – and a basin for washing the dishes. What more do I need?" she asked as she shepherded Frank to one of the two chairs at the table. "Sit there till I get you a towel, then you can go and take a wash.

Monty knew she was addressing the young boy, but for some impish reason he couldn't help himself. "But I took a bath this morning." He grinned at her, much the same way that Frank was grinning at him as he sidled over to a chair and tentatively perched on the edge.

"I wouldn't do that Mister, if you wanna live. She's got a right temper on her if you talk cheeky to her," Frank said and ducked to avoid the towel that was sailing towards him.

"You. Wash. In there. Now," Teddy said with a grimace on her face, pointing to the door of her bathroom. "And you Charlie ..."

"Yes? What about me?" He gave her a lopsided smile.

"You'd best take the other chair."

"Take it where?"

Teddy looked around for another missile to send and harrumphed when she couldn't see anything handy. "You are

incorrigible, as much a fish out of water here as you were back at
Calinda." She looked at him sideways as she moved to the kitchen
area. He might be uncomfortable in her small flat, but if he was
joking with her, then he was losing some of his English reserve, and
she glimpsed the Charlie that she had known back in Australia when
his stuffing had been disposed of. And she liked that. She picked up
the electric kettle and gave it a gentle shake.

"Wait up Frank, I need to get to the tap," she called.

"Charlie, sit down for goodness' sake, you're taking up too much
floor space standing there." She manoeuvred past him, knocked on
the bathroom door before opening it ajar. "Here Frank, fill this for
me. And toss your clothes out. I'll find you something clean to wear."

She waited till first the kettle, then a pile of clothes appeared
through the gap in the door. Teddy tossed the clothes onto the floor.

"Your mum kick you out again did she?" she called out over her
shoulder as she carried the kettle back to the kitchen.

A muffled reply floated out over the sound of running water.

She shook her head. "His mum locks him out whenever her
'gentlemen callers' visit. Poor kid almost lives on the stairs and he's
not the only one. A shame really."

"You mean you are living in a ... 'lively' neighbourhood?"

"Oh Charlie. Really? You are being polite." Teddy laughed. "Too
polite for the neighbourhood. If you were an American, you'd have
said 'Den of Iniquity' wouldn't you? I mean, that's what you're
thinking isn't it?"

Monty felt himself starting to colour. She was doing it again,
only this time it did not sound as malicious as when she'd taken the
mickey out of him back in Australia. "Well, I don't know what else
to call it. I didn't want to tread on toes." He nodded towards the
closed door behind which Frank could be heard enjoying the hot
water clean-up. Monty despaired at the watery mess Teddy would be
left with when the ablutions were over.

"Frank? Never mind him. He is more aware and comfortable with what goes on in this collection of flats than you ever would be."

Monty sat watching Teddy as she busied herself with attending to the kettle and setting out some mugs. Trust Teddy to be the one to open his eyes to another world. She seemed to be adept at that. Australia, Art, and now this. He tried, but couldn't help himself consciously making comparisons. Teddy and Melanie were literally worlds apart, and so was he when with one or the other. There was a freedom which he felt when he was with Teddy that he knew could never be replicated with Melanie. Take today for instance. While Melanie would have gone overboard to dress to impress his parents, Teddy had worn a simple blouse and skirt, with no hint of ostentatiousness. He almost laughed out loud thinking back to the previous weekend when Melanie would have thought Teddy's attire to be totally inappropriate for a day at Brighton; and she would not have been interested in going anywhere near The Pier or eating fish and chips. She would have expected – and he would have obliged – a full meal at *The Salt Room* or some other, equally fashionable establishment. And as for venturing onto the beach and taking off her shoes, well ...

"Hope you like instant coffee." Teddy placed a mug and a plate of sliced up fruitcake on the table in front of him. "What are you smiling at?" she asked as she sat down on the only other chair at the table.

"I was recalling you trying to walk on the beach this afternoon."

"Yes, that was an experience. But I had to do give it a try. Couldn't very well say that the beaches over here are rocky and not be able to vouch for it from personal experience, now could I?" Teddy laughed and Monty knew that he could never tire of the trilling of her laugh. He wondered how Melanie's laugh would compare, and nearly choked on his coffee. Now was not the time to be thinking about Melanie, even if he had only been comparing her with Teddy.

"Frank!" Teddy called out. "Don't use all water, I'll be needing a wash later." She turned to Monty. "I'm sorry Charlie, but I'd better get some clothes for Frank and get him something to eat."

She got up from the table, went to a plastic garbage bag propped up in another corner, and tipped the contents out over her bed. Monty watched as she then rummaged through the assortment of clothes.

"Is that your wardrobe?" Monty asked, tongue in cheek.

Teddy laughed.

"No, mine is in another bag, under the bed."

"I did think that they looked a little small for you. Where'd they come from? Don't tell me that you brought your outgrown clothes over from *Calinda* especially to clothe the down-and-outs of Hackney."

"Don't be daft. Why'd I do that? There are plenty of charity shops here, already filled with good quality cast-offs. Come on Frank. I've got some clean clothes for you, I'll put them just outside the door. Hurry along now."

Monty looked at his watch, then drained his mug and picked up a slice of fruitcake. "I'd better get moving," he said raising the cake in salute to Teddy. "Back at work

tomorrow. How long are you here for?"

"The exhibition runs for another week, then it'll be time to pack up the pieces that haven't sold, and then I'm off."

"Back to Australia? Or are you going to see something of the UK first?" He wasn't sure why he was hoping that she'd be staying on. It wasn't as if he had any leave available, and if she was touring he wouldn't be able to see her again anyway. Then his train of thought stopped. Did that mean he wanted to see her again? He shook his head, stuffed the last couple of bites of cake into his mouth and scraped the chair back from the table. He stood up, dusted his hands over the table, and looked at her enquiringly, waiting for an answer.

"Not sure yet. Probably go home. I've things to do, people to see ... I know I can always come back, but it's such a long way so it would make sense, while I'm here, to trip around a bit. So I'm not sure. Tink I'll just wait until the exhibition's over then decide. Still, it's been beaut to catch up, and spend some time with you this visit." She turned towards the bathroom door where gurgling and the clanking of pipes could be heard. "Frank! Get dressed and get out here!"

Teddy turned back to Monty. "Sorry about that Charlie, if the water runs for too long the plumbing starts to complain. As I was saying, I've really appreciated you letting me get my feet onto English soil – it's been a wonderful experience. Catching up with my UK fans has been great too. I might come back with another exhibition, with an English influence courtesy of this weekend."

She took a step towards him, stood on her toes and pecked his cheek. "You said you had to go, and I've got a little English ragamuffin to feed. I'll come with you to the front door and see how many more I can scrape up before I feed Frank." She laughed. "Come on, won't keep you. Don't want your father blaming me if you are late to work tomorrow."

THIRTYTWO

Melanie spent the week after the dinner party implementing Phase One of her plan to win-over Monty. When she arrived at work the following Monday she was pleased to see that, as she had arranged, a huge vase of red and yellow long-stemmed roses was sitting on her desk outside Monty's office. A large white card, strategically placed, protruded from among the wispy asparagus fern, and written prominently on the card were the words 'with all my love xxx'. She smiled. Phase One of her planned strategy to win-over Monty was in place.

The flowers did not go unnoticed by the others in the office, and admiration was not short in coming, with unguarded speculation as to who had sent them to Melanie. She sat at her desk and basked in the attention as she waited for Monty to arrive.

Monty arrived at work at his usual time and walked the gauntlet of gossip towards his office, stopping at Melanie's desk. He was at a complete loss by the array of roses commandeering a large portion of her desktop – he'd never known her to have flowers on display.

Melanie, meanwhile, felt her pulse quicken, pleased that, as she had anticipated, he noticed the flowers.

"I see you have an additional admirer," he said, bending down to smell the roses, and in so doing missing the card and message. "Nice. Yellow and red – friendship and love. You're one lucky woman. Two admirers. It's not Valentine's Day is it?" He smiled at her and walked on into his office. Who could be sending his PA flowers? he mused as he walked across his office to place his briefcase on the sofa. On the way back to his desk he stopped in front of the mirror behind the office door to check that he was presentable for the clients. He frowned at his reflection, bewildered at the realisation that he felt no pangs of jealousy over Melanie having someone who thought enough about her to send her roses. Was that an indication that his feelings for her were only superficial?

Melanie stared after him, inwardly fuming. That had not been the reaction she had expected. Where was the curiosity? The envy? The jealousy? She slowly counted to ten, then waited a few minutes to allow Monty to go through the morning's ritual of shedding extraneous clothing and briefcase before settling himself at his desk. She then pushed her chair back, picked up the day's mail and followed Monty. Did he not want to know who cared about her enough to fork out a considerable amount of money to lavish on her? She left the office door open and walked to Monty's desk.

"The mail," she said, holding it out towards him, waiting for him to look up and take the letters.

Normally her routine was to announce the mail and then lay it down on the desk, so Monty didn't immediately respond to her. When there was no swish of paper on the desk, he looked up, perplexed. He reached out to remove the letters from Melanie's hand. "Thank you, Mel," he said and smiled. "Was there something else?"

She shook her head. "No, your first appointment is not for another couple of hours. Would you like your tea now, or later?"

Monty was shuffling through the mail and simply waved his hand in dismissal. "No thanks, I'll have it later, when ..." He pulled his desk diary towards him and turned the page, "When Angela and Alf Bois are here, thank you." He smiled up at her.

It was a smile that normally melted her innards, but today, while it started to work, she reminded herself of the purpose of this week, and resisted. Her returning smile would have chilled Monty if he'd been looking. Melanie turned and walked out of the office, pulling the door closed behind her with as much force as she could muster, but it still swooshed slowly and quietly closed.

Phase One appeared to have had no effect other than depleting her own bank balance. She had already taken steps to initiate Phase Two, maybe she ought to bring forward? But in the end, she decided to stick with her original plan. She would allow the roses to remain. They might still prove to be effective.

Melanie implemented Phase Two the following week glad that she had been privy to Mr Charles' schedule. Thanks to her buttering up of Mr Charles' PA Veronica with hollow compliments and tempting sweet morsels that had taken every vestige of Melanie's limited generosity, and further dented her funds, she had planned the day down to the minutest detail and had taken exceptional care in choosing her attire. Today was not the day to arrive at the office looking her usual efficient and demure PA. No, today she was an enticing siren. Plenty of leg and cleavage were being exposed to more air than usual; her makeup was impeccable, and her raven hair now had auburn highlights. Yes, she was dressed for the kill.

She entered Monty's office, closed the door behind her and leant back against it, her hands behind her back. She had, under Fiona's tutelage, practised the alluring pose to perfection. She waited till Monty looked up and she smiled sweetly. She was enjoying what she was about to do, and had rehearsed every minute to exactness. All she needed to do now was execute Phase Two. She could feel the adrenalin coursing through her body and wondered if the excitement she was experiencing was anything like that felt by a murderer about to kill. She calmed herself and let her tongue slip out of her mouth and slowly lick her lips.

"What is it Melanie? Has Mr Argyll cancelled his appointment again?"

Monty held his pen, a hand either end and up to his face so that for a moment it appeared that he had a green caterpillar wavering side to side over his upper lip. Under normal circumstances Melanie would have been amused, and made some comment about a mouldy moustache. But not today.

She sashayed towards him, arms now swaying gently at her sides, moving in tandem with her hips. She was enjoying this moment of suspense and it showed on her face.

Monty put his pen down. "Come on Mel, I don't have time for this. I've a busy day, as you well know. For heaven's sake you jammed the appointments in. I've barely time for lunch. What is it?"

Melanie was now standing in front of his desk. Slowly she placed her hands on the desk and leant forward.

"No, Mr Argyll has not cancelled his appointment, though he did phone to advise that he is running 'just a tiny bit late' and would most likely not make it till later this afternoon." She once more ran her tongue over her lips. "But that works out well for you as Mr Charles has just now asked for you to join him in his office."

Monty, mesmerised and not immune to the view that was being displayed in front of him, pulled his thoughts back away from the distraction of Melanie, and turned them to his father. It wasn't often that his father asked to see him without it being scheduled in advance. That was how the man, and the firm, worked. He looked up at Melanie's face, trying to read beyond the obvious to see if she knew what was happening.

Melanie's lips formed themselves into a smile which did not reach her eyes. Oh, she knew what was going on. Not only with the effect she was having with Monty, but also with what was most likely going to happen once he was sat in his father's office. If he ever managed to be seated.

She sighed seductively and slowly straightened herself up, then half turning away she looked triumphantly at Monty.

"Immediately," she said almost threateningly, and walked back to her desk, leaving the office door open.

Monty sat back in his chair. "Well, what to make of that?" he whispered as he ran his fingers through his hair. His thoughts first mulled over what had happened to cause Melanie to take on the persona of a siren, or was that a vixen? Did it have something to do with the sender of roses? Whatever it was, he'd never seen this side of her in the office before, and he wasn't too sure that he liked it. Then his father. What was it that his father could possibly want to see him for so urgently? That too was totally out of character.

He put his hands on the edge of his desk and pushed his chair back, stood up, then walked over to the door. He closed it so that he could check himself in the mirror fastened to the back of it. He gulped.

There in the mirror, almost mocking him, was the reflection of Teddy's charcoal sketch, and his eyes lost their focus as once more he was transported to another time. A time which he had, until recently, quashed from his being, but was now paramount in his thoughts. Damn and blast Teddy bringing it all back to his consciousness. Yet ...

Monty refocused. Staring in mirror and recalling less taxing times did not answer the question of what Melanie was playing at.

His reflection smiled back at him – it must be Melanie's new admirer that had brought about the change in her. He looked at his eyes in the mirror, did he feel cuckolded? He took a step back, surprised at the thought that filled his being. No! He didn't even feel jealous. What he felt was relief.

Stunned, he burst out laughing. He had thought his world was complete since Melanie had arrived at the firm and become his PA. Never had he imagined the relief that he was feeling now, knowing that he had been usurped. He must remember to ... oh, he'd think of something he could do, or get for her to thank her for showing him the light. Or maybe he ought to thank the admirer who was sending her the flowers.

He quelled the desire to laugh again and turned his thoughts to his father. What could he be wanting? But he didn't dwell on the contemplation. 'Immediately' in his father's terminology meant just that, so he had best hurry and meet him.

Melanie was briefly disappointed to see Monty breeze past her desk without looking at her. Still, she knew what he was going to encounter in his father's office, and knew that the smile on his face and the jauntiness in his step would not last long. And a smile of satisfaction infused her face. She would have danced a jig, office or no office, if she had thought her clothes would have been up to it.

Instead she sat up straighter and pulled her blouse down to expose even more cleavage as a kaleidoscope of thoughts started to meld into focus. A conniving smile spread across her face. Yes. She knew what she would do to help ease and secure Monty for herself.

After the meeting with his father he would need an understanding shoulder and intimate condolence. She would clear his diary of the remaining appointments for the day (Mr Argyll would just have to make another appointment) and tantalisingly suggest that the two of them go out for a cozy lunch. After all, she *was* dressed for more than a day at work.

THIRTYTHREE

Monty was not overly perturbed by the summons to his father's office, though it was unusual for it to be unscheduled. He ran the possible scenarios through his head, wondering if he had made some error of judgement, or neglected to follow up on something. But he could not come up with anything. He ran his fingers through his hair and straightened his shoulders before he tapped on the door to his father's office and walked in. Mr Charles' office was almost a mirror of Monty's, the major differences being the view from the window his father was standing in front of, and a wall display of numerous photographs of his father with a bevy of prominent figures.

"You wanted to see me, father?" Monty asked as he walked towards the seating area where his father stood, hands behind his back, looking out the window.

His father took his time turning around to face Monty. But when he did the scowl on his face brought Monty up short, and he frowned. That scowl brought a whole new dimension to this meeting.

Slowly the scowl was joined by other contortions as Charles Chinthurst's face turned puce, and his jaw quivered menacingly.

Monty knew instantly that whatever it was, he was in for a verbal thrashing. The last time he'd seen his father so filled with venom he'd found himself on a plane to Australia. Monty shelved all his previous conjectures for the invitation to attend his father, and he frantically rewound what had been happening in his life of recent times that would have brought this on. But all that came to mind was the recent afternoon at *Whytecliff Manor* with Teddy, but how he could be culpable for that disaster was beyond him.

"You!" His father pointed a shaking finger at Monty, then at one of the chairs that fronted the large desk. 'Sit!" Charles demanded as he strode across the room to sit heavily at the desk. He glared at Monty who was still standing as though impaled to the carpet, staring at his father.

"I said 'sit', now sit!"

Monty felt much like he had each time he'd been hauled in front of the headmaster. Only this was far worse. This time there would be no parent to bail him out. Feeling defeated before the battle ensued, Monty knew that there was no recourse but to comply. He walked back to his father's desk and sat down.

"I will have you know that I shall not have you undermine the integrity of this firm. It has been in the family for generations and has a reputation to uphold." He clenched his fists and thumped them on the tabletop so hard that the regimental line of pens jumped.

If Monty had not already been intimidated, he might have found the activity amusing. But he had been moulded to subservience when it came to interviews with his father so sat stone faced opposite him and waited for the revelation of his misdemeanour.

His father was in no hurry, and Monty kept his clamped hands in his lap and stared belligerently at a point on the wall behind and slightly to the left of Charles' ear. To do anything else would only add fuel to his father's antagonism.

"Have you got nothing to say for yourself?" Charles barked, fists sending his pens into another dance.

Monty blinked and looked his father in the eyes. What the heck was the old man on about? Monty had not been able to think of anything that he had done, in or out of the office that could be construed to manifest the cloud of anger emanating from across the desk.

"I have absolutely no idea what you are on about, sir."

"I'm talking about your galivanting around the country."

Galivanting around the country? The only times he'd been out of Cambridge for more than a year had been when he had taken Melanie to the gallery opening in London, which he wouldn't call a galivanting episode, and the other weekend. Surely his father wasn't meaning those two days when he had taken Teddy to see something outside of London? He stared at his father incredulously. How could he know about that? And besides, what harm was there in that? It was a most natural thing to do – reciprocate Teddy's sharing of her life all those years ago. And that opportunity had been orchestrated by his father, so how could he now ...

Monty let out the breath which he hadn't realised he was holding. Of course. That had to be it. His being sent to Australia was a punishment, and punishments were not to be rewarded with kindness. So was that the source of his father's current anger?

"What are you talking about?" Monty asked, trying to hold his resentment at bay.

"I'm talking about you associating yourself with that woman you had the audacity to bring to *Whytecliff Manor* for lunch the other week."

"But father, you wanted to meet her. Mother said that you insisted that I bring her."

"Don't you tell me what I did or did not said, and don't you dare bring your mother into this. This has nothing to do with her." Charles opened his fists and placed his hands, splayed fingers, flat on the desk. Then raised himself up to lean menacingly forward towards Monty. Breathing heavily, he raised one hand and wagged a pointed finger in Monty's face. "And I am telling you now that you are to have nothing further to do with Ms Delany."

He then straightened up and glared at Monty. "Do. Not. Sit. When I am standing! You know better than that." He waited. Glaring at his son.

Monty swallowed, and, attempting to display control, determined to not visibly quail, slowly pushed his chair back and stood up. His father nodded in approval, harumphed and, hands clasped behind his back, walked over to once more look out the window.

Monty didn't know what he was supposed to do. Did he follow, or remain where he was? His knees felt as though they would fail him at any moment, but there was no way that he was going to sit back down. Or show how he was feeling, although he wasn't sure how he was feeling, other than discombobulated. Who did his father think he was, telling him who he could or could not associate with? For goodness' sake, he was no longer a child. Then again, Monty felt his shoulders slump, no one ever stood up to the mighty Charles Chinthurst II. His father was so unlike the first Charles Chinthurst, Monty's grandfather. Now there was a man who could be reckoned with. Monty remembered the man with fondness, an emotion that did not sit comfortably on his successor. Unfortunately.

Monty sighed and walked slowly toward his father, stopping to rest his hands on the back of the sofa. The dark brown leather felt cold to his touch, much like how he thought his father's heart must be.

"Surely what I do in my own free time out of the office is of no concern of yours, sir." Monty said, keeping his voice as neutral as he could. Then he held his breath, waiting for the onslaught that experience had taught him to expect whenever he broached topics he knew to be kindling to his father's precious and precarious pyre. Honestly, trying to have a personal and serious conversation with his father had always been akin to tiptoeing through a minefield. Only today it would appear that this minefield had no ordinance map to accompany it.

"Let me tell you a thing or two about my employees' free time activities. And yes. On this occasion I am calling you an employee. You might think that you are in line to succeed me, or, in the interim being made a partner. But until that time arrives, based on your current, and previous behaviour, let me just add, that you had best think thrice before assuming that such a promotion is anywhere near secure."

While this speech was being uttered Charles had slowly turned around and was now facing Monty, his eyes, bulbous, piercing and dominating his livid face, were focused on Monty's hands.

"That animal is already dead, it does not need you to strangle it." Charles almost yelled, "Get your hands off it."

Monty let go of the sofa, took a step back and held his breath.

"I will have you know that what you do in your spare time, and with whom, is very much my concern. My very own grandfather, your great grandfather, built this firm up from nothing. You hear me? Nothing! And I shall not have the likes of you and your hussies, brick by brick dismantle it."

Monty tilted his head slightly to the side and gaped at his father. Hussies? The family firm? What was his father going on about? He opened his mouth to ask, but was brought up short when Charles pointed his finger at him and took a step forward.

"You will not interrupt!" Charles moved to one of the armchairs that matched the sofa, indicating the one opposite him. "Now sit!" he demanded as he himself settled into the chair.

Monty, still puzzled, walked around the sofa and sat, somewhat uncomfortably, opposite his father.

"Your behaviour has sullied our family's name once, and I will make sure that you do not do it again. And I shall not have you fraternising with the likes of Ms Delany."

Monty stared at his father, not quite sure how to respond, or even if he should, but he wanted to know what his father had against her. And how he knew about his recent involvement with her. Did his father not realise that by trying to impose a ban on their friendship he was potentially swaying Monty towards her rather than away? Not that he had any romantic feelings towards her. How could he, when he remembered her as a precocious and rumbunctious pre-teen, hell-bent on making a mockery of him?

Still, he had to admit, seeing her now as a mature adult, she was proving to be a refreshing change from any of the women he had known since his return to England. And, to his surprise, he realised that included Melanie. There was something about Teddy that was making him feel alive. And he didn't want his father to shut that down. It had now been a fortnight since he had had any contact with Teddy and the release he had experienced in her company had been quietly eroding away, and he was feeling his old English self seeping back. Who knew how much longer she would be in the country? He could not let her leave before he saw her again. He needed a re-charge from her vivacity before she left.

"But ..."

"There will be no buts," Charles growled, his eyes shooting the proverbial daggers across the intervening space.

"I only want to know what it is that you have against Te... Ms Delany? Why so much angst?"

"What do I have against the woman?" Charles spluttered. "You have to ask me what I have against her? She's a colonial for starters. And have you heard her voice? That irritating twang and nasal vowels. Totally unrefined. They might pass for something down in that godforsaken country of hers, but here? Oh no, such a voice would never stand up in the circles where you belong. You ought to know that. No, no. I do not want, no, I demand, that you have nothing further to do with her."

Enraged, Monty stood up and drew breath. "Sir, who do you think you are to tell me who I can and cannot have as a friend? I am no longer a child, and well past the age of my majority." He stopped as he saw his father grip the ends of the armrests and his eyes once more bulge and jaw clench.

Monty momentarily imagined that if his father were a steam engine, then he had just stoked the firebox and his father would be emitting steam any minute, and decided that it was not a good time to be standing.

Charles agreed. "You will not stand while I am sitting!" he roared, mindless of his voice possibly carrying beyond the confines of his office.

So much for standing up to the old man, both literally and figuratively, Monty thought as he dutifully sat back down in the armchair and rubbed his hands against his temples.

"And while you are at it, you can also do something to rid yourself of that PA of yours."

Monty shook his head. First Teddy, and now Melanie? Where'd that come from? "What's wrong with my PA? She is extremely efficient, and speaks English with the cultured accent you seem so set on."

"You call her accent cultured? How long has your head been in the sand boy? She's nothing but a jumped-up trollop. She might not have a face marred by scars, but you can do far better for yourself than a money-grabbing, gold-digging upstart the likes of her. Have you seen what she is wearing today? One would think that she was working at *The Cow and Calf* or some such, and not here. No, I say you need to get rid of both of them. You should be associating with the likes of Sybil Forbes. Now there's a wholesome woman for you. Comes from good stock you know. The Forbeses."

With a faraway look, Charles' gaze drifted past Monty toward the pictorial array of notoriety on the wall, then returned to him "You might remember her, her brothers were about your age. She'd be just right for you. Might ask Mother to host a party for you."

Oh, Monty remembered Sybil. In their youth he and her brothers called her Insipid Sybil, and he smiled. The nickname was a more accurate descriptor than malicious taunting. The poor girl's physical attributes could be tempered at a substantial cost – the braces had helped keep her buck teeth in check. He doubted that science or psychology had yet devised a cure for her startling absence of charisma or compelling personality He wondered if she still crinked her little finger like a hook when drinking from a cup, and restricted her conversations to the social pages. Monty mentally shook his head, bewildered to think that his father thought she would be a suitable partner for him.

Charles' tone might have mellowed somewhat but he was far from settled. He stood up, walked towards Monty and once more aggressively waved a finger at him.

"You will stand when I'm talking to you, boy."

Monty jumped to his feet, ensuring he suppressed the urge to stand at attention and salute – he doubted his father would appreciate the humour in such a gesture.

"Just remember, I've got my eye on you, and I will be actively looking into what needs to be done with you. You need to be kept in line. Can't have you wrecking the good name of this firm over unsuitable companions. All this," Charles waved his right arm around to encompass the family empire. "All this will be yours, one day. Hopefully in the distant future, but we must prepare you for that outcome. And the likes of those two women do not come into the equation. Now get and do what has to be done. Go!"

Charles shook both his hands dismissively towards the door, and Monty, feeling as though he had been slam-dunked, left his father's office.

THIRTYFOUR

Melanie had been furtively watching the door to Mr Charles' office since Monty had entered, and that was ages ago. What could be taking so long? She had wondered about walking over and engaging his PA Veronica in conversation on the perchance of hearing what was being said behind the closed door, but one look at Veronica efficiently working had been enough to know that such an action would not have been welcomed.

She looked at her watch, again. Time was running out if she was to execute her plan and spend the lunch hour commiserating with Monty. She was now in two minds as to how she should respond when he did make his appearance. No doubt he would be feeling chastened, but would he blame her for the summons? Would Mr Charles have told Monty that it had been she who had 'casually mentioned' that Monty had spent the weekend with Ms Delany. He had given her his word that the disclosure would not be placed at her door. She had explained to Mr Charles that she had only thought it her place to alert him, the head of this illustrious firm, that the heir apparent was mixing with dubious company. And he had been grateful for her interest in the wellbeing of the firm.

Now she was feeling nervous. Should she maintain her businesslike aloofness or be solicitous and carry on with her idea of commiserating over a meal?

What she was not expecting, was to see Monty walk out of his father's office almost in a daze, walk through the open office without acknowledging any of the staff and disappear out the main door.

It was a couple of hours before Monty returned to work. Melanie was relieved to see that his demeanour had been restored to what she was used to seeing.

"I see that the flowers are holding up; or are they a new bunch?" he asked flippantly as he passed her desk and entered his office, still smarting from the meeting with his father. During the time he had spent traipsing the streets of Cambridge, unseeing of the buildings being gawped at by the myriad of tourists cluttering his path, he'd thought about his father's ultimatum.

Teddy would be returning to Australia any time now, so that was a fait accompli. He just needed the opportunity to say goodbye, and thanks.

Removing Melanie from his life might be harder. Then he remembered the flowers and her admirer. He wondered who it might be. Mel was certainly a woman who would catch any eye. He speculated that it was highly likely to be George. The chase of another's woman would be just the thing that George would enjoy. He remembered Mel's cocktail party and felt sorry for George's wife.

Melanie gritted her teeth. Phase One still wasn't working. But Phase Two had been initiated and no doubt the seeds had taken root. She frowned. She couldn't yet see that there had been any growth. She supposed time would tell on that one. After all, germination took nurture and time. But did she have the patience to wait? She was missing being the only female in Monty's life, and to share his attention with another weakened her position to the prospects of being his next wife. She needed to act.

She stood up from her desk, picked up the day's mail and walked to Monty's office door. She stopped and ran her tongue over her lips before knocking. She ran her hands down her skirt, licked her lips again, opened the door and walked in seductively.

Monty looked up and smiled as she entered. He had to admit that his father was correct on her dress sense today. There really was a lot of skin showing, more than necessary, or appropriate, for their office, and he wondered what any earlier visitors must have thought. He grinned. They probably thought that all their Christmases had come, if they could only get her to come to them. Either that, or they would be thinking that he himself was onto a good thing.

"Yes Melanie?" he asked, seeing that she had not entered emptyhanded. He had to admit that he was glad that it looked as though she had a legitimate reason to enter, and that she had not simply come to pry information out of him. To ask him about the summons from his father.

His father might have made the mandate, but Teddy, standing up to his father had shown him that, just because his father had demanded something, it didn't mean he had to comply. Though, in this instance, with his future being brought into the play, he wasn't too sure how he could avoid it. His walk around the city and contemplation of the River Cam – not that it posed a threat – had left him with no solution. He had always known that he was being groomed to step into his father's shoes when he retired. Though it seemed far off — his father appeared indestructible — he was in no hurry to assume that responsibility especially if the grooming included the supervision of his social activities. He had a life to live before then. Though he should have realised, after his time at *Calinda,* that his father's reach was immeasurable.

"The mail," she said as she sauntered towards Monty. She was tempted to walk around and stand beside him, but decided to play the part that she was paid for – his PA, not the partner she envisaged as her future, now that the artist woman was out of the picture. Or at least she hoped, after this morning's meeting with Mr Charles, that would be the case.

She stopped and stood on the other side of the desk, waiting for Monty to look up. To look at her.

But Monty didn't look up. He occupied his hands shuffling through the papers that were already in front of him.

Melanie let the mail slowly, and individually, slip from her hands and slide onto the desk. She shuffled her shoulders, straightened her blouse and leant forward, resting her now free hands on the desk.

Unable to delay any longer Monty gave a quiet and resigned sigh before looking up at Melanie, avoiding the cleavage struggling to be released. Yes, Melanie definitely presented an eye full. Maybe George did know a thing or two about mixing work and pleasure, and his father was right. In his position he was ill-advised to fraternize with the staff. A shame really, Meanie was good company out of the office. He frowned, What should he do?

"Is there anything I can do for you?" she asked, and Monty could almost see the syrup dripping from her lips as she smiled solicitously at him.

"A coffee would be nice, Mel." He mentally kicked himself for the familiarity, and quickly corrected himself. "If you could fetch me one, please Melanie?"

When she had left, Monty sighed, and, with his head in a fog, walked over to look out the window in the hope of easing the see-sawing of his thoughts.

It didn't help. Rain bleared the view.

He walked back to his desk but stopped to look at the two framed pictures. He smirked. Melanie must, at some time, have seen and been inspired by the wall in his father's office which was adorned with images of his father alongside esteemed personalities. He didn't need that sort of public affirmation. His eye rested longer on the second frame.

Every time he looked at it he was reminded of his pompous stupidity. No matter how much Teddy professed to not being angry with him, he could not rid himself of the knots that tugged at his innards whenever he thought about that incident.

He didn't hear Melanie enter and put the tray of coffee on his desk, until she stood by his side and interrupted his musings.

"That is a lovely photograph, isn't it? We all look so impressive – you, me, George and Fiona." Melanie gave a melancholy sigh and touched his sleeve. "Don't you worry, there will be others joining it soon enough, I'm sure." Enough to replace the stupid rendition of the kangaroo. She couldn't wait to see it being relegated to the rubbish bin.

Monty looked down at her hand. It was a very personal and possessive gesture, and such familiarity was, now, totally inappropriate for the office. Not that anyone would know, but it would be those little things that would give away their relationship.

"Your coffee. I put the tray on your desk," she said sweetly, her fingers crossed – she had put a second cup on the tray, for her.

Monty looked again at the kangaroo, and thought of the framed picture in his drawer. Then he looked Melanie. She was standing as demurely as her outfit would allow, her hands now clasped in front of her. He knew that he could, and should, just dismiss her without explanation, but he couldn't bring himself to be so unkind. Besides, Melanie was his only avenue for a respite from work.

She was the woman that his father wanted him to dismiss, from the office and his life. He had no idea how he was he going to do that. Or even if he wanted to. He blinked. Was he wanting to hold onto Melanie out of the comfort of familiarity, or in defiance of his father?

"Tray?" Monty quizzed. "Am I expecting a client?" He hoped not. What he wanted was some more time to himself. His mind was cluttered and battling with the emotions that the bubble-wrapped picture in his drawer ~~was~~ engendered. Teddy, who had awakened memories of the freedom he had felt in a community less constrained by society and tradition would be leaving, and so his newly found anchor would be gone.

"No, not for a while. I just thought that you might like some company so I brought one for me. Would you prefer to have it on the sofa?" she suggested, hoping for a cozy time– With her plans for a soothing lunch having been scuppered due to his long absence, she was frantically formulating Phase Two-point-one. There had to be some way for her to secure Monty for herself.

He smiled. "Thank you, but no, the desk will be fine, he said, indicating the chair opposite him. Maybe the company would appease the maelstrom in his brain and he would then be able to think straight.

Conversation stagnated as Monty sat at his desk while Melanie sat in the guest chair opposite him. She had been tempted to pull it round to sit beside him, but one look at Monty's preoccupied face had her stay where she was. Being forward was one thing, but maybe not right now. She was feeling decidedly uncomfortable, and her attire was not helping. She was much more comfortable in her usual skirt and blouse. Besides, the siren effect had not worked; she'd flag that approach in future. She was still anxious to find out exactly what had transpired between Monty and Mr Charles, and how she could best help Monty Now, rather than her planned intimate consoling there was the expanse of the desk separating them, and she had no idea how to broach the subject. To make matters worse, Monty, with his uncharacteristic frostiness was not creating any openings for her. He was, by all appearances, in a world of his own, and she didn't know what else was in her arsenal to help breach the world he was in.

Monty took another sip of his coffee, wishing that there was a piece of shortbread or a biscuit to go with it. It was good coffee. It would be, he knew it would have been made with the aid of a barista machine in the staff kitchen. But he was remembering how he had been more comfortable drinking Teddy's instant, drunk from a chipped mug while a ragamuffin splashed about in the bath-cupboard. He wondered what she had done with the pot of tulips.

THIRTYFIVE

A month had passed since Monty had stood in his father's office having strips torn off him. A month in which he had not achieved much in the way of removing Melanie from his life – work or social. He simply didn't have the heart to sack her, she was just too good at her job. And he liked her. A lot, now that Teddy wasn't around for him to make comparisons.

He missed being with Teddy, she was rejuvenating and a welcome change to the reserved circle that he frequented. But between his increased workload, his children, and a social life with Melanie, there had been no time for trips to London. And Teddy hadn't bothered to contact him either.

The situation with Melanie was proving to be more difficult to resolve. He had spoken again with his father, hoping to negotiate an equitable and agreeable solution, to somehow retain Melanie in his life, but to no avail. His father was adamant that only someone of the calibre of Sybil Forbes would be acceptable as the future 'lady of the firm'. Monty had had a hard time keeping a straight face when his father had made that pronouncement. Since when were wives considered part of the firm? He'd never heard his mother being referred to in such a manner, nor had she taken any part in the business other than as an appendage to his father in social settings.

Migraines were not something with which Monty was overly familiar, but the headache festering behind his temples were angling on becoming one. He'd been trying, unsuccessfully, to concentrate on the file on his desk, but the words kept merging into one another. So he was pleased when he heard the knock on his door.

Melanie sauntered in, a package balanced in front of her in such a manner that it was pushing her bosom up as if in salute. Monty quickly averted his eyes and lowered his head to hide the grin that had leapt onto his face. He knew that she suspected that he was struggling to dismiss her. He could only assume that her suspicions had been fostered by her frequent tête-à-têtes with Veronica that he'd witnessed. And he was finding it amusing, observing how she was doing everything in her power to make that action extremely hard for him.

"This just came. Special delivery. It's addressed to Charlie Hirst, again," she said as she walked towards him, leant forward over the desk and proffered the package. She had been very, very tempted to open it, but didn't know what Monty's reaction would be. His moods had been hard to read after his meeting with his father, usually aloof in the office yet not when out socialising, though even then there were moments when intimacy seemed a thing of the past. She had given up on formulating any more Phases to initiate and had fallen back onto expanding Phase One. "Are you sure he has gone?" she asked, running her tongue over her lips.

Monty took the parcel, but chose not to answer Melanie, mainly because he could no longer be sure that Charlie Hirst had gone. Since Teddy's reappearance it felt as if Charlie Hirst was also making a comeback. And Monty was feeling quite disconcerted that it was such a welcome comeback.

He put the parcel on his desk and almost caressingly placed his hands on top of it before looking up at Melanie, avoiding the cleavage struggling to be released. "A cup of tea would be welcome about now, thank you Melanie."

"But ..." Melanie wanted to protest. She wanted to stay and ask again about Charlie Hirst.

Monty looked at her severely and she quickly straightened up.

"Right away Mr Chinthurst, would you like a biscuit with it?"

If Monty had not been so preoccupied with the package under his hands he might have registered the sarcasm and venom that had tinged Melanie's reply.

"Just the tea, thank you."

Monty made sure that Melanie had shut the office door behind her before he picked up the package and played it through his hands. What could Teddy be sending him now? And did he want to open it to find out?

He stood up, carried it to his briefcase, and put it inside. Whatever it was, he would discover in the privacy of his own home.

He was sitting back at his desk when Melanie returned with his cup of tea.

"Who is Charlie Hirst?" Melanie asked, as she put the cup down.

"Hmm?" Monty looked across to her.

"Charlie Hirst? Are you ever going to tell me who he is?" She tried to decipher the hurt that spread across Monty's face, and wondered if she now wanted to know, if it pained him so much.

"All you need to know is that he is someone I knew a long time ago." No matter how many times Melanie, or anyone for that matter, asked who Charlie Hirst was, he would not divulge the secret that was so special to he and Teddy. He could only imagine how scathing anyone would be of the juvenile insult that meant so much to him.

"Then at least tell me if he worked here?" Despite working for Monty, and latterly getting to know him more personally, she still knew very little about his personal life. No matter how surreptitiously she tried to delve into his past life, Monty gave nothing away.

"Then if he never worked here, why are things coming here for him? What are you going to do with this latest one?" she asked, looking around the desk for it. "What have you done with it?"

"You don't need to worry about it. I've taken care of it."

Melanie looked around. "Where? How?" She couldn't see the package anywhere, and Monty hadn't been out of the room. "Don't tell me you threw it out the window?" She looked over to the window and, panicking, started to move towards it as she had the momentary vision of him opening it and hurling the package out over the busy street below. She hadn't heard any screams from accosted pedestrians, or the scrunch of it being run over. Then remembered that the windows didn't open, and relaxed.

"But it came from that artist woman, didn't it?" Melanie, fed up with not getting any satisfactory answers, was fishing. "She must know that he is not here, so why'd she send it here?"

Monty mentally shook his head and sighed deeply, Melanie was like a dog worrying over a bone.

"He once used the office as his point of contact." He felt like snapping 'satisfied?', but restrained himself.

"Now, please Melanie, don't ask me any more about Charlie. And as for today's package, like I said, I've taken care of it."

Melanie looked around. "Where? How?" She couldn't see the package anywhere, and Monty hadn't been out of the room. "Don't tell me you threw it out the window?" She looked over to the window and, panicking, started to move towards it as she had the momentary vision of him opening it and hurling the package out over the busy street below. She hadn't heard any screams from accosted pedestrians, or the scrunch of it being run over. Then remembered that the windows didn't open, and relaxed.

"But it came from that artist woman, didn't it?" Melanie, fed up with not getting any satisfactory answers, was fishing. "She must know that he is not here, so why'd she send it here?"

"Please Melanie, don't ask me any more about Charlie. And as for today's package, like I said, I've taken care of it."

THIRTYSIX

Monty waited until he had eaten his dinner before psyching himself up to open the package from Teddy. He knew, from the form, that it contained one of her pieces of art. He just wasn't sure if he was ready to see which one it was. He was fearful of it being another incriminating rendition of one of his escapades, and if it was, he had not wanted it to see the light of day in the office.

Even now, sitting in his favourite armchair, he had a glass of Dutch courage on the side table beside him. He reached out for the glass and brought it to his mouth, only to find that it was empty. He sighed. He didn't feel like getting up to refill it. He looked across the room to the mantle clock. The news would be coming on TV soon. He could delay opening it till after that. Not that he held much store in the often prejudiced reporting, it was still a good idea to know what was being fed to the viewing public.

He reached for the remote, turned on the TV, and froze. He sat up straighter and leaned forward, straining to hear the report, before turning up the volume – Australia was on fire.

Well, not exactly, but large swathes of three states were experiencing numerous late season bushfires. He raked his brain for where *Calinda* lay in relation to where the blazes were eating up hectares of pasture, bush and forest. He had not experienced the effects of bushfires while he'd been there, but he recalled the precautions Ralph Delany took to prevent and prepare for such an eventuality. He'd been forever grateful that he had been spared going through that ordeal. Now, late in the season fires were ravaging the land. He hoped *Calinda* and the surrounding stations were being spared.

He'd have to ask Teddy. He wondered if there was still time for him to get to London or if it was too late to visit. But first he'd better see which picture she was sending him, so when he got to her place he'd know what he was thanking her for.

He picked the package up from the floor where it had landed after falling off his lap when he was watching the news. He pried the package open. As he suspected, there was a framed picture, but an envelope was obscuring it. With trembling fingers he opened the envelope and and smoothed the page open.

Dear Charlie,

By the time you are reading this I will be several thousand feet in the air on my way home. I am so terribly sorry that we did not have a chance to say goodbye in person.

The exhibition closed up with great success, and I have very few pieces to take back with me.

Thank you so much for giving me a marvellous time. I really did enjoy catching up with you again and wish you all the very best in any and all of your future endeavours.

If you ever do make it back to Australia in the future, hopefully not in similar circumstances to the first time, please, please, please do make the effort to look me up so we can catch up again.

Please accept the enclosed as a momento of the lovely weekend we spent together. You will notice that I have taken the opportunity to deviate from my usual mediums and styles, but that is what the weekend, and England did for me.

I hope you are as impressed with it as I am pleased.

All the very best,

Your one and only and ever more shall be so,

Teddy xx

Monty put the page down and let out a sigh. Teddy had left, and he felt totally bereft. It was as though someone had pulled the plug on his lifeline. He wondered if she had heard about the fires, and that was why she had left so soon. Teddy had gone. And she had left without giving him the opportunity to say goodbye.

Monty wiped the back of his hand across his eyes, pleased to be on his own as he was not prepared to admit that they were tears he was mopping up. What would his father have to say about him having tears, and tears over 'that colonial'? Damn his father. Then he wondered if his father had actually spoken to Teddy and that was why she had left without letting him say goodbye. He wouldn't put it past his father, not unless his father had spoken to Teddy before having it out with him in his office. If he had, then Teddy would have had the time to tidy things up in London and be on that plane. He hoped that had not been the case. He clenched his fists at the thought of his father brow-beating her into submission, then remembered that Teddy was not likely to be intimidated by his father, unlike himself. He sighed, no, his father's hand was not in this subterfuge. It was more likely that Teddy had chosen to leave this way, the way that he had left her, and Australia. There was a certain irony there, and he laughed. Typical Teddy. But what was her motivation for the cowardly exit? Or was it cowardly? Had she been avoiding an emotional goodbye? It would certainly have been one for him as, with surprise, he realised that his feelings for her ran very deep.

Slowly he picked up the frame, and looked at the offering Teddy had left him. It was in coloured pencil and indeed different to any of her other pieces that he had seen, and he wondered what Melanie would make of it.

This one was an infusion of just about every colour of the rainbow. It was bright, the images more precise than those at the gallery. And represented a real mish mash of memories for the two of them. She had managed to incorporate their weekend's outings with some Australiana.

He held the edges of the frame at arm's length. It was as if he was looking down at a whirlpool of colour, ringed with bright orange and red that could only be flames. Had she known that Australia was about to ignite? When had she created this piece of artwork?

Smatterings of seashells, pebbles, sand and deckchairs intermingled with flowers, deciduous trees, gumtrees and anthills. A man with a dog was traipsing between these and across the whirlpool as they chased a kangaroo, and a stag. He could make out something that looked like the pier at Brighton.

He couldn't describe it as anything other than colourful—a kaleidoscope of memories. It was brilliant how she had infused it although, and he suddenly missed her. Not with the passion of a lost love, but with the emotion that went with losing one's compass.

He laid the picture back down on his lap, and once more wiped the back of his hands over his eyes. There was so much in there to see and to remember. How he wished that he could thank her in person. Then with a sinking heart he realised that he did not know *how* he could thank her. He did not have her address, although he supposed he could always send it via those at *Calinda*. It no longer mattered if word came back to his father.

Monty's head was in a muddle. After fifteen years of trying to repress anything to do with Australia and Teddy, there was now no denying that they were both an integral part of him. She had awakened something in him that he had forgotten, and now did not want to lose again. For fifteen years he had played the part that his father, society, and even Melanie had channelled him into. Teddy, in the short time she had been here, along with the memories that she had enabled to escape, had infused him with life as he wanted it to be. And now she was gone. His support had vanished. And without Teddy handy he did not know how he could cope.

Well, he thought, his father would be pleased. That only left Melanie. He still had to dismiss her as his PA, and his father had made it equally obvious that he had to also remove her from his social life. Well, if there was one more thing that he could thank Teddy for, it was that he did not have to comply with the strictures of society. He was able to be his own man. He took a deep breath, and squared his shoulders then wiped his fingers across the picture. "Thank you, Teddy."

And on that note, he took himself to bed, to toss and turn and dream.

THIRTYSEVEN

The next morning Monty woke with resolve paramount in his mind. He knew what he was going to do, and was uncharacteristically very late arriving at work.

Monty stopped outside the firm's office and composed himself before pushing open the main door. He was starting to realise the magnitude of his resolve to rebel, but there was no going back now. He was determined to let go, one step at a time, of what he thought of as his old life. But it would be a struggle. And today's change from his routine was making itself felt. Not that he was about to admit the reason for his almost drunken movement. He plastered a smile on his face, opened the door and stepped inside. No one appeared to notice his entrance and he let out the breath that he had not been aware he was holding.

Melanie alone had been watching him struggle through the open office, his briefcase swinging by his side, bringing a brief grimace to his face each time it bumped into his thigh.

"Whatever have you been doing?" she asked solicitously as he came level with her desk. "Are you all right?" She made to get up from her seat. "Can I get you anything?"

Monty slowed his steps and grimaced. He'd rehearsed what he would say, knowing that she wouldn't be fobbed off with a casual excuse such as tripping over something. 'Racquetball."

"What?"

"Racquetball." He couldn't be bothered explaining it beyond that.

"Why?"

That question he could handle better. "I decided that I needed to improve my energy levels; now that the children are getting older," he said, confident that at the mere mention of his children Melanie would find something else to talk about. He mentally shook his head. Did his father know about her aversion to children, and was that what was behind the mandate? Maybe pursuing Melanie would not be the wisest move. His children were an important part of his life.

Monty smiled when Melanie started to shuffle the papers on her desk.

"Looking at you, I think that you might have left the rejuvenation a bit late. Are you planning on taking up racquetball as a frequent activity?" Melanie said, furtively looking up.

"No. After this morning I'm inclined to admit that today was a one-off. Roger can find someone else to partner him – the floor, walls and ball are too much for me." He grimaced as he turned to move towards his office. "I think your flowers are needing some attention," he said putting his hand out and lifting a drooping bloom. "You could try running their heads under some lukewarm water, might revive them."

Melanie gaped as his audacity. Then glared at him. She refrained from replying with the acerbic retort that sprang to mind, reminding herself of her ultimate goal.

In the sanctuary of his office Monty limped to his desk, judiciously bent down and took the framed charcoal out of his drawer. It was time that it saw the light of day. He then slowly made his way to the sofa, and, when he had deposited his briefcase there, he turned to look where Melanie had hung the photograph.

Monty smiled, his expression tinged with triumph and a hint of malice. Clutching the framed charcoal in one hand he hobbled over to the wall. Once there he gleefully removed Melanie's revered photograph and tossed it towards the sofa, grinning when it slid off and hit the carpet. Then with gleeful defiance he replaced it with Teddy's charcoal stick figures. He stood back, admiring the two framed artworks of Teddy's and felt the weight of the last fifteen years miraculously dissipate, and he felt liberated.

He then slowly made his way back to his desk. He was just cautiously lowering himself into his chair when Melanie knocked and entered.

"Mo... Mr Chinthirst!" She almost sprinted across the room, and reached out to help Monty sit down. "Here, let me help you."

"I'm fine Melanie, thank you." He tried to smile as he eased himself onto the seat, willing the beads of sweat on his forehead to remain under his hair.

"Are you sure you are all right?" Melanie asked, her face puckered in concern. There had to be something which she could do to help ease the pain. Then, without thinking she blurted out "I could massage your legs for you. I'm sure that would help."

Monty almost laughed as he imagined Melanie kneeling down beside him, rubbing her hands up and down his leg. No doubt she would want him to roll his trouser legs up and all. Then he did splutter thinking how that would look should a client, or his father walk in on the action.

Melanie cocked her head to one side, and looked at him strangely. "Did you injure your head as well? Can I get you some paracetamol? There's bound to be some in the First Aid box."

Monty grimaced as he settled into the chair, and shook his head. "No, I said I was fine, and I am. Some tea would be nice though, thank you." Monty turned the page of his desk diary to the right day and looked at it, then up at the clock above the door. "Yes, I've time before Mrs Sedgely's due. A cup of tea now, and then maybe you could join us when she arrives."

"Will you be conducting business at your desk or ..." Melanie turned to indicate the informal seating arrangement near the window, and to admire once again the media photograph, mentally preening herself to think that if the meeting was to be held there, Mrs Sedgely would see her nestled in between Monty and George. She stopped mid-sentence.

Monty watched, his pain forgotten, as Melanie, her face infused with disquiet and pending anger clasped the edge of his desk. She then turned to face him,

"What is that ... that thing doing there? And where has my ... the, photograph gone? You can't have that, that indecent monstrosity on public view."

"Why not? It was on public view when you first saw it."

"That's different. It was in a small and dark room in an inconsequential picture gallery. No one of importance would have seen it there."

"I thought you spent the evening talking with people that you claimed were important?"

"Yes, but they were people who may be important for you to know in the future. I'm talking about the people who come into your office who are already important. What will your clients think? They are the ones that you need to impress if you want them to stay as your clients. You simply cannot have it on display. Where is the photograph, so I can return it to its proper place?

Monty wasn't quite following her logic, and found her attitude amusing. And he marveled to himself that he should find it so. Times were definitely changing and he was feeling enlivened by them.

"I take it you do not approve of how I decorate my office then?" he asked, mischief in his voice, and he blinked. When was the last time he'd heard himself sound like that? And then laughed as he calculated that it would have been some time in his preteen years, before he'd been sent away to school and had the accepted societal norms stuffed into him. "They stay. I like them."

"Well then be it on your head when Mrs Sedgely arrives and sees them. You realise that she, and all your other clients will only complain to your father, and then what will you do?"

Monty looked up at Melanie. What the hell did his father, who rarely if ever entered his office, have to do with how he decorated the room?

Melanie's face coloured as she watched Monty scrutinise her and she took a step back. Had she gone too far? She knew that the décor of the place did not come under her job description, but didn't Monty realise that she only had his best interests at heart? What was that adage about a better woman being behind every successful man? When would he comprehend that she was that woman for him?

Monty was studying Melanie, but not as a potential source of superior support. Was it possible, with the mention of his father, that she had been the one to divulge to his father the about time he had spent with Teddy?

"I'd appreciate that tea now, if you wouldn't mind. Just a quick one before Mrs Sedgely arrives," he said dismissively as he waved her away with his hand.

Melanie controlled the snort of disapproval she was feeling, lifted her head and turned and walked away, hoping that she had not caste the die to her detriment.

Monty watched her go, her hips provocatively swaying, and he shook his head. There had been a time, only a few days ago, when he would have been captivated by her movement. But that had been before the euphoria of liberation that he had felt with the simple act of asserting his own preferences for what to display on his walls.

Monty made sure that he was already at the sofa and armchairs when Mrs Sedgely arrived. It would not have made a good impression to be seen wincing and hobbling from his desk. But he made sure that he was standing when Melanie escorted her in.

Before he had the opportunity to welcome his client she had detoured to stand and view the two pictures. Breathless, for different reasons, Monty and Melanie both waited.

"What wonderful taste you have in art, Mr Chinthurst. They look like," she took a step forward and peered more closely. "Yes, I was right. They *are* Delanys." Beaming, she turned to look at Monty. "You are so fortunate to have two of her masterpieces. I do like her work, they are so full of mystic, and energy." She stepped back from them. "These two are different – this one's subject is more recognisable," she said indicating the doe and joey. "But I do find the stick figures quite amusing, and so very lifelike. It must have been some party she was depicting. Almost makes me wish I'd been there," she laughed, then turned to Monty. "Have you ever met her?"

THIRTYEIGHT

In the two months since Melanie had handed Monty the package for Charlie Hirst, he had not heard anything further from Teddy. He was missing her vivaciousness in his life. He knew that he couldn't be in her company, physically, but felt sure that if he could at least correspond with her – a letter, or email, or anything, then that would help him feel the way he had when she had been in England. That weekend when he had felt so liberated. He was desperate to feel that way again.

In desperation, he drove to London in the hope of finding someone with a forwarding address. Failing that, he could always write to her via *Calinda* but that would also open a potential avenue for his father to find out what he was doing. Between his father and Ralph, who he had left in the lurch, he preferred his chances in London

He had first visited the art gallery, only to be told that they couldn't help him. Her exhibition had been very successful, with most of the pieces being sold and those that had not been, Teddy had taken with her. And, as he had suspected, they could not give him the names of any of the guests at the opening, privacy and all that. He had then driven over to Hackney to the flat she had stayed in, but when he had turned up to ask about Teddy, the only person he could rouse was Frank. All he could share with Monty was that the only thing Teddy had left was a pot of tulips which she had given to his mother.

The only other option that he could think of was to approach the Manninghams. No matter how much he wanted to know where Teddy was, there was no way that he was going to do that. George would gleefully tell Melanie that he was looking for Teddy before he had time to get back to Cambridge. And that would be disastrous.

Melanie was already driving him to distraction with her relentless and unwavering determination to ingratiate herself.

No, he just had to acknowledge that Teddy had come and gone out of his life much in the same way as he had in hers all those years ago. All that was left was for him to resume life as normal. Only he had no idea what his normal was any more. And making a choice between letting go of his staid English way of life and reinventing himself along the lines of the freedom that Teddy espoused was being made more difficult with Melanie doing her best to help him overcome what she perceived as his melancholy.

It still rankled his father that Melanie had not been replaced. But he had, what he thought, was the solution to that, and Monty in general.

It was another month when Monty arrived at work to find the place abuzz. The entire staff were not seated sedately working at their desks but rather they were conducting what looked like a festive free-for-all, with his father taking centre stage.

"Ah, Monty, my boy," his father exclaimed, raising his hands above the heads of the those milling around him. "I was wondering when you might deign to arrive."

Monty, who had been wondering what was causing the joviality in the air felt his heart sink with the greeting, and he wondered what he had done wrong this time. Though the tenor of the room suggested nothing too disastrous. He tried to smile as he walked tentatively over to his father as a way was made for him. It was rare to see his father in the outer office, usually he timed his appearances to be before, or after the usually regarded office hours.

"Father, sir, Mr Charles?"

"Come, come, no need to stand on ceremony. Here." He thrust out a stiff buff card the size of a typical memo pad.

Monty took it and turned it over to see what was written on the front, then looked up at his father, puzzled.

"Yes, my boy. Everyone in the office and more besides, is invited. No exceptions, and no excuses. All our clients, and our friends. It's going to be a special occasion. You can bring the children. They might enjoy themselves. There will, no doubt, be other children for them to play with. Of course, your old nanny will be on hand for the littler ones."

He then leant in closer to Monty and, sotto voce, just for him, added "Sybil Forbes will be there." He winked, and with that, Mr Charles twirled around and pompously strode back to his office, which was taken as a sign for everyone to return to their desks and start the day's work.

Monty, still puzzled, walked to his office with the card in his left hand, tapping it against the handle of his briefcase. His father was inviting everyone to a soiree at *Whytecliff Manor*? Everyone. Since when did his father socialise, at his home, far less invite the staff?

"Isn't it exciting?" Melanie gushed as she caught up with Monty just before he got to her desk. "I'll have to take a longer lunch won't I?" she continued, picking up the mail and following him into his office. "You'll let me do that, won't you?" she cooed.

Monty glanced at her. "Why's that?" he asked.

"I'll need to buy something special to wear, won't I?"

Monty let her prattle on. What she was going to wear was of little interest to him. His thoughts were taken up more with the reason or reasons behind this abrupt departure from his father's usual protocol.

And prattle on she did, "An invitation to *Whytecliff Manor*. Can you imagine? It's a very nice invitation too. It's what would be nice for a wedding invitation. I must ask Veronica where Mr Charles had them done. She will know, won't she? Bound to. Funny how it's taken your father, not you, to invite me to your family home."

Monty shook his head. She was like a giddy schoolgirl, he thought as he deposited his briefcase and the invitation on the sofa and walked back to his desk, smiling at the two framed pictures. The pictures had been his anchor, and his workday didn't start until he had acknowledged their presence. The memories they invoked kept him grounded and, for some reason, feeling free.

"Do you know why it is that we're being invited?" Melanie continued with her inquisition.

"I have no idea," Monty said as he took the mail from Melanie's hands and sat down at his desk. "And speculation is useless. When is it, by the way?"

"Mo... Mr Chinthurst. Really! It's there on the invitation. Didn't you look? Where is your invitation? It's a very nice one too. I'm going to keep mine safe. I might even have it framed. What do you think?" she asked, pointedly looking at the wall where her photograph had once hung. She still quietly seethed over that.

Monty traced her gaze. Gosh he was missing Teddy.

He turned his attention back to the mail, wishing that one of them would be from Teddy. Knowing her, and going on her previous communiqués if she wrote to him, she would address it to Charlie Hirst, and Melanie would be on his case, again.

"It's this Saturday."

"What is?"

"This party that your father has invited us all to."

"I'm not that sure it is a party," he said, marvelling that his father might extend himself to holding a party. At *Whytecliff Manor* no less, with the staff, and children included.

"Then what is it if it's not a party?"

"I have absolutely no idea. Most probably it'll be something innocuous." And he hoped that his father wasn't planning on announcing any nuptials for him and the illustrious Miss Forbes. With his father, there was no knowing. Anything was possible. And he would not put it past his father to put the cart before the horse to gain his own ends.

"But you must know, he is your father, he must have told you something."

"Not necessarily. You've worked here long enough to know that. Mr Charles is very much the man in control and keeps things close."

"Maybe he is going to announce his retirement, and that you are going to succeed him. Imagine, you, the head of the firm." Melanie's eyes sparkled at the prospect of becoming the wife of the head of the firm.

"Hardly," Monty scoffed. His father too young to retire. He turned to rifle through the mail.

There was an envelope with an Australian stamp, and he felt himself catch his breath. He wanted to pick up the letter, but not while Melanie was in the office. Just in case it was from Teddy. A letter from Teddy needed to be opened and read in private.

"Tea would be nice, thank you Melanie," he said as he looked up at her.

"But," she felt dejected. She wanted to talk about the upcoming event, and Monty was only interested in the mail and work.

Monty glared at her.

"Yes Mr Chinthurst. Right away," she said as she backed away and walked out.

Monty watched her as she left, his fingers itching to pick up the letter with the Australian stamp. But now was not the time. If the letter had something to do with Teddy, he wanted he wanted a clear mind, free from any thoughts of what his father might be planning. He flicked it across the desk and watched as it tipped off the edge. If he left it there he would not be tempted to open it, so he turned his attention to the rest of the mail, which proved to all be business related and of less interest.

Melanie breezed back into the office with his tea. She had balanced a biscuit on the side of the saucer, hoping that it would butter him up.

"Oh, what's this?" she asked as she placed the cup and saucer on the desk. She bent down and picked up the letter that had dropped. "From Australia?" Her mood took an immediate dive. If it was from Australia, was the artist writing to *her* Monty? She took a closer look, the post mark read something, "Western Australia?" She frowned. She didn't know much about the geography of Australia, nor where that woman was from, but she didn't think it was Western Australia. She looked at Monty, but he was busy opening another envelope. She placed the Australian letter next to the cup and saucer.

"May I go for an early lunch now? Or are you needing me?"

Monty looked up from the last letter to be read, expecting to see a seductive posture to go along with what he took to be an inuendo. But Melanie was standing demurely, hands held together at her waist. He raised an eyebrow in query.

"I'd really like to get started on finding something to wear on Saturday."

Monty frowned. "I thought the invitation stated that it was casual dress? Surely you don't need to buy something new, your existing wardrobe would be adequate, wouldn't it?"

"Really Mr Chinthurst. I can't afford to wear something I've already worn before – there might be someone there who's seen me wear it. Can I take an early lunch?"

Monty, keeping his face blank, and deciding that he would never understand her, dismissed her with a wave of his hand. "Yes, you may go."

THIRTYNINE

Monty collected his children from Lyndall and drove to Whytecliff Manor, wondering the whole way what was behind his father's party and what surprise he was going to spring. His father was not known for magnanimous gestures, so there had to be some deviousness at play. It was mind boggling that whatever was being planned required the attendance of all the staff members and their families.

In the entire existence of the firm, except for the one-time staff picnic at Anglesey Abbey – he still had no idea what the purpose of that had been – no one had ever hosted a staff activity. There had never even been a Christmas bonus – the Chinthursts didn't believe in such frivolity. Admittedly there had been a few occasions, very few, when select clients and staff were invited to a meal at a restaurant to match the clientele's social standing. They had never been easy or enjoyable encounters. He was hoping that today's event would be more palatable, but was having difficulty believing that would be the case.

The children, sitting in the back of the car, suddenly squealed, excitedly pointing out the window. Monty's mouth gaped open as he saw what the two were on about.

"Well, I'll be," he said as he saluted the gatehouse keeper. The stone and wrought iron entrance was festooned with helium balloons. He looked in the rearview mirror and smiled at his children. "I think that granddad has forgotten that he is an adult, don't you?"

Two heads nodded fiercely, jogging up and down as best they could in their car restraints. Monty laughed, and continued driving towards his family home.

Being family, Monty drove slowly past the front of the house, amazed at the collection of cars that littered the available parking spaces, and followed the gravel path that snuck around the side. He then parked the car in one of the garage bays.

Children in tow, Monty walked towards what would have at one time been designated 'the tradesmen's entrance'.

"Hello Mavis," he greeted the middle-aged woman whirling around the kitchen like a manic orchestra conductor. "I see that you have not lost your touch, this place smells delicious," he laughed.

Mavis stopped mid-stream in her ministrations to the several young women busy preparing platters of hors d'oeuvres, charcuterie board and canapes, and turned around.

"Mister Monty," she almost screamed as she wiped her hands down her apron and almost ran across the tiled floor towards the three who stood just inside the door. She stopped in front of Monty, then bent down to face the children. "And you have brought Master Chas and Miss Lottie with you. Hello there cherubs," she said clucking under their chins and standing up. "My, how they have grown. Are you all moving back in? Oh, silly me. You're here for this shindig that Mr Charles is putting on, aren't you."

Monty put his hand on her shoulder, "I doubt that I will ever permanently move into the wing that my mother set up for me. But you are correct on the other hand. We have been invited to attend whatever it is that my father has planned." He smiled, released Mavis and put a gentle hand on each child's head. "Come on kids, we'd better get moving and let Mavis and her crew get back to work," he said, shepherding the children through the kitchen and out into the house proper, where he met his mother standing at the bottom of the staircase.

"Mother?" Monty said, leaning in to plant the required kiss on her cheek, and wondering why she was dressed as though this afternoon was a formal occasion.

"Monty dear." She smiled, then absent-mindedly ruffled the children's hair.

Monty smiled, it was only to be expected that his mother would not lower herself to embrace her grandchildren. No wonder they never expressed any desire to visit their grandparents.

"What is the reason for the gathering?" he asked. He watched as a sporadic stream of guests were greeted at the door by the family butler and ushered into the foyer, where local youth, dressed in black and white like penguins, held trays of assorted drinks.

Your father has something very special to announce, and wanted to share it with everyone. And, you should know better than to ask, no I do not know what it is. Come along now, the children are all gathering in the nursery, and I have someone I want you to meet."

"Not Sybil?" Monty asked, tongue in cheek.

"Good heavens no, that is in your father's providence. You will see her shortly. No, this is someone that has been asking after you. Seemed most anxious to catch up with you.

Come along now."

"I'll meet up with you shortly mother. I first will make sure that Chas and Lottie are settled in the nursery."

After taking his children to the nursery and introducing them to Betty, his old nanny, and to some of his remembered toys that he knew they had not seen on previous visits which had never included the nursery, he followed the waves of voices to the larger of the reception rooms.

He smiled. Of course the event would be held here. Not so much because it could accommodate all the guests but because the walls were festooned with portraits of his ancestors, sedately frowning across to where the floor to ceiling windows opened out onto a terrace and then the manicured lawn. An array of oil paintings commissioned from the 'old masters' were strategically placed to catch favourable natural light. Along the wall under the family tree a long row of tables had been placed to accommodate the delicacies that Mavis and her players had created. Already guests, mainly the office staff, were busy piling their plates. He could only guess what they were making of it. The clients would be more at ease with the offerings and environment.

He saw his mother standing on the terrace with a couple of people just outside one of the patio doors. He didn't recognise who was with her, their backs being to him. He made his way over to her, stopping to exchange brief pleasantries with familiar faces, and wondering where Melanie was. He could do with her company, his father be damned. He wanted to have Melanie on his arm when he met Sybil. He looked at his watch. She ought to be here by now, and he hoped that nothing had happened on the way. He had offered to bring her, but when she knew that the children would be with him, she had caustically declined.

His mother saw him approach and while Monty still had a couple of yards to traverse, the couple with her turned.

The Manninghams. What the hell were they doing here? They were neither staff, clients, nor friends of his parents, as far as he knew, so how did they wangle an invitation? The only common denominator that he could think of was Melanie, but why and how, she would have managed to get them included on the guest list was beyond him. Monty composed himself and reluctantly joined them on the terrace.

George, radiating effulgent bonhomie, grasped Monty's hand. "Monty! So glad that you got here." He released Monty's hand and grabbed his elbow instead, "Come over here will you. Excuse us, girls," he said as he twirled Monty away from the women.

Monty disentangled himself and shook his arm, ridding it of George's touch as they walked towards the end of the terrace. What had got into the man?

"I hear that you are in a bit of bother," George said as he reached for Monty's arm again.

Bother? Monty stopped walking, released himself from George's grip and turned, puzzled, to face him. "What are you talking about George? Bother? With whom?"

"Oh, you know. Things get talked about. Have I let something out that I ought not to have?" George laughed and kept walking.

Typical, Monty thought. George, the perpetual purveying monger of rumours that he had no authority to be privy to, and was only too anxious to share. Monty shook his head and in a few strides had caught up to him.

"Where's that PA of yours? Melanie? Thought she'd be here, hanging off your arm." He dug an elbow into Monty's side. "She's a goer that one. Have you heard from Theodora? She seems to have disappeared. She was always good to have babysit. Jolly good thing that your father included children in the invitation, might not have managed to get Fee to come with me otherwise. Didn't want to miss out on seeing your place."

"It's not my place," mumbled Monty as he stared at George. Drugs had never been part of their student scene, but he sure seemed to be high on something right now. George grabbed Monty's arm again and starting walking further along the terrace. "If you ever get tired of that Melanie, do us a favour and head her my way, will you?"

"George!" Monty stopped walking and George, still holding onto Monty, was swung around sharply.

"What?"

"What are you on about? Can't you choose one subject to talk about and then keep to it? My mother said that you wanted to see me. So tell me this – what are you doing here, this afternoon? How did you come by an invitation? And why did you want to see me?"

"Now who's changing the subject? Which question do you want me answering first?"

The two of them were now standing at the end of the terrace where there were a couple of benches. Monty steered George to one and they sat down.

"What are you doing here?"

"I'm here, along with Fee and the kids, because we received an invitation."

"How did you come by being sent one? My understanding is that they were sent to our staff, clients and select friends, of which you are neither, nor is your wife. And I doubt very much that my father has any recollection of you. Or would want to. So how is it that you are here, today?"

"Ah," George said, taping a finger on the side of his nose. "Where's Melanie?" George stood up and started to walk quickly towards where his wife was still engaged in conversation with Mrs Chinthurst by the open patio-window.

"George!" Monty called out in exasperation as he stood up and followed him. The man was incorrigible. And what was his obsession with Mel? Did she have something to do with the Manningham's invitation?

FORTY

Monty caught up with George as he reached the women and waved to someone inside. The women turned to look and Monty followed their gaze to see Melanie walking towards them. It appeared that she had not heeded the dress code for the afternoon. The gold lamé-like figure-hugging cocktail dress with its ruffle, chiffon sleeves, and keyhole neckline left little to the imagination. Monty stepped through the patio-window and met her.

"For a while there I thought you weren't coming. Is everything all right? You found the place easily enough and didn't have any car trouble?" He knew he was overreacting, but felt that he had to say something, if only to establish his priority over George who was now by his side, grinning fit to burst.

"Yes, here I am," she said, smiling at Monty and slipping her arm proprietorially through his, before turning to George. "Good to see you George, where's Fiona? Ah, there she is," she said, straining her head beyond the men, then dragging Monty towards the two women who were now entering the room.

"Mother," Monty said. "I'd like you to meet my Personal Assistant, Melanie Carruthers."

The two women made each other's acquaintance, and Monty could tell from the discrete sniff his mother gave that she was not impressed. Melanie on the other hand was gushing like a groupie meeting her crush for the first time.

Monty didn't know if he was flummoxed or intrigued. The whole afternoon was enigmatic and leaving him totally perplexed. He looked around to see if he could see the Forbeses and Insipid Sybil among the sycophants gracing the room and gorging themselves on gossip and food, and wished that his father would hurry up and make his announcement.

No sooner had this wish surfaced into his consciousness, than a hush rippled through the guests and Monty saw his mother move serenely towards the main door to the room as his father made his appearance.

So much for the edict that dress for the afternoon was 'casual' – his father had obviously not written, or read, or had conveniently forgotten, what was on the invitation. Typical. There he was, not exactly white tie, but certainly ensuring that his guests would be feeling decidedly under dressed. Dressed in his best dinner suit and bowtie the only thing that was missing was the cummerbund. He smiled broadly and raised his hands in a gesture commanding attention.

Oh, he had everyone's attention, Monty thought as he watched his father walk through his guests to meet his wife. He wondered if he and Melanie had been in cohoots when they dressed for the afternoon. The sense of unease that had taken up an uncomfortable residence over the previous few weeks increased in intensity. What was he missing?

He looked around at the faces surrounding him. They were all intently following the convergence of his parents. All except George.

George was standing, alone, near the windows. His eyes were quizzically riveted to Monty's left, where Melanie was latched onto his arm. What was going on? Monty watched as she smiled serenely at George, and inclined her head ever so slightly. Monty frowned and looked back towards George, who jerked his head up in acknowledgement. Was there something going on between the two of them? Where was George's wife? Monty scanned the guests. She and Veronica were standing near the tables, heads close and in conversation.

A general quiet shuffling of feet brought Monty out of his musings and he watched as Charles took his wife by the elbow and the two of them walked through the passage that the guests opened up for them, stopping every few feet to engage in hand-shakes, head nodding and trivial exchanges with select attendees. Monty watched as his father reached out and grasped the arm of a woman, drawing her to join him. Could that be Sybil? He strongly suspected it was when his father craned his head, obviously searching for him among the faces around him. Monty instinctively found himself rounding his shoulders and bending his knees, hoping to be absorbed into the throng.

Melanie tried to haul him upright as she watched his parents and the young woman walk the remainder of the way to stand in front of the tables now well depleted of food, under the portrait of Monty's grandfather – the first Charles Montgomery Chinthurst. Charles kissed the strange woman's cheek before releasing her and giving her a gentle push towards the crush of guests standing in an arc around him.

"Thank you all so very much for coming here today. Welcome to *Whytecliff Manor*. I would like to be in a position to say 'We are gathered here today ...' but sadly that happy event has yet to grace this house." He glanced after the woman then stared fiercely at Monty whom he had now located among the guests. Everyone turned their heads to look in Monty's direction, and a titter of laughter rippled around the room. "But I will save that announcement for another time, hopefully in the not-too-distant future." More laughter followed.

Monty felt Melanie give his arm a squeeze. He looked down at her. Surely she was not entertaining the possibility that such an innuendoed proclamation would include her. Or did she know more about today than she was letting on? After all, the Mannighams were here, no doubt at her instigation, and he knew that she had been talking to Veronica about the invitations. He frowned. What else could they have discussed? All he knew was that since he had started dating Melanie his life and emotions had been battered and buffeted about worse than anything a hurricane could generate.

He turned back to look at the three people standing facing the guests. The young woman who his father had just released could only be Sybil. She was unperturbed by the gentle push and went to stand with an older couple that he recognised as the Forbeses. So this was Sybil. She was most definitely no longer a young girl to be tormented and teased, but time had done nothing to improve her appearance. Until his father had brought attention to her presence no one would have paid her any notice. There was nothing to distinguish her from any of the other women in attendance, with maybe the exception of Melanie – Sybil, in figure hugging jeans and polo-shirt, had adhered to the dress code. And this was who his father saw as a potential wife for him? He looked back at his parents. His mother the perfect foil, his father definitely the man of the manor. The two of them smiling out to capture the attention of their guests. He could see that they were enjoying the moment. And he wondered yet again what was behind the gathering. Whatever it was, he had the feeling that it was going to be something that he'd not be welcoming.

"As you will all appreciate, the firm, our firm, your firm," he spread his arms out expansively, "has been in my family for generations and we have been a sought-after paragon." Charles beamed over his guests. Monty could see his chest expanding with pompous pride. Monty felt himself shrivel in embarrassment while the guests applauded, their smiles mirroring his father's.

"But now we must move with the times," Charles continued after bringing his arms in front of him and motioning downwards with his outstretched hands to lull the accolade.

Monty frowned. What did his father mean? Moving with the times? And why was this the first time he had heard about potential changes?

Then he remembered the letter from Australia that Melanie had included in the letters she had brought into his office. He wondered if today's event had anything to do with that? When he'd finally felt composed enough to read it, he'd slit the envelope open and withdrawn the letter, but as soon as he'd read the salutation and first line ...

Dear Charles,
    In reference to your last communiqué ...

... he'd realised that writer was addressing his father, and now he cursed that he had not bothered to read further.

What *had* the letter been about? And if it was what this event was about, how was it that he was only hearing about it now? Didn't his father trust him? Or was he on the outer as punishment for not toeing his father's line? He sighed and shuffled his feet.

"And, today I have invited you here to share with you how the firm is going to make that timely move."

An undercurrent of excited murmuring rippled around the room like a Mexican wave. Melanie gave a little bounce beside Monty and looked up at him, expectation brightening her face. He slowly shook his head. "Don't look at me like that. I have no knowledge of what he's on about."

"Doesn't matter. I mean, 'moving with the times' that must mean something big, and big is always good. Whatever your father has in mind, it's going to have to include you."

Monty looked again at Melanie, puzzled by what she was prattling on about. He knew how his father worked. He did not enjoy being anything but in control and if anyone stepped out of line he did not hesitate to apply, often excessive, retribution. Oh, he could well attest to that. He subconsciously rubbed his backside.

It was the 'it's going to have to include you' that had Monty worried. His father had given him an edict, and he had not wholly complied. The evidence was there for all to see, hanging onto his arm. Under normal circumstances, being here among staff, friends and clients would provide one with immunity from reprisal, but he knew that his father was likely to take pleasure in public humiliation.

"I have decided it is time to expand."

There was a collective gasp from the guests, followed by a wave of chatter. Melanie was trying hard to contain her own excitement, while Monty stood gaping at his father. So this was the rationale behind today? The firm was expanding. And he knew nothing about it? Wasn't he the heir apparent, and potential partner? But he had been kept in the dark over this? He glared at his father, who grinned back and gave a small nod. His father was really rubbing in his procrastination over ridding himself of Melanie. He sighed and felt a tense coil tightening in his chest, and he clenched his fists while his stomach twisted uncomfortably, both at the news and at the smirk on his father's face—a silent taunt.

"Expansion Monty! How exciting," Melanie said, clutching Monty's arm tighter.

Monty looked down at her and felt sick.

Charles waited for the quiet exclamations to settle before smiling and reaching out to Sybil, "Come here my dear."

Sybil turned to her parents, clasped their hands in hers, and gave them a tentative smile. They nodded their heads and smiled proudly. Sybil let go of their hands and slowly looked around at the sea of faces before walking to stand beside Charles, who put his arm around her shoulders, pulling her closer.

"May I present to you, Miss Sybil Forbes. She is to be the new face to our new branding. Now," Charles speared Monty with a chiselled gleam, and Monty felt a gazillion eyes swivel and zero in on him. "Come here boy," he demanded.

Monty cringed. He didn't move. He couldn't. Flashes of memories from years of previous summons when he had disappointed his father cascaded through his head, along with the consequences that followed. Though he didn't think that his father would be so dictatorial as to embarrass him in public, if that's what he had in mind this time.

Melanie gave him a dig in his ribs, "Monty! Pull yourself together and get on up there," she hissed.

Monty looked down at her, but with his mind still centred on his previous deportation, instead of seeing Melanie, he saw Teddy. She would not be standing beside him bubbling with excitement at possible personal advancement and telling him to suck it up. Teddy would be spitting chips. He smiled, recalling one of the many colloquial terms she had bombarded him with, and had then laughed at his confusion. She'd have told him to 'man up' and turn the command into a challenge.

Monty squared his shoulders. He was ready.

As Monty reached the spot where his parents and Sybil were waiting, his father grabbed hold of his shoulder, his fingers transmitting the message that Monty had to behave, and spun him around to face Sybil.

"You remember Sybil Forbes, don't you?" his father said so quietly than no one other than the three of them heard, and dug his fingers meaningfully into Monty's shoulder again, and gave him a little push towards Sybil.

Monty looked at Sybil more closely. The orthodontic work had paid off. Two lines of perfect teeth showed between the muted lipsticked lips that struggled to form into a smile. Her arched eyebrows were enhanced to augment the hazel eyes which mirrored his scrutiny. For his own part he was still wondering why his father would suggest she might be of any interest to him, especially romantically.

Monty could feel the waves of animosity that the woman was generating – surely she was not still resenting him from all those years ago? But he could not imagine why else Sybil would be harbouring such loathing towards him.

Charles then turned to his guests. "I'll let these two get reacquainted while I continue with how having Miss Forbes and my son up here with me has anything to do with us moving on. The firm is expanding. And that expansion is not a matter of moving into bigger or better premises. The firm is going international." Charles' smile was fit to split his face in two. "Yes! International," he repeated, then paused to allow the clamour of voices to settle down as friends, staff and clients turned to each other and exclaimed all manner of opinions.

Monty, only half listening to his father, watched the small flicker of triumph escape Sybil's otherwise composed and almost hostile demeanour. She knew something that he didn't, and that was not sitting comfortably with him. First Melanie, and now Sybil. Was he the only one floundering in the dark? Hoping for moral support, if not answers, he looked towards where he had left Melanie. George was now beside her, looking very chummy without his wife beside him.

Monty watched the two of them together. He still didn't know what was behind the Manninghams being present, but one thing was obvious, and that was that George was not to be trusted, and nor apparently, was Melanie. And he was getting tired of it all. Ever since seeing the first envelope with Charlie Hirst's name on it in Teddy handwriting, his life had been pulled him into a veritable vortex with what felt like only a child's Styrofoam paddle board to keep him afloat. Kicking got him nowhere.

Charles on the other hand, was in his element. He had succeeded in solving the problem he had with his son's choices. Expanding had been an idea he had been toying with for a number of years, but not internationally. No, that had come about with the combination of realising Monty was not heeding his directive to remove his PA from the scene, with the proposal of a merger from an acquaintance in Canada. Charles had not liked the idea of merging, after all, his firm was a family firm and merging would diminish his control. But to set up a branch offshore, that, he thought, was worth investigating.

Once his guests were again focused on him, and settled, he continued. "This coming week will see the highly accomplished Sybil Forbes fly out to Australia to set up a branch of the firm there in Perth. And my son, who is well versed in international travel, having taken many a holiday abroad, will be accompanying her."

Monty's head snapped around and he gawped at his father.

"I'm quite capable of travelling on my own," Sybil muttered, and Monty looked at her. He knew what was happening here; did she? But her expression gave nothing away.

"Miss Forbes here will head up the new office," Charles held his arm out to indicate Sybil, and smiled. "While my son Monty here, will be there to man-handle and supervise things," Charles said, almost off-handedly.

Monty did a double-take. That sounded as though it was more than a temporary assignment. So what did that mean for his children? He knew, growing up, that there were families who lived abroad while their children remained in England, only seeing each other on home-leave, or during the long summer school holidays when the children would be unaccompanied passengers. But he did not know if he liked that arrangement, besides, his children were still too young to travel like that. Would Lyndall consider bringing them out for a holiday? So much to think about, and so little time. Sybil was leaving this coming week and he was meant to be going with her.

There was no time to think beyond getting sorted himself. Damn his father.

Sybil glared at Monty and hissed under her breath, "I'll have you know that I am a university graduate, and have an MBA from Cambridge. I do not need anyone supervising me."

Monty looked at her in surprise, as much from her accomplishments as from what his father had revealed.

"Did you know about this?" Monty asked as his mind took in the possibility that he had been kept out of the loop.

"Of course I did," Sybil replied scathingly.

"Since when?" So she had known about the appointment, though it made sense that she would have if his father was announcing it. Not even he would be confident enough to pull that off without knowing in advance that it was an indisputable fact. Monty didn't know whether to feel enraged or resigned.

Sybil slowly and carefully curled a strand of her shoulder-length hair. "Enough time to organise myself," she answered, sounding almost bored.

"How long?"

"At least a month."

"A month?" She, and his father, had been privy to this arrangement for a month and he was only hearing about it now?

"Before you ask, I did not apply, I was head-hunted," she said with a deadpan face.

He smiled thinking how much Teddy would have laughed at her articulation. She had loved taking the mickey out of the plum in his mouth, and now, for the first time he was suddenly aware of how pretentious it sounded. And his father had disparaged both Teddy and Melanie. The hypocrite.

And now he was sending him to Australia, again.

He looked at Sybil. She was no longer insipid, but she did look a trifle prissy. And Monty almost burst out laughing. His father might thing that by sending the two of them to the other side of the continent to his last visit to Australia he would forcing he and Sybil together and the match could be made. But if that was his thinking, he would be seriously mistaken. Had his father forgotten that 'the colonial' was also in Australia? Teddy might be in a different State, and on the other side of the continent, yet she wouldn't be out-of-the-way.

When only moments ago he had felt put-upon, and furious at his father's constant meddling in his life, he was now almost bubbling with excitement that he had an opportunity to regain the freedom that he had unknowingly been missing from his life. He wanted to hug Sybil and kiss his father. But he controlled himself. For the time being.

He smiled as an idea formed in his mind. Melanie could have George, or the other way round. He just felt sorry for Fiona, but then again, maybe she had brought it upon herself in the first place. He didn't know, nor did he care. In the meantime he'd let his father wallow in his moment of glory.

White-faced, Melanie was shell-shocked, and, feeling faint, she was being supported by George who had his arm around her waist. This was nowhere near where she had hoped her underhand schemes would lead to. And certainly not what she had been expecting when she had spoken to Mr Charles.

Her mind whirled as she tried to grasp what this announcement meant for her now that her scheming was crumbling. She took a deep breath and looked at George, and smiled. Yes, that could be the solution. He was her saviour in more than just this momentary lapse in her composure. As for his wife, well ...

Fiona ought to have known better. She should have worked harder at holding onto George. After all, Fiona had been 'the other woman' to woo George into her arms. Melanie looked across the room searching for her erstwhile friend. Their eyes locked, and they both read the signals. Melanie might have a mission on her hands, but she knew that it would not take much to get George on her side. She smiled at the woman who was now her rival, and gave George's arm a suggestive squeeze.

"This, therefore, is a great day for us all. Who knows where or what will be next. I have every faith in Miss Forbes' capabilities and expect to see great things coming out from Australia after this. Now, let us all show her what it means to be part of the Chinthurst family firm," he said as he once more opened his arms wide in invitation.

It did not take the guests long to comply and, while Charles reached across Monty and gave Sybil a gentle push forward, boisterously applaud her, with even some wolf whistles joining in, which brought a frown to Charles' face.

"And let us not forget my son," Charles continued, breaking into Monty's reveries. "Come here son."

Monty, standing beside his father, wasn't sure where he was meant to go. He smiled sardonically and stood where he was.

"This, after a fashion, will be my son's last opportunity to share some words with us all. When he returns to our shores, and what will then be our Head Office, he will be a changed man, and who knows what his status will then be." Charles beamed and gave a hearty laugh, carrying a not-so-subtle innuendo masked in innocence. Charles pushed Monty forward.

Monty gave a slow smile as he looked out over the see of faces. These were the people that had worked for him, or were clients, some had become friends. He gave Melanie and George a nod, and watched as George shuffled, uncomfortable and shamefaced. Melanie looked at the floor. He turned his eyes to Sybil, who was standing stoically beside him. She gave nothing away, although he was surprised that the barbed vibes she was generating were not visible to everyone. He gave a little laugh. Travelling and working with her would be challenging. But if that time spent was going to provide him with the opportunity he was imagining, it would be endurable.

He turned to see how his parents were bearing up. His father wore the beginnings of the smirk that Monty was familiar with. The scheming dictator. He looked at his mother. She was clasping onto her husband's arm as though they were joined at the hip while he showed no emotion.

It was as though a veil had been lifted from Monty's eyes and he realised that the social strictures that he was expected to maintain were not him. And he took a deep breath, composing himself for what he was about to say.

"Miss Forbes, I am sure that we will make a good team." He could sense his father puffing out his chest and mentally congratulating himself, and Monty smiled again, before continuing. "I might even say formidable. And for that I need to thank you," he said as he turned to his father, aware that the gratitude was not for what his father, and the guests expected. He moved his hands to hitch into the waist of his trousers as though to pull them up.

"All you here I suppose, like me, had no idea what the occasion was, or what to expect. I know, for me, it has come as a complete and mind-blowing surprise to learn that in a week I'll be on the other side of the globe. I was totally taken aback and it's natural for me to have mixed emotions when faced with such a significant transition. While some might view it as a departure from what they expected, I see it as a chance to grow, to challenge myself," he looked markedly at Sybil, who, with the typical stiff upper lip he'd expected from her, didn't show any reaction. "But I am excited about the possibilities that lie ahead and," Monty was seemingly nervously fiddling with his belt, "other than saying goodbye to everyone, all I have to add is I'm glad to have already made the first step." Then as an aside to Sybil, he added "See you at Heathrow."

Monty turned his back to the room, dropped his trousers and pulled his shirt up to reveal ... a collective gasp, along with some more wolf-whistles, applause and laughter from the guests had Charles turn and stare at the source of amusement, while his wife grasped more firmly to his arm and hyperventilated.

Monty made himself presentable again, then, laughing, turned back to face the room. The tattoo of the Boxing Kangaroo on his right buttock back out of sight. He then walked away from Sybil and his parents. Smiling broadly, he made his way through the mass of the guests, who were generous in their congratulations, accompanied by back and buttock slapping. He needed to get out of the room, collect his children and explain to them, and Lyndall, that he was letting go of his old life and starting a new one in Australia.

Don't miss out!

Visit the website below and you can sign up to receive emails whenever Leigh Leslie publishes a new book. There's no charge and no obligation.

https://books2read.com/r/B-A-DWOM-APGXC

BOOKS 2 READ

Connecting independent readers to independent writers.

Did you love *Monty*? Then you should read *Eenie, Meanie, Minie, No!*[1] by Nolan MacKenzie!

DID THEY FALL OR WERE THEY PUSHED?

EENIE, MEANIE, MINIE, NO!

NOLAN MACKENZIE

[2]

The diaries of a dead man call. Can Sandie resist? Where will reading them take her?

Sandie's husband and his university nemesis compete for the affections of a man long since gone. She turns to the old man's diaries for assistance. It began in academia but it won't end there. Because university can be murder.

Sandie uses the diaries to decode a mystery stretching across decades and continents. She might pay with her marriage and her life.

Kidnapping and murder form the backdrop for this fast paced thriller set in 1990s New Zealand.

1. https://books2read.com/u/bzeYA9

2. https://books2read.com/u/bzeYA9

Also by Leigh Leslie

About the Author

Leigh lives in the South Island of New Zealand but still calls Australia home, even though she left when she was twelve. Educated in Australia, Africa, Europe and New Zealand she has seen a lot of the world.

No matter where in the world Leigh was living, she has always been surrounded by books. As a child, when she was not being read to, she would be an avid listener to the tales that either her maternal grandmother or her father would weave.

Leigh never considered writing until she was encouraged to attend a U3A Creative Writing course in the 1980s. She has been writing ever since. Now, after many years of traveling, teaching and working in a school library, among other careers, she is ready to share her writing with the public.

Leigh writes under several names –Leigh Leslie, Nolan Mackenzie (Thriller, Mystery); Jacklyn Harris (Romance).

Leigh has two adult children, who are also voracious readers and write when they can find the time.